PHIL WHITAKER has written four novels. He
won the John Llewellyn Rhys Prize, Betty Trask
Award and was shortlisted for Whitbread First Novel
Award for his novel, *Eclipse of the Sun* in 1997 after
graduating from the UEA creative writing MA. He
went on to win the Encore Award with his second
novel, *Triangulation*, in 2000 and published two other
novels, *The Face* (2002) and *Freak of Nature* (2007).

D1100937

BRISTOL LIBRARIES
WITHDRAWN
SOLD AS SEEN

SISTER SEBASTIAN'S
LIBRARY

ALSO BY PHIL WHITAKER

NOVELS

Eclipse of the Sun (1997)
Triangulation (1999)
The Face (2002)
Freak of Nature (2007)

PHIL WHITAKER

SISTER SEBASTIAN'S LIBRARY

CROMER

PUBLISHED BY SALT PUBLISHING 2016

2 4 6 8 10 9 7 5 3 1

Copyright © Phil Whitaker 2016

Phil Whitaker has asserted his right under the Copyright, Designs and Patents Act 1988 to be identified as the author of this work.

This book is sold subject to the condition that it shall not, by way of trade or otherwise, be lent, resold, hired out, or otherwise circulated without the publisher's prior consent in any form of binding or cover other than that in which it is published and without a similar condition including this condition being imposed on the subsequent publisher.

This book is a work of fiction. Any references to historical events, real people or real places are used fictitiously. Other names, characters, places and events are products of the author's imagination, and any resemblance to actual events or places or persons, living or dead, is entirely coincidental.

Every effort has been made to trace copyright holders and to obtain their permission for the use of copyright material. The publisher apologises for any errors or omissions and would be grateful to be notified of any corrections that should be incorporated in further editions of this book.

First published in Great Britain in 2016 by
Salt Publishing Ltd
12 Norwich Road, Cromer, Norfolk NR27 0AX United Kingdom

www.saltpublishing.com

Salt Publishing Limited Reg. No. 5293401

A CIP catalogue record for this book is available from the British Library

ISBN 978 1 78463 078 2 (Paperback edition)
ISBN 978 1 78463 079 9 (Electronic edition)

Typeset in Neacademia by Salt Publishing

Printed and bound in Great Britain by Clays Ltd, St Ives plc

Salt Publishing Limited is committed to responsible forest management. This book is made from Forest Stewardship Council™ certified paper.

for Hilary

SISTER SEBASTIAN'S LIBRARY

One

S HE ROLLED ON to her side, meeting the plump caress of an unused pillow. Its cotton cover was cool and dry and soothing. The sun had travelled some way since she'd fallen asleep - it was shining directly on her now, causing her to squint when she opened her eyes. Overhead, the ceiling fan dragged itself uselessly round. She imagined the humid air flopping and folding in the wake of the blades, more doughy mixture than evanescent gas. Fresh perspiration beaded, and crawled across her skin.

The white muslin drapes over the open French doors billowed softly. Elodie swung herself out of bed and made her way towards the whisper of refreshment. She pictured herself, sweeping the curtains aside and stepping out into the afternoon and its breeze. If the balcony had opened on to the inner courtyard, with its azure tiled pool fringed by sun loungers, then she would have done so. The norms of behaviour within a hotel can be very different from those outside its walls. But on the street below her room everyday life laboured on: revving, parping, shouting out; bursts of shrill Arabic music Doppler-shifting as cars passed. Her appearance would be a transgression.

Her alarm sounded behind her, dreamy seashore waves over a gentle acoustic guitar. She retrieved her phone and silenced it. There was only one text, a simple 'Good luck!' from Seal that had come through just as she was switching it off at

Gatwick, and which she hadn't yet cleared from the notifications bar. She'd decided not to arrange roaming; she wanted to be removed from her normal life, to be in control of how and when she made contact with home. Endless missives from university colleagues, social media updates from friends and acquaintances – all would make it difficult, painful even. And unexpected calls or emails from family would be a thousand times worse. She clicked off the display and tossed the phone on the bed. It felt liberating, but also a little scary, to be cut off from the world she knew.

She peeled off her t-shirt and pants and dropped them at the door to her en suite. A fixed shower head jutted from the wall. She turned the valve and was hit, square in the chest, by icy grapeshot. She shrank into the corner, the water ricocheting off the tiles, needling her shins and thighs. That there could be anything so devoid of heat in the entire city. Eventually, having waited for warmth that never came, she dipped cupped palms into the torrent and sluiced herself with a few handfuls. The extremes of temperature defeated her. Perhaps hot water, like air conditioning, was intermittent. What was the phrase the man on reception had used? *Certain times* – air conditioning would only be available at certain times. She'd asked when these were. He'd shrugged and said that depended on when there was electricity; the generator couldn't power it alone.

Back home in UK time the children would be starting afternoon lessons. She felt a cramp of longing but quickly righted herself – it would be business as usual for them, in the thick of it with friends. To them, this was no different than Mummy being away at one of her conferences. That was how she wanted it.

Not for the first time she wondered how it would feel were she doing this for one of them. If she allowed that train of thought she quickly became swept up in ferocious gusts of maternal care – imagining Maddie or Ollie alone, afraid, ill, or in danger. The protectiveness, the anger, the fear – the strength and purity of the emotions evoked simply by *imagining* her child in peril. She knew with clear-eyed certainty that she would risk anything to keep them safe. Her feelings for Bridie were strong and unsettling, too, but more complex; more malleable.

Elodie dried herself and unzipped her suitcase, letting what little English air was trapped inside escape. She dressed in an ankle-length skirt, bought specially for the trip, and an oversize shirt she'd not worn for years. The cotton was affected by the change of climate, its fibres swollen with the humidity, making the buttons stiff to push through their holes. Standing in front of the full-length mirror she laid a silk scarf over her head and tied it securely at her throat. She noted the effect with flat curiosity. Face, hands, feet the only exposed flesh. A collision of impressions: Bridie in her scapular and veil; anonymous women in hijabs glimpsed on the ride from the airport. Now her. Cloaking herself, obscuring herself. Conforming herself.

᪥

The *petit taxi* took her weaving through the nouvelle ville, past pavement cafés, low rise apartment blocks, shop fronts with huge plate glass windows – but for the Arabic signage she could have been anywhere in southern France. Eventually they emerged on to a grand, wide boulevard, traffic running either side of a broad esplanade shaded by lines of trees. As they drove, Elodie caught glimpses of overgrown flower beds and a couple of dry fountains. Here and there, men were grouped loosely around concrete benches, some in suits, others in white cotton robes, seemingly everyone smoking.

'Le voilà!'

The driver pulled up outside a set of high gates wrought in blue-painted metal, intricate detailing picked out in gold. Firmly closed. Through the bars she could see what must be the consulate building itself, some thirty feet back: Moorish arch set in the centre atop slender pillars, the walls that stretched either side rendered in perfect white stucco, date palms planted at orderly intervals to left and right. She was struck by the absence of regalia. The embassies she walked past in London were invariably bedecked in national flags and brass plates. Here there was no Union Jack, no ostentatious indication that this was UK territory. And between the gates and the building, a series of monstrous concrete roundels, each the size of a hot tub, arranged in such a way that no vehicle larger than a motorbike could possibly swerve a path through them.

She passed a twenty dinar note forward to the taxi driver, waving aside the coins proffered in change. He looked at her over his shoulder, and issued a stream of Arabic that sounded like a question. She smiled apologetically and shook her head.

He joggled his hand a couple of times, making the money chink in his palm. 'Merci, madame!'

'Ah! De rien.' She reached for the door handle. 'Au'voir.'

Out on the pavement, she couldn't immediately see how to gain access. A pair of impassive sentries in battle fatigues, each cradling a submachine gun, flanked the archway into the building itself, but if it were part of their job to walk forwards and open the outer gates to someone evidently wanting entry then clearly no one had told them. She looked around for a buzzer or intercom. A sign on the wall caught her eye, blue lettering on a white panel, detailing the opening hours of the consulate and the ways of contacting duty staff when closed. *If you are a British national in distress, and having difficulty reaching us on the emergency telephone number, please call the FCO Switchboard in London on +44(0)20 7008 1500 for assistance.*

Unbidden, she had a fleeting vision: a woman in profile, torrential rain dripping off curly brown hair, standing in front of these gates in the dark of a night time, clumsy fingers trying to punch those digits into a phone, her head and shoulders hunched forward in an effort to keep the screen dry. Bridie. In distress. A couple of thousand miles from home. The slenderness and tenuousness of the connection to someone of her kind, someone who might be able to help her.

The image made Elodie anxious. Next to the sign was a small recess in the wall, inside which she saw a telephone receiver. There was no keypad: when she picked it up and held it to her ear the ringtone was already buzzing.

'British consulate. How may I help?' The female voice was heavily accented.

'Hello, it's Elodie O'Shea. I have an appointment with the consul.'

⚬

The ante-room was empty. Elodie spent a few moments savouring the respite from the humidity and heat; she could actually feel her skin beginning to dry as the perspiration evaporated. She loosened the knot of her scarf and let it slide into her hand. She shook out her hair. What she would give for her hotel to be this gloriously cool.

The chairs were of dark wood, upholstered in red leather; wider, more substantial, plusher than those she'd found in the equivalent government waiting rooms back home. They had a feeling of age about them. In contrast, the walls were decorated with prints of contemporary London landmarks: the Gherkin, the Eye, the O2. On the table was a selection of British magazines. She was surprised to see they were the current editions. How amazing – yet, as soon as the thought occurred, how utterly likely – that there would be someone whose job it is to keep diplomatic outposts around the globe supplied with the latest glossies. She smiled to herself, and took a copy of *Ideal Home* over to a chair.

She flicked through, trying to find an article to capture her attention. Her thoughts kept drifting. She was aware of her shoulders dropping an inch or two. Ever since touch-down she'd been assailed by otherness. She'd disembarked down open steps directly on to the concrete of the taxiway, the idling jet engines loud in her ears. There was no bus; she'd had to walk from plane to terminal building in blistering heat, feeling conspicuous in her Western clothes. A group of bearded and blue-clad workmen, leaning on shovels, stared blankly at her and her fellow passengers as they straggled past. The relief she'd felt negotiating immigration without a hitch, only to find herself surrounded by a crowd of men claiming to be taxi drivers, pressing forward, calling out their stock phrases – *Hello! Yes, please! Bonjour, madame! This way, please!* – each jockeying with the others, hands trying to displace hers from the handle of her suitcase. She'd felt the full force of her vulnerability: none of the men had official ID, and few of the waiting saloon cars were even liveried as taxis. This clamour was about money, of course it was. The worst that could happen would be gross overcharging, and maybe a verbal tussle over being taken to the hotel she'd booked, rather than one that would pay the driver a commission. Yet what if the car she got into was driven by someone with another agenda? Someone for whom a solitary Western woman would be a prize beyond measure?

She hated that she even thought this way. She'd travelled a couple of times between the early rungs of her academic ladder-climb. Of course there was the occasional unfortunate who came to grief - a missing person, a body found, a rape ordeal - but these were the kinds of things that could happen anywhere, to anyone. There was a sense of being one of millions of young people criss-crossing the world, travelling cheaply, forming short-lived confederacies before parting company just as casually again, open to new experiences and ways of being. She'd felt part of a determinedly multicultural generation, one united around humanism and internationalism, one in which music and ideals combined into a force powerful enough to relieve famine and end apartheid. There'd been guilt to wrestle with: the poverty she encountered in India, particularly, was incomprehensible. There'd been hassle to deal with, too: with such disparity of wealth there couldn't be otherwise. But not fear.

When had that come? After the twin towers, but not straightaway. Perhaps fear crept in once she became a mother, once she had her children's futures to preoccupy her. Maybe fear had come when London was assaulted just days after

Make Poverty History, just a day after winning the Olympic bid. Or was it no single event? More the drip drip of a hostage-taking here, an execution video there, a piracy and ransom elsewhere. Whenever it had come fear was now here, and she was upset by her seeming inability to prevent its distortions of her perception. The suspicion, the anxiety it engendered.

She closed the magazine on her lap; she wasn't going to be able to read. When had fear come for Bridie? *Had* fear come for her? Maybe that was what faith had done – blunted, reduced, removed her capacity to be afraid.

The door opened and a woman entered the ante-room. She was dressed in a cream linen skirt with a plain white blouse. Blonde with hints of grey, cut in an impeccable bob.

'Dr O'Shea?'

Elodie nodded.

'I'm Anne Armstrong. Peter's wife?'

'Oh! Pleased to meet you.' She got to her feet. 'Elodie.'

Anne's handshake was firm: 'I thought I'd pop my head in and say hello.'

'Thank you.'

'This must be awful for you. I'm so terribly sorry.'

Anne's eyes were a crisp blue. She had the confident air of a barrister; her voice was warm and slightly low in pitch. Elodie guessed she would be in her mid-fifties, would have been a formidably attractive proposition in her youth.

Anne nodded, as if acknowledging the silence. 'When did you get in?'

'Just this morning. I couldn't get a direct flight. I've been travelling all night.'

'You must be exhausted. Can I get you some tea?'

'No, I'm fine, honestly, thank you.'

8

Actually, she would have loved some tea. What was that about? Not wanting to be a nuisance? She was irritated with herself.

'We didn't know your sister. Peter only took up the posting in April.'

'Of course.' It hadn't occurred to Elodie that the consul or his wife might actually have met Bridie. 'Are there many ex-pats out here?'

'There used to be, in the petrochemical industry – agriculture, too. Numbers declined dramatically during Peter's predecessor's time. There's a few teachers left, and, of course, a few other missionaries.'

'I'm not religious myself.'

Anne smiled. 'Medical?'

'Molecular biologist. At UCL.'

'Ah, then you must know Brian Deerham. He's a very dear friend.'

Anne gestured that Elodie should sit, and took the chair next to her. They fell into anecdotes about the vice-chancellor. How extraordinary to have come all this way and to meet someone with a common acquaintance. Then again, Elodie had the suspicion that wherever she'd happened to have worked or lived Anne would have been able to rustle up some kind of connection. The more she talked, the more Elodie could detect an echo of the teenage girl Anne must once have been – fresh-faced, enthusiastic, a palpable appetite for life. Elodie liked her; Anne reminded her of a certain sort of female academic – Rosie Glenn at Manchester, Penny Newton at UCL – who had been her inspirations and role models. Women whose brilliance was matched by an unremittingly outward focus – no place for self-importance or pomposity, there was simply too much to get stuck into and be determined over. Ever since she was an undergraduate, Elodie had aspired to the same – to succeed in her field, if that was what she was capable of, without aggression and without treading on anyone on her way. It saddened her to think that she may never realise it, that the vagaries of her life might mean that was now no longer possible. She began to wonder about Anne, whether she was where she had always dreamt of being, or whether she too had been blown off course by some ill wind it was impossible to resist. She began to formulate a question, some vague enquiry as to whether being a diplomat's wife allowed a career of one's own.

Before she could ask, the door opened and the receptionist appeared again to say the consul was free. Anne touched her arm.

'I've got to head out, but we should talk some more. Leave a note of your hotel with Peter and I'll get in touch. Perhaps you'd like to come for dinner?'

'Thank you, that would be lovely.' Elodie felt a flush of gratitude – something about that gesture of kinship amidst her current dislocation. Anne's skin felt warm against hers as they shook hands in parting.

'Bridie?'

Peter Armstrong looked momentarily confused.

'That's her real name – her baptismal name, I should say. Sebastian was the name she was given when she took her vows.' Elodie spread her hands. 'She's named after a third century male martyr.'

'Forgive me - I'd assumed it was a feminised form. You'd prefer me to call her Bridie?'

'I've never call her anything else.'

Peter Armstrong transpired to be a slightly plump Scot, soft Edinburgh accent, sandy hair, his eyes pale blue. Elodie had him down as ex-Army - he had the same air about him as so many of Adam's family's friends - some sort of middle-ranking officer before leaving to join the diplomatic corps. Even though there were three small armchairs arranged around an occasional table at the far end of his office, he had elected to stay sitting behind his desk. Elodie felt scrutinised.

'So what, in broad terms, do you want to achieve during your time here? And how we might be of assistance?'

It wasn't that his tone was unfriendly. Just a contrast to his wife's. She guessed he had to be businesslike in these sorts of things.

'I'm really here on behalf of the family. To be sure that everything that could be done, has been done - is being done.'

He made as if to speak but she continued over him. 'I know it is, the Foreign Office have been pretty good at keeping us updated, and Missing Abroad have been fantastic. But you can imagine what it's like for my mother.'

'Sure, sure.' Peter looked at the pen held like a bridge between his hands. 'My staff have been in liaison with the police in Beb, and have contacted every hospital and clinic in the region. If your sister were to turn up anywhere, we'd be informed. We've also, through our French counterparts, made extensive enquiries in the Ardennes, though there's nothing to suggest that she's left the country. Certainly not through any of the major ports or airports, anyway.'

The phone call from the convent in Reims, the first inkling

that there was a problem. The Mother Superior, through a translator, asking Mummy when she had last heard from Sister Sebastian.

'Was there a history of health problems?'

The euphemisms. The delicate skirting round.

'She was one of the most robust characters you're ever likely to meet,' she told him.

'You're not convinced about the idea of a breakdown?'

'Bridie had some pretty tough stuff happen to her. She always took it and did something good with it.'

Peter upended the pen, resting it on the desk so it was like a rocket. 'Things can change, though, can't they? As I understand it, her order had been noticing erratic behaviour for some time. They tried on several occasions to recall her, but she refused to leave. That's unusual, isn't it?'

'Well.' Elodie crossed her legs; rearranged the folds of her skirt. 'We knew nothing about that. My mother saw her in the spring, the last time she was home, and there was nothing amiss then. That's only six months ago.'

His eyebrows - even his eyelashes she noticed - were also blond. So pale as to be almost invisible. It gave his eyes a peculiarly exposed look. It must be hard sometimes for him not to appear to be staring.

'I want to go to Beb myself,' she said. 'Probably in a couple of days, once I've been in touch with the bishop. Could you arrange for me to meet with the police there, so I can get a briefing in person?'

She could read the look on his face, the absence of any surprise. Of course he would have been forewarned.

'I can arrange a teleconference with the Beb police for you.'

'I have to go there. Actually see where she lived. Where she disappeared. Talk to people who knew her.'

'What did London say?'

She exhaled. 'Oh, they strongly advised against. Of course they're going to say that – what else *can* they say?'

'They might have a point.'

'They might. Or they might just be making it up, taking a precautionary approach. They weren't fantastically keen on me coming here, even.' She shook her head. 'Anyway, it's non-negotiable.'

Peter raised the pen, pressed its barrel against his lips. She was aware of a rising irritation: why couldn't he just put it down? It wasn't as though he was actually writing anything. The pen was like some token of his authority, something for him to hang on to.

After a moment he let his hands drop. 'The last thing London wants is for you to run into trouble.'

'So you're saying Bridie has run into trouble, then?'

'Of course not. We have nothing to suggest anything—'

'Well.'

'Look.' He leaned forward slightly, resting his forearms on the desk. 'The Arab Spring here amounted to a handful of street protests and some hurried constitutional adjustments – more like an April shower than an Arab Spring, in fact. This has always been a moderate country with a secular government. But it's not immune to what's happening elsewhere. The official line is there's no Islamist threat, but we are aware of unrest. There've been demonstrations in the south and east, small scale civil disturbances, and at least two car bombs that have gone completely unreported in the official media. The president is a strong leader, and the security services have been very successful at disrupting the jihadis to date, largely because they don't currently enjoy popular support. But the further away one gets from the capital, the less governed the space is. To be perfectly candid, it's only a question of time before we see more. And when they do come we will very likely see them in areas such as Beb, well away from the centre, and they will very likely target Western interests of one sort or another.'

He laid his pen quietly on the desk in front of him. 'Until we know for sure what has happened to your sister, we have to be precautionary.'

She sat staring at him for a few moments. His hair was thinning at the temples, just like Adam's. It was curious how men receded at different ages.

She'd been through all this with the FCO. No one would press the alarm button over Bridie because there was nothing to say anything dreadful had befallen her. There had been nothing on any backchannels, she had been assured, but in the same breath she was told that meant little. In past instances of hostage-taking it had been months or even years before word was finally received. Sometimes word never was received; sometimes just a body turned up in some random place. These things weren't about kidnap with a defined aim; they weren't part of any tight tactical plan. They were about seizing assets when the opportunity arose. About having birds in hand. Or they were about engendering fear. Or generating a sense of senselessness.

The thought of Bridie. Caught up in something like that.

'I don't expect you to understand,' Elodie told him, aware of the curtness in her tone but giving into the flash of anger. 'We're in a complete vacuum. As a family we saw nothing wrong, yet once it became clear Bridie had gone we hear all this stuff from her order about problems going back years. It's impossible, back in the UK, to shed any more light on it. If I can go to Beb, talk to her parishioners, people who knew her day to day, I can at least get some idea of what's gone on.' She ran a hand through her hair. 'I'm not some starry-eyed romantic – I don't imagine I'm going to get there and track her down or anything, but at least if I can talk to people we might get a better idea of the truth.'

'And this can't be done remotely, through phone calls or email?'

'No one seems to have the first idea who I should contact. It's incredible, really, but her order don't seem to have kept any records as to who her congregation actually were.'

He nodded his head very slightly, several times, as though counting something.

'Will you be travelling alone?'

'I've got a friend arriving in a couple of days. He'll accompany me.'

'Well, that's something.' He looked down at the blotter in front of him. 'I would like to send one of my people with you, but I can't.'

Was that a chink? 'Can you put me in touch with an interpreter, a guide – someone local I can trust?'

'I'm sorry.' He breathed out. 'It's not that I'm unsympathetic.'

He looked at her directly. She found it hard to read his expression.

'Listen,' she said. 'I understand your dilemma, but can we go off the record? Any assistance you give me would be strictly confidential. No one back home would ever know about it, there'd be no come-back on you, I promise. I'm responsible for myself.'

He pressed his lips together ruefully. 'I do hear what you're saying, Dr O'Shea, but I simply can't. I'm sorry.'

There was no point antagonising him. But no point in prolonging the meeting if it was to be as fruitless as every other official contact she'd banged her head against before flying out.

'OK, well, thank you for taking the time to meet with me at least.'

He got to his feet and accompanied her to the door.

'Goodbye,' he said, holding out his hand. 'And good luck.'

'Oh, I nearly forgot,' she said. 'Your wife asked for my contact details.'

'Anne?'

She nodded, fishing a pen from her handbag. Peter stood silently while she wrote the name of her hotel on the back of one of her cards. He glanced at it when she handed it across.

'Thank you. I'll be sure to pass that on.'

Something about his expression looked discomfited, like that was the very last thing he was intending to do.

Two

S HE WAS ONLY vaguely aware of the build-up, but there must have been a lot of preparation in the parish beforehand. The sort of thing that concerned only grown-ups. As a child she was carted along to mass every Sunday morning, and there was the youth club on Sunday evenings – the dread feeling as it came to an end each week, and she knew nothing now lay between her and the next day back at school. But that was the sum total of her involvement in parish life, leaving aside special classes for first holy communion and confirmation, and occasional outings to the social club, upstairs above the church hall, when her parents felt like venturing out for a drink.

The Jesuits arrived one Sunday, a team of three of them, invited by Fr Constantine to lead a parish mission. How old would she have been? Twelve maybe – so Bridie would have been about fourteen. An impressionable age. She supposed her parents must have gone to various adults' events, though she had no recollection, but the fortnight saw a flurry of activities for the youth – games nights, art evenings, youth choir, Bible storytelling, folk group, morality Q&As. Twenty or thirty kids, all of them in their teens – the next generation. They worked up a special mass to be celebrated on the final weekend of the mission, everything done by the young people – they rehearsed dramatised versions of the readings, wrote the bidding prayers, decorated the church with the work they'd been doing in the clubs, appointed ushers and readers and collectors and musicians from within their ranks. Priests were always known by their surnames – Fr Smith, Fr Jones – but not the Jesuit who led the mission's youth ministry. Fr Gerry. Gerry, really. An energetic nexus, full of vigour and vim and creativity. He played guitar. He was funny. Always willing to get stuck in and make of fool of himself: hopeless at rounders, toppling over at Twister, playing a goofy Pharaoh in the re-enactment of the Moses story. She couldn't really remember what he looked like, beyond the fact that he had shortish brown hair and a moustache – the things that one remembers from child-hood – but she could still recall the affection he inspired, the example he presented of what faith could look like away from the dour dry rituals of the everyday church.

She guessed it was what he was there to do: make connec-tions, forge relationships. Inspire. In the space of those two weeks, Gerry became something to every one of the parish youth. He was a pied piper, a bewitching impresario. To some, perhaps, a massive, unattainable crush.

They were given Bibles at the start of the mission, a brand new copy for each of the parish's youth. Good News trans-lations, they were covered in fawn leather, a Celtic cross em-bossed in gold leaf on the front. They used them at several of the youth sessions, opened and shut them many, many times. There could have been no mistake.

Sometime after the missionaries had departed – soon enough that she was still missing Fr Gerry and all the colour and vitality he'd brought; was still in the same anti-climactic mood that she struggled with after the last nights of end-of-year shows – she'd opened her Bible again and found the inscription inside the front cover. Neat ink pen, the exact words long since lost to her, but their gist still with her all the same: *Elodie, It has been such a blessing to get to know you, the wonderful person God has made in you. You are special in His sight. Listen carefully to Him; follow Him all your life, and He will lead you to fulfil all the promise He has for you. Bless you, Fr Gerry.*

She may have been unable to remember the exact words, but just revisiting the memory caused a faint echo of the intense warmth that had bloomed inside her tummy when she'd stumbled across the dedication left for her to discover at some future, unspecified time. She'd been sitting on the stairs at home, the Bible open on her knees – that was her recollection, anyway. The sheer unexpectedness of finding the message, where no message had been before. The magical thrill of the words. Wonderful person. Special in His sight. All the promise He has for you.

She harboured the secret, didn't tell a soul. She was special. So much so that Fr Gerry – jaunty, dashing, charismatic Fr Gerry – had gone to extraordinary lengths somehow to leave her an inscription in her personal Bible.

How on earth had he done it? She couldn't work it out. She was sure there'd been nothing written in there as late as the last Sunday, when the mission had culminated in the youth mass. And after that the Jesuits had departed, moving on to the next parish, to their next mission. In the end she decided her parents must have been involved. It was the only explanation she could think of. Gerry must have asked them; they must have stolen the Bible away after she'd gone to bed, presented it to him. Perhaps he'd called round. Had he sat in their living room, pen in hand, writing while she'd been soundly sleeping?

She didn't ask her mother, though. It was preferable to fantasise, to speculate, to dream. If she heard how it had happened – if her mother confirmed her idea – the words would have crystallised fantasy into concrete reality, and the lustre would have been lost.

A jealous thought began to take root. If he had done it for her, might he have done it for others? She dare not reveal her secret by asking her friends – the ground-swallowing embarrassment if she proved to be the only one – but there was a way. Next time Bridie was out, and when Mummy was busy downstairs, Elodie slipped into Bridie's bedroom. Ears straining for any footfalls on the stair treads, she'd started to search for her sister's Bible, trying to suppress a sudden and urgent need to pee. She found it in Bridie's smalls drawer, took it out, carefully opened the front cover, and found the handwritten inscription inside. The virtually identical inscription.

She was crushed. She was not special. And while it was virtually identical, one word in this message for Bridie jumped out at her, a word that hadn't appeared anywhere in hers. *Vocation.*

I believe you may have a vocation. Listen carefully to God; follow Him all your life, and He will lead you to fulfil all the promise He has for you.

That's where it had all started. For Bridie. For her. She was sure of it.

Did Bridie ever sneak into her room, search out Elodie's Bible when she wasn't around? Did she notice the absence of the V-word and understand that, though duplicated, her inscription was beyond the ordinary? Or had she simply harboured her own secret, content to believe that she was the only one, kept the knowledge of her specialness closeted within her heart?

Three

A CHAMBERMAID MUST have been in while she was
at the consulate – the sheets were smoothed and the
superfluous lightweight quilt was folded back neatly. She took
her case and laid it on the foot of the bed, beginning what
limited unpacking she was going to do.

The photos were always the first thing. Maddie, in Speedo
cap, goggles up on her forehead, beads of water and a look
of unadulterated delight on her face after winning the gruel-
ling county two hundred metre freestyle final. Ollie, equally
joyful, with a bundle of brown and white fluff on his lap, two
button eyes peeping nervously out from the fur, taken just
minutes after getting home from the breeder with eight-week-
old Pogo. She placed the pictures on the table beside her bed,
Maddie on the left, Ollie on the right. It was like writing a
sentence: first-born at the start, second-born coming after.
It was a ritual she'd observed throughout the years: every
conference, international symposium, research seminar she'd
travelled to attend. The photos were updated from time to
time, but she always brought them – even though she had a
zillion on her phone these days. Something about the physical
presence of framed memories, making a hotel room a home
from home.

She hung a few clothes in the wardrobe, hoping the creases
would drop out in the hot, humid atmosphere. A few layers
down she excavated her laptop, and the continental adaptor;

found a socket near the head of the bed and plugged it in to charge.

The receptionist had given her a code when she'd purchased an hour of wifi. She piled pillows against the headboard, and settled herself back with her knees raised, computer propped against her thighs. When she opened the laptop, she found Bridie's dedication card where she'd sandwiched it between keyboard and screen. It was face down, the inscription on the back dated to commemorate Sister Sebastian O'Shea's entry into the Sisters of the Divine Mercy. She turned it over, spent a moment looking at the painting reproduced on the front, some Italian master's depiction of Saint Sebastian's martyrdom. He was shown as a beautiful youth, naked except for a loin cloth, bound by ropes lashed round a tree. Multiple arrows pierced his flesh, protruding through calf, thigh, flank, neck, each wound unrealistically bloodless, the expression on his face bizarrely serene.

She opened the drawer in her bedside table and put the dedication card away. She'd found it when searching for a photo of Bridie to bring with her. She'd been chastened to discover that the most recent picture she had of her sister was years old, snapped outside the tent they'd just pitched at Glastonbury when Elodie had been pregnant with Maddie, and when Bridie had been on the brink of taking her final vows. Aside from blurry family group shots at special occasions since, she had nothing more up to date.

She started up her laptop, entered the wifi code, and set about what limited contact she was going to allow herself with the world she had left behind.

Dear Mummy
    Please stop worrying. I've arrived safely and am settled

into the hotel, but communications are erratic and I may not be able to get news to you as often as I'd like. I've met with the consul today and he couldn't have been more helpful. It'll take a couple of days, but he's going to fix me up with one of their local people who'll come with me to Beb and smooth the way. He had nothing new to report – there's still a complete absence of information. But no news is better than bad news, so keep faith.

I will update you as often as I'm able. I'll email the children but do give them my love and a hug from me.

Much love, Elodie

Dear Maddie

You would love it here, it's hot hot hot, I haven't seen a cloud since I arrived. The hotel is lovely, I haven't tried the pool yet but it looks gorgeous and I think I'll go for a swim before supper. The only thing you wouldn't like is the wifi situation – it makes me appreciate what we take for granted at home – you have to buy time online here in little chunks, and the power is erratic to say the least, so I may not be able to contact you as often as I'd like. I doubt Skype will be a starter, though I will try before I set off for Beb. Everyone is being very kind and helpful, and I hope to see Aunty Bridie soon.

I hope you had a good day at school. Work hard, and do help Nana whenever you're able.

Love you darling, Mummy xx

Dear Ollie

The journey took all night, and I saw the dawn out of the window as we flew in. I thought of you, how you love the sight of the world below when you're in a plane, how tiny everything looks. They produce a lot of olives here, and I could make out rows and rows of regimented groves during the descent to the airport. They looked like nurseries growing crops of model bushes for Hornby train sets!

I'm off to Aunty Bridie's soon, and I'll be in touch as often as I'm able. Be good for Nana, particularly with Pogo – Nana's legs aren't what they used to be. I hope you had a good day at school. Don't forget to practise your guitar!

Lots of love, Mummy xx

Dear Henning

Just checking everything's OK at your end. I can't wait to see you. I'm feeling more than a little lost, and more than a little daunted. The consul was an utter waste of time. I'm off to see the bishop tomorrow and hoping for better things from him.

Send me a message by return if you can. Unless I hear otherwise I'll be at the airport Monday at three.

El xxx

Hi Adam

Just to let you know that I got here OK, and am finding my feet. I don't really know what to say beyond that. I've emailed the children, and Mummy, but send them my love in any case. Please be kind to Mummy – try to remember that, whatever it might look like to you, she's only trying to help. I know you're upset about the situation, but it won't be for long, and I am asking you

*to respect what I need at this time. I'm sorry for my part
in what happened between us.*
  Elodie

She sat there for a short time, re-reading the last email
twice through, trying to decide whether to send it, amend
it, or delete the whole thing and just let him get on with it.
Or whether to write something completely different, only she
didn't know what that might be. She was so tired of trying to
anticipate his reactions, so tired of trying to avoid the next
blow-up or the next interminable days-long silent treatment,
so tired of being the one always trying to make peace. She
couldn't decide what to do. In the end, she hit send, and there
was no longer any decision to make.

There was a faint smell of drains emanating from the
shower room. And God, the heat. She was aware of a tight-
ness in the pit of her stomach. She was exhausted, but she
needed to keep going till a reasonable time to get her body-
clock in synch. Images jostled in her mind. Adam shouting,
screaming, furious at her for going at short-notice, his brittle
ego turning it – as he somehow managed to turn virtually
everything – into a slight against him, an unwarranted disrup-
tion and burden. Ollie crying; Maddie sullenly withdrawing to
her room. Memories from another era: her own father raging,
smashing a stool down on the floor, breaking its wooden leg.
Herself the crying one when they'd been growing up; Bridie,
the scornful withdrawer. It was happening again, over and
over again, like some unstoppable video loop.

She opened her eyes with a jolt. There was that brief dislocation in time – just for a second she must have fallen asleep.
Her finger moved the laptop cursor and she called up the

Missing Abroad homepage, bookmarked on favourites. She sat watching the Currently Missing column refreshing itself every ten seconds, focusing on each new photograph as it appeared in front of her. The faces were familiar by now; she even knew there would be thirty-two of them – assuming neither a miracle nor another disaster – fading in and out, one after another, a visual roll call of the lost. It was mesmerising, a comforting ritual. Was that wrong, to find solace in other people's tragedies? Since Bridie disappeared, Elodie had learned surprising things: that it felt somehow shameful, almost sordid, to have someone in your family go missing. That when you spoke to people you could practically hear the thoughts and judgements tumbling round their heads. This was either some dreadful crime from which there could be no happy end – but in that case, where was the body, the blood, the eyewitnesses who'd seen something, however trivial, out of the ordinary? Or else it was a damning indictment of a family: what in the background, the upbringing, the formative years, could lead someone to vanish with no word to those they supposedly loved?

Some people – even a couple of formerly good friends – had shunned her. She tried telling herself they simply didn't know what to say, that they were uncomfortable with the prospect of emotionality. But she knew she'd become a plague carrier; that by keeping Elodie at arm's length these erstwhile friends felt they could protect themselves from becoming tainted by her gross misfortune.

The others on Missing Abroad helped: knowing that she, Bridie, their family, were not the only ones. That others had been struck by this same plague.

Most of the pictures showed cheerful people: crinkly eyes,

smiling mouths, bright clothes, sun-flushed skin. Snapped on holiday or at parties or on special occasions, nothing in their demeanour suggested that life was anything other than a breeze. There was no clue that they would, on some unforeseen day in the future, simply vanish, leaving nothing but a flotsam of possessions and memories bobbing on the surface of the life they'd left behind. Chris Rowland, a Scottish mining engineer, living in Brazil for the past twenty years, last seen some fifteen months ago. Lucas Garrett, a stocky twenty-nine-year-old, photographed in front of Buckingham Palace, not heard from since boarding a ferry to visit on old pen friend the previous September. Nineteen-year-old Kerry Andrews, lips frozen in mid-pout as she blew a kiss to the person behind the lens, texts home abruptly ceased five days into a fortnight in the Serengeti.

Elodie wondered at the lives stretching out behind the photographs, the complex histories condensed into these single pictures and the accompanying brief lines of context. David Saunders, a man in his fifties who'd spent three years travelling in Asia, whose infrequent but reliable missives home had stopped coming over a year ago. How long until it had dawned on his family that the next letter or phone call or email was never going to come? Three years travelling. Was that a success story: a packet made from selling a rapidly growing start-up, no need to worry about money again, time to get out there and see the world? Or was it the closing chapter of a life gone unbearably wrong: a broken relationship, a shattered family, no hope of picking up the pieces again? Who goes travelling for that length of time at that stage of life? Who did he leave behind, what family, what friends? What did they mean to him; he to them? There was no clue in

27

his photo – a bluff sort of face, the smile understated, thinning hair tousled by wind blowing in from whichever sea was in the background. He looked like a Yorkshireman. Looked like he might be one of those no-nonsense head teachers who get parachuted in to sort out failing schools.

She'd done this for all of them at one time or another – searched their features, their expressions, tried to work out what kind of person each of them was, what their story might be, the story behind the brief details supplied by concerned family or friends. She could find out easily enough, if she really wanted – a quick search on a name would turn up local news articles at the very least – but she didn't want to. She preferred conjecture. A couple of the biogs did give more detail: one mentioned 'vulnerability', another gave a candid diagnosis of schizophrenia in someone who'd been traipsing Europe from one holy shrine to the next in search of a cure. Much as she sympathised she didn't want to think about the other missing people in this way. She wanted them to be hale and hearty, to have been suddenly and unexpectedly overtaken by misfortune, however tragic or violent. She wanted them to have been wrenched out of happy families and successful, satisfying lives. The alternative felt infinitely more dispiriting.

Guy Baverstock, forty-nine, on a two-week diving holiday in Mozambique, emailed friends to say wouldn't be able to make a trip in the UK planned for shortly after his return. He had not been seen or heard from since. Guy Baverstock. A regular-sounding name. He could be an old university friend, a colleague, a neighbour from along the street. What had happened to him? Had something befallen him, or had he created this himself, disappearing so as to start over, so as to leave behind an intolerable mess? She stared at Guy for the slow-running seconds until his picture abruptly faded. Then, appearing into the briefly vacant area of the screen, the face of her own sister, Bridie. Sister Sebastian O'Shea.

Mummy had wanted to use this photo, taken that spring when Bridie had last returned to the UK, dressed in full habit for the family gathering. Bridie's tentative smile, her eyes looking past the camera somehow. She looked ill-at-ease; disconnected – or was that just Elodie's supposition? What must it be like, to be living in an alien culture, to have aligned your life with people in real poverty, a poverty few in Britain could truly grasp? Then to be whisked by plane back to the world you once knew, the sheer easiness of life, the availability of things? To be transplanted from north African heat, dirt, toil and difficulty and landed back in middle-class English comfort? It was the first holy communion for cousin Tom's eldest. Bridie had been guest of honour, the true religious in the family. Elodie hadn't gone. A clash with a research seminar in Milan.

'We can't use this,' she'd said, when Mummy had produced the print.

'What's wrong with it?' Mummy had taken the photo back, was looking at it again as if searching to find the fault.

'Look at it.'

Face like a moon, hair completely hidden beneath the veil, neck masked by the bland whiteness of her wimple.

'And?'

'People don't remember faces like that, Mummy. They need the hair to frame things, the neck and shoulders to give proportion.'

'Your sister is a nun, darling. We need to show her as such. People will be much more likely to remember her.'

'Yes, if she's wearing her habit when they see her.' Elodie paused. 'But if she's not, they're never going to put the two together.'

Mummy had prevailed. Mummy always prevailed somehow, her poor-me pathos never failing to hobble Elodie with guilt. Bridie – Sister Sebastian – faded from the laptop screen, and the first of the thirty-two missing faces reappeared to start the cycle again. Elodie hibernated her computer and put it to one side. From the next door room came the sounds of pieces of furniture being scraped across the tiled floor. Drifting above the traffic noise outside her window, the amplified ululations of the muezzin sang the call to afternoon prayer. She felt the need to get out of the room, to march about, to do something. Elodie swung herself off the bed and began to search the contents of her suitcase for the costume she'd brought when she'd learned the hotel had a pool.

❧

The water was bracingly cold. Elodie started a vigorous breast stroke, focusing on each surge forward, her eyes fixed on the far end. A couple of children – Americans, from the accent – were playing in the shallower water, splashing each other, shouting and shrieking delightedly, their mother reading on a sun lounger, shaded by a parasol. Elodie wondered why they were here; this couldn't conceivably be a holiday destination. Probably visiting a father working for an aid agency or an international body. Since getting to know Henning she'd come to appreciate the huge numbers of people scattered around the developing regions of the world, employed by the WHO, or any of the legion UN branches and offshoots, the World Food

Programme, the World Bank, to say nothing of the countless charities and development bodies, and private companies seeking profits abroad. To attract and retain the right people the packages had to be attractive – flights and accommodation for families, school fees for children to be educated back home. Even Bridie's order, espoused to frugality as it was, would cover two return trips each year.

She neared the children, and felt her heart warmed by the innocence of their games. They were two girls, must be about five and eight, she thought. Presumably it was no different to them whether they were having fun in a pool out back in a Florida villa or in the courtyard of a North African colonial hotel. What did they really know of the world in which they were moved around? Perhaps this felt just like normal life to them: their father away for long stretches, then they get flown out for a few weeks during the holidays, living the life of riley in some exciting hotel or other. If she were to ask them, would either of them know more than that? Even though they must be near enough twice the age of these American kids, neither Ollie nor Maddie really had much interest in what she or Adam actually did in the countless hours they spent at work. Mummy's a scientist, she does experiments with horrible insects; Daddy works in an office doing something for the running of the country.

She reached the shallow end and stood for a while, catching her breath. The older girl was cradling her sister in her arms, both of them giggling in anticipation of the moment when she would let her sibling go and she would duck briefly under the surface. Again and again. It seemed to be the most hilarious thing on the planet. Their humour was infectious; Elodie found herself smiling. She was wistful, too. The mother was lost in her paperback, paying no attention to her daughters' game. Wasting something precious. This era was behind Elodie now; it belonged to a different time, a time when her kids were younger, when they were all still a happy family, a time before the problems began. Or before she'd come to appreciate that the problems had always been there, fermenting and growing, initially unseen, like microbial life on agar.

She launched herself forward again, gliding past the kids who were oblivious to her presence. She noticed that the water was no longer anything like as cold; how swiftly her skin thermoregulation had kicked in. She stayed with breast stroke, not wanting to wet her hair at this time of day.

What did that mother tell her children, she wondered? About where they were, why they were here, what it was that their father did in such a faraway land? She hadn't been straight with hers. There seemed no point in worrying them, not at this stage. Not till there was anything to worry about. Some vague stuff about Aunty Bridie being unwell and needing her to visit; Mummy wouldn't be away for long; Nana would come to help look after them. That had been enough for Ollie. Life always was straightforward for him. Maddie, that bit nearer adulthood, had asked a couple of questions, but seemed satisfied that Mummy going to visit Aunty Bridie was not going to impact on her sporting pursuits, nor her being able to hang out with her friends. It had saddened Elodie, the ease with which she'd been able to pull the wool over their eyes. Then again, Bridie had lived abroad for the entirety of their lives, and was more a concept than a real person to them, someone who turned up every now and again around Christmas time or for family functions. But not someone with whom they had any real connection.

What would it be like if she were to go? Mummy's going to live abroad. She could feel the thud of the depth charge exploding deep beneath the surface of their lives. She would be ripping them away from everything familiar – their friends, the neighbourhood they knew so intimately, their school and clubs and activities. Their father, their extended family. But what if they stayed behind? Would Adam even want them; could he even cope? The thought of them living with perpetual meltdown. You'll be fine; Mummy will see you every holiday. You'll be able to come out and visit. Switzerland is such a fantastic place.

She lunged for the side at the deep end, outstretched hand finding purchase on the smooth tiles. She hung on, breathing a little heavily. From the neck down her body felt cool, refreshed. Just her head was still hot, felt like it was baking in the relentless sun. She craved ducking beneath the surface, to taste that deeply delicious cool. Sod the hair. She held her breath and let go of the side, slipping underwater, her eyes closed against the chlorine. Her scalp felt icy, such a contrast to the rest of her skin now so thoroughly acclimatised to its new environment. Sound muffled. The voices of the American children still reached her ears but were quieter, indistinct, far far away. She stayed suspended like that for a moment, then bobbed up again, wiping water and her fringe from her eyes.

She struck off in crawl, no longer restricted to breast stroke. She settled into her rhythm, feeling her arms skewering the water, breathing to the right every fourth stroke, exhaling streams of bubbles as she powered along. She thought of Maddie, her determination to be the fastest, the best. No way could she do anything to disrupt that, to deprive her daughter of her chance of a place in the national squad.

The more she swam, the more urgently she wanted to swim. Within the space of a single day, she'd begun to feel confined, trapped in boxes: aeroplane, taxi, hotel, taxi, consulate, taxi, hotel. Yes, they were safe; yes, they were secure. Her hotel was a bubble of normality and comfort in this otherwise entirely strange city. Tomorrow she would set out on foot. The Catholic church was just a short walk away according to the map she'd downloaded. She thought of her younger days, her travels before Adam, before children, before tenure, before settling down. The invigoration of being in new places, seeing new people, fresh sights and insights, different cultures and ways of being. She yearned for even just a tiny reminder of that feeling. And much as she was impatient for Henning to join her, a part of her wanted a taste of that freedom before he came, while she could still experience it alone.

She reached the shallows again, found that while she'd been immersed in her front crawl, the American woman had begun wrapping her daughters in their towels, her paperback spread face-down on her lounger. The two women's eyes met and Elodie smiled. The mother smiled back, though briefly, quickly busying herself in attending to her children again.

Four

THERE'D BEEN A single the previous December, some of the world's biggest rock and pop stars joining forces as Band Aid, selling a million copies in the first week and dominating the charts throughout the holiday. The TVs that sat in every living room brought footage of swollen-bellied, tear-streaked, fly-blown Ethiopian children to trouble the conscience of the nation. Elodie and Bridie had gone carolling with their church. For that year only, traditional songs were disregarded. Breath clouding the evening air, fingers numb on guitar strings, the folk group choir performed a continuous loop of *Do They Know It's Christmas?* from house to house to house. The donations, which ran into the hundreds, were sent to help the famine relief effort.

As the summer term wore on, news came of what was to be the greatest concert ever. Simultaneous shows in London and Philadelphia, performers, promoters, technicians, roadies, all giving their services pro bono. The day itself, a gloriously sunny July Saturday, saw them in front of the telly from the outset. Bridie was fifteen, Elodie thirteen; they drank in the pictures of the build-up, scarcely able to comprehend the size of the crowds steadily filling each stadium, and the estimates of two billion others watching with them around the planet. Then, at midday in London, came the start. The British national anthem, played by the band of the Coldstream Guards. Then the real start, Status Quo, *Rockin' All Over the World*.

The sense of utter elation as those chords crashed out, and tens of thousands in Wembley sang along, sending a message of solidarity and hope around the globe.

Spandau Ballet, David Bowie, The Who. Elodie and Bridie's favourite, Alison Moyet, in a blistering duet with Paul Young. Interviews with stars between the acts, shots of the youth of the world basking in the sunshine, partying with a purpose, partying to feed the world. Elodie would have given anything to have been there. Bridie, too.

'This is it, El,' Bridie said at one point, as the total donated passed a significant landmark. 'This is absolutely it. Our generation's coming through! Governments, churches, all the people who said you can't do anything – we're cutting through the nonsense and just *doing* it. Nothing will be the same again.'

Sting, U2, Queen. A throat-constricting video to the soundtrack of The Cars. They stayed with it for hours, nipping out for drinks and snacks and to use the loo in the lull times, one always staying behind to shout for the other if it looked like something big was about to happen.

And being aware, from time to time, of their father's presence in the doorway of the lounge, tutting at acts of frivolity, exhaling loudly when concert-goers caught sight of themselves on camera and waved and whooped for all they were worth. He came and went, making it hard to relax, to enjoy themselves. Periodically there would be raised voices in the kitchen, or out in the garden: Dad, increasingly irate at their spending a whole day cooped up in front of the TV; Mummy, trying to placate him, soothe him. Elodie did her best to block it out, but from time to time his objections pierced her defences: it was disgusting, this whole spectacle of millionaire rock stars strutting and parading themselves on the backs of abject suffering. It was enough to make him sick. If they felt that strongly, there was nothing to stop them donating their obscene fortunes and having done with it. This, this was pure self-aggrandisement.

'God!' Bridie said, low enough that only Elodie could hear. 'Why can't he just shut up?'

Then, at some stage during the afternoon, Bob Geldof, perched in the BBC commentary box, frustrated by the sluggish rate of giving, shouting at them – at the world – out of the screen: *Give us your fucking money.*

The flurry of footsteps, the abrupt jab at the switch. The concert cut off.

'Right! You two, that's enough. Out. Now.' Their father, lips compressed with rage. The shell-shocked silence. The end of that amazing day.

'Dad, that's completely out of order.'

Mummy, behind him. 'Bridie! Don't talk to your father like that!'

Bridie, on her feet. 'This is the single most monumental thing that's ever been done in the history of the world and you want to switch it off just because he said one swear word?'

'I will not have language like that in my house!'

'Bridie, please!'

'What? Language like fuck?'

'Bridie!'

'Fuck fuck fuck! Language like fucking fuck in your fucking house?'

She was heading out of the door. Her cheeks were smudged red. Elodie was shaking, watching her sister go. He made a feint for her, a lock of his swept-back black hair falling forward with the sudden movement. She shied away, nearly made it past him. He lunged a foot out and caught her shin, sending her flying. He bent down, grasped the top of her arm roughly, and pulled her upright, her face wincing with the pain from his grip.

'Get up to your room, you foul-mouthed young woman, and stay there till I've decided what to do with you.'

Bridie, propelled out of the doorway with a shove.

Mummy, standing off to the side, forlorn.

Their father pulled back the heavy velvet curtains with one, then another, whip of his arm. The sun streamed into the room, its brightness harsh after the half-light. Elodie stared at the now blank screen. Her mother came over, once he'd gone, and rested a hand on her back. It's not his fault, she told her, for the hundred-thousandth time. He isn't very well.

An awful foreboding hung over the house. Everyone splintered off to their private spaces. Mummy closeted herself in the kitchen, banging about, preparing food. Their father disappeared to the garage, sawing furiously some wood for some project or other. Bridie, her door firmly shut, made no response when Elodie knocked, ever so quietly. She went in anyway, and found her sister lying on her back on her bed, her nostrils flared, wetness streaking the skin round her eyes, staring at the ceiling.

'Leave me alone.'

Elodie wanted to do something to comfort her, but didn't have the first idea what. She went quietly away again.

The rest of the day passed in pained silence. Bridie remained upstairs while the three of them had supper, hardly a word passing between them beyond the grace that marked the beginning of the meal. Elodie felt increasingly worried when she came to go to bed and there was still no break in the impasse. And it continued the next morning: the first she saw of Bridie was when she was marched down the stairs by Mummy, eyes fixed on the floor, in readiness for going to mass.

The silent car drive.

The four of them, sitting through the service.

Their father, as usual, taking the offertory, processing with the other collectors up to the altar and bowing before he gave his laden leather bag with its metal handle to Fr Constantine.

Mummy and him, sitting, standing, kneeling in all the right places. Lowering their heads in prayer. Shuffling up to communion, taking the host on their tongues like they'd always done for years before anyone was allowed to use their hands.

The silent car drive home.

She heard the footsteps on the landing from her bedroom. She knew with a sick quake in her stomach what was about to come, as it always came. She listened anxiously, but couldn't really make out the words. Bitter experience told her what he would be saying, though: how this was for Bridie's own good, that it would hurt him more than it hurt her, that it was for the good of her soul. She prayed fervently in her head that Bridie would just submit, that she wouldn't goad him by talking back or trying to resist. Elodie felt terrified of what he might do if she did.

She heard each thwack clearly enough as the belt landed on her sister's buttocks, the sound piercing two wooden doors and the corridor space between them. She counted them, each one seeming to sting-out more loudly than the last. One, two, three, four, five, six, seven. She could picture him, his whole torso twisting with the effort of each blow. She could replay in her mind exactly what Bridie had said. She knew then that he had done so, too. A lash for each swear word that had passed her sister's lips.

Five

HER ROUTE TOOK her through a zigzag of intersecting side streets. The shops in the immediate vicinity of the hotel quickly petered out in favour of drab apartment blocks, linen hanging from open shutters, the cables from satellite dishes looping loosely across expanses of wall. Here and there, apparently arbitrary metre-long sections of kerbstone were painted in the yellow, blue and green stripes of the national flag. Some boys were playing with a football up ahead; there were no cars to interrupt their game. Elodie pressed on, phone in hand, tracking the series of lefts and rights. The main roads on her map were marked in French, commemorating both the colonial and the indigenous – Rue D'Orsay, Rue Djallat el Habib, Rue Sainte Claire Deville, Rue Cherah Mohamed – but these smaller streets were unnamed. Even if they had been, it would have been of no help: she quickly discovered that the blue-enamelled street signs at each junction were rendered in Arabic, the script incomprehensible to her. At some point since independence, all trace of French had been expunged.

The city's sole Catholic church was on Avenue Fertas Mohamed and, by her reckoning, Elodie should easily have been there by now. Something was wrong with the map – perhaps it didn't detail the smallest roads; what she thought she'd been following on the screen didn't seem to correlate with reality on the ground. Whatever the reason, she was lost. She looked up and down the street: how quickly she'd become cut off from the bustle of the city, marooned in this backwater area. She couldn't decide whether to retrace her steps or go further in hope. She'd allowed herself plenty of leeway, but to turn back now would surely make her late for her appointment. She felt a flush of irritation with herself. The bullish mood of the previous evening had dissipated with the restlessness of her night – the unfamiliar bed, the oppressive humidity. She'd reconsidered her plan over morning coffee, had been tempted to take a *petit taxi* after all, but the stubborn bit of her, the bit that had been determined to break out of the boxes, would not be overruled.

An old man was watching her from a doorway across the road. He was leaning his weight on a tall stick, both hands resting on its handle. He had a black fez on his head. His white cotton robe was stretched tight over his rotund belly, and hung in loose folds beneath.

'Good morning,' she called as she approached him. 'Bonjour.'

He raised his chin briefly in acknowledgement. His skin was deeply lined and tanned. She showed him the map on her phone, pointing to where the church was marked.

'L'eglise Saint Francois d'Assise?' she asked.

He lifted a hand, his fingers fishtailing as he rehearsed the route. 'Tout a droit . . . a gauche . . . a droit . . . a gauche . . . enfin, c'est derriere de la mosque. Ce n'est pas loin.' His voice was deep. Grey stubble peppered his cheeks. She caught the smell of tobacco and spices on his breath.

'Merci, monsieur. Vous êtes très gentil.'

His face, impassive till now, softened into a lop-sided smile – the legacy of a stroke, or some sort of past trauma, she wondered. It made him suddenly appear vulnerable. 'Bonne journée, madame.'

'Au'voir, monsieur.'

The encounter meant nothing – a dozen words exchanged over the course of less than a minute. Yet the simple humanity of the transaction buoyed her; her step was more purposeful as she walked on. Something about being lost in a strange place a long way from home, seeking and receiving help from someone, the courtesies of life being constant across countries, continents, cultures.

A final chicane brought her out on to a wide avenue, tree-lined, traffic criss-crossing in front of her once again. Directly opposite was a mosque, its gold-domed minaret stretching high above its green-tiled roof. Behind, the old man had said. The mosque had been built at an odd angle, oblique to the road – orientated towards Mecca, she supposed. On the plot to its rear, half hidden by ebulliently fronded palm trees, there was a whitewashed building, a simple latticework frieze around the tops of its façades. A metallic frame had been mounted on the front parapet, housing a single bell, and topped by a plain white cross.

She hated to be late. Her watch told her it was exactly ten thirty. She sought a gap in the stream of cars and motor scooters, and hurried towards the church.

A tall priest was standing at the entrance, his robes white and his chasuble emerald green. He was in his sixties – French, she imagined – and had a round face, strikingly large black-framed glasses, and a broad smile as she came up to him.

'Bienvenue! Welcome! Welcome to our church!'

She took the proffered hand, suddenly unsure from his

manner whether he was expecting her, or whether he had taken her for a generic visitor.

'I'm Elodie O'Shea. Sister Sebastian's sister? I have an appointment with Bishop Bonouvrie.'

'Yes, yes, of course. I'm Father Tellier. Bishop Bonouvrie asked me to attend you. He is celebrating this morning.' He half-turned, sweeping an arm behind her to usher her inside. 'You are familiar with reading?'

'Sorry?'

'It is Mission Sunday. We would be honoured if you would read our English language bidding prayer.'

They were through the double-doors. The church was at least three-quarters full, a sizeable congregation gathered inside. Six lit candles were arrayed on the altar, three either side. A flute and guitar were playing a gentle instrumental.

'I'm sorry,' Elodie said again, lowering her voice. 'I'm here to meet the bishop.'

'Yes, yes, of course, he is expecting you.' The priest paused momentarily. 'Please, it is very simple.' He gestured to an empty space a few rows from the front. 'We will call up a representative from every nation present. If you would say our English prayer, then light a candle for the UK, then show everyone where is the principal city of your country?'

She followed the direction of his gaze. To one side of the altar there was a large easel on which a world map poster, A1 size, had been mounted. A banner across the top had the word RENCONTRE handwritten in felt pen capitals. Elodie's confusion crystallised into realisation: she'd been invited to meet the bishop after Sunday mass, but the time she'd been told to arrive was evidently its start.

Fr Tellier was thumbing through a sheaf of papers,

whispering to himself as he did do, then he drew one out and presented it to her.

'Here it is, the English prayer.'

She could go along with it, or she could protest, explain that she hadn't set foot in a church for twenty years, that she'd had no idea they were planning this. Fr Tellier was beaming at her, his face shiny with perspiration, the prayer sheet wavering barely perceptibly with his slight tremor. The altar bells suddenly chimed, a high-pitched *trrring!* All around her congregants rose to their feet. She took the prayer, managed a swift smile, and eased herself sidewards into the vacant pew.

She didn't take in much of the opening hymn. She could see with awful clarity how it had evolved. *Of course* Sister Sebastian's sister would wish to attend Mass. And how wonderful that her visit coincided with some kind of international service; she could represent her home country. Elodie glanced around at the gathered faithful – virtually every face was black African. The singing was lusty, resonant harmonies springing up from different places to left and to right of her. The words were projected onto a screen at the back of the sanctuary. *Belota mbutta Nganga, Yandi Yayi ke Kuissa.* She had no idea of the language; the phonics suggested a sub-Saharan dialect.

The procession passed her as it made its way up the aisle, Fr Tellier and another priest slightly behind and flanking the bishop. She had a glimpse of a romanesque nose in profile, a studied solemnity on Bishop Bonouvrie's face. The clergy had evidently assumed she would be a practising Catholic, just because she was Bridie's sister. Certainly no one in the congregation would have cause to think anything different. She could pull it off, no problem: go up there, recite this two-line prayer, point to London on the map if that's what they wanted her to do. But *she* would know. She would know that the words she was speaking were issued into a void. She would know that there wasn't anyone, anything, to hear them. She would know she didn't believe.

Elodie had a sudden image in her mind: Bridie, her dark waves of hair, her bright green eyes, laughing: *I'll get you back in a church one day!* Was it an actual memory, a recollection of a real day? When had it been? Outside somewhere, in a garden perhaps, a pub garden; talking – debating – arguing. Bridie teasing her, telling her that one day she'd go back. Yes, the more she thought about it, the more sure she was that it was a real memory. But had Bridie said that? Had she actually said *she'd* get Elodie back in a church? Or was it simply a prediction of what Elodie herself would do?

The procession had reached the sanctuary. Bishop Bonouvrie was behind the altar, arranging his accoutrements. He drew himself upright and spread his arms wide, and started to intone the opening prayers, the congregation responding to his incantations. Elodie's O-level French, the embers of which had been kept glowing by Haute-Savoie holidays over the years, was unable even to supply her with the gist. Instead, jumbled English phrases, dimly remembered from childhood church-going, jostled in her memory: *The Lord be with you; And also with you. Let us lift up our hearts; We lift them up to the Lord. Let us give thanks to the Lord our God; It is right to give Him thanks and praise.*

҉

She'd had no idea there even was a country called Burkina Faso. Yet another person – this an attractive young African woman in a turquoise dress, her braided hair tied back with a matching band – came to the front, recited a short prayer in her native language, lit a votive candle, and placed a red sticker over the capital city of her country. The twenty-first candle; Elodie was counting, amazed at the cosmopolitan composition of the congregation.

Cote D'Ivoire, Congo Brazzaville, Soa Tome, Cabo Verde, Guinea Equatorial, Guinea Bissau. What brought all these people here? Was it study? Work? This was not a wealthy country, but could it be that it was a better prospect than even more grinding poverty elsewhere? Most of the congregation seemed to be West Africans in their twenties, more men than women. Elodie had a sense of an entire continent in flux. How many millions were chasing how few resources, travelling from country to country in search of a better wage, or any chance of earning at all? What were they doing? Labouring, serving, constructing? This church must be like a life-raft – a measure of familiarity in the Muslim world in which they'd come to live, an arena in which to forge friendships and meet others with a common heritage.

Finally they finished Africa. Fr Tellier called forward nationals from India, the Philippines, France. As each one left the sanctuary – another candle burning, the world map adorned with another red sticker – Elodie prepared to be summoned. Each time it was another country's turn: Canada, Italy, Portugal, Spain. She experienced a moment of piqued defensiveness for her homeland: how peripheral and insignificant Britain evidently was when viewed from here. Were all these other places of more importance? Or perhaps the priest had forgotten her – not an unwelcome thought – the last-minute nature of her arrival meaning that she'd slipped his mind.

But then he announced, 'From the UK.' Elodie got to her feet and joined him on the raised area at the front of the church. She turned towards the congregation. The faces watching her. She realised she had no idea if any of them knew who she was, or why she was here. Had any of them met Bridie? She supposed some of them must have. How did they feel about her? What did they think had happened to her?

She looked down at the slip of paper in her hands. Took a breath.

'So that the whole Church to be "missionary" and its people to see their own history in a worldwide perspective, in order to think and act on a worldwide level. Let us pray ...'

The prayer left her curiously cold. It wasn't the grammatical error. It wasn't even the feeling of being a fraud. It was something about what was written there. She couldn't articulate it, was just aware of a sense of anti-climax, a was-that-it?

She felt Fr Tellier's hand on her elbow. He moved her across to the table, ablaze with candles now, their flames dancing in synchrony whenever a draught caught them. She took the taper and lit a fresh wick, adding one more light to the many. Then placed a sticker over the south-east part of Britain on the map, wondering, disconnectedly, whether anyone watching was as ignorant as to the whereabouts of London as she had been of the geography, or even existence, of several of their own homelands.

Back in her seat, she leaned forward, resting her elbows on her knees, her hands on her forehead. She was self-conscious; aware that she was echoing the posture of someone at prayer, yet at the same time powerless to resist the urge to close her eyes and withdraw. She felt overwhelmingly tired. The prayer she'd recited was bothering her intensely. What were her feelings? She tried to focus in, shut out the sounds from the church around her.

She was aware of anger. She was angry. It was a stupid prayer. She'd handed the slip back to Fr Tellier before lighting the candle, and now she couldn't even remember what it was she'd read out loud. Some blandishments about the church and the world. That was it, surely; that's what was so upsetting. That the prayer she'd been given to read was so utterly unmemorable. The more she thought about it, the more she realised she wanted the words to have actually *meant* something. That she actually wanted them to have been for Bridie, for her missing sister's safe return. And even as she thought this, she was aware of her self-contradiction. It didn't matter what words there had been, how eloquent or powerful or significant they might have sounded, because she didn't believe they would actually have meant anything in any case.

She sat back in the pew, opened her eyes, taking in the colourful wall-hanging behind the altar, a tapestry of a cross composed entirely of interwoven flowers and birds. She was shocked by how she felt, that this unexpected involvement in the service should have stirred such deep emotions. Perhaps it was memory. Even though so little had been in English, the rituals and performances were utterly familiar, awakening long-buried experiences of a world she had rejected and had left behind. And a world her sister had espoused.

The offertory was being taken. A tall lean youth was working the pews on her side of the church, passing a wicker basket along the row in front of her. She felt another wave of indecision. She wasn't wealthy, but she suspected she had more than many of the congregation would ever have in their lifetimes. She was struck by a sudden appreciation of how important this church must be to them, this disparate group of dislocated young people so far from their homes. When the basket came to her she gave in to a sudden impulse and placed a bureau-de-change-crisp two hundred dinar note on top of the slew of coins.

Halfway through the service. The eucharistic prayer still to go – memories of childhood masses, her and Bridie, bored out of their skulls, hoping and praying it would be the shortest of the four versions, and dreading it if it were to be the very longest. What was the really short one – Eucharistic Prayer Two? She was pretty sure Two was the quickest, and One was the most interminable. Hopefully the prayer today would be short. Then just communion to get through. What would the priests expect of her then? Would they even notice that she didn't come forward? Finally, the dismissal. After which would be her chance to meet with the bishop, collect the keys to Bridie's chapel, and enlist his aid for the journey she was about to make.

⚘

'We are, of course, very concerned for your sister, and are holding her in our prayers daily.'

Bishop Bonouvrie's English was impeccable. Elodie confined herself to a nod. She couldn't help thinking he looked a little like pictures she'd seen of General de Gaulle. The chair he was sitting in had impressive carved wooden arms; she was on a stackable visitor's chair, metal legs and moulded plastic seat.

'Have there been any further developments?'

'I saw the British consul yesterday but they have no new

information. They tell me they've exhausted their lines of enquiry. There's been absolutely no word of her for over six weeks. It's like she just disappeared into thin air.'

The bishop shook his head. 'It is most perplexing and most troubling.' He shifted his weight slightly. 'You will be travelling to Beb?'

'That was one of the things I hoped you would help with. Her order in France told me you hold the keys to her church?'

'Her chapel, certainly. We have the masters.'

'Would you allow me to borrow them? I may need to look around. In fact, I *do* need to look around.'

'The police will have conducted a very thorough search.'

'It's not that. I need to see where she lived and worked. It's difficult to explain. It will help me to have some picture of her life out here.'

'You've never visited?'

The bishop's office was adjacent to the sacristy. She could hear Fr Tellier and the other priest talking on the far side of the connecting door. They would be divesting themselves of their ceremonial robes. She remembered the mysterious allure the sacristy had held for her as a girl. A male domain she was barred from entering, where ordinary men and boys were transformed into priests and altar servers. She and Bridie had trespassed once - an occasion when there was some big parish do on, and everyone else was in the church hall. How old would they have been? She wasn't sure, thought maybe it had been during the parish mission fortnight. They'd opened vestment closets, found stores of incense, unguents, altar wine, and unconsecrated hosts. She'd been so nervous and excited by their transgression she'd been gripped by an irresistible urge to pee, so much so she'd almost wet herself, and had to leave abruptly to get to the loo. Bridie had been calmer, unflustered, every inch the older sister.

Girls were allowed to serve on the altars these days. Mummy had told her. At least, they were allowed to in some parishes but not in others, and Mummy's was one that moved with the times. The church was pulling in different directions, trying to figure out its historical differentiation between the sexes as the cultures in which it existed changed and evolved. She couldn't remember whether Mummy had been for or against.

Elodie's gaze had drifted. She looked back at the bishop.

'I'm sorry, what did you say?'

'Sister Sebastian was in Beb so many years. You never visited?'

'No!' Elodie gave a little laugh. 'It's terrible, isn't it? I had my first child not long after she took her vows. It isn't like Beb is somewhere to bring kids.'

'This is something you regret?'

She felt uncomfortable under his gaze. He reminded her of a therapist she'd been to, years ago, when things had first started getting really unpleasant with Adam. He'd always seemed to know exactly the questions to ask, too.

'Life is so busy – work, children, all the stuff of home. The years just ran past.'

Elodie looked at the bishop. He nodded slowly. She had never once contemplated coming out here. This had been Bridie's choice, Bridie's decision. If she had wanted to spend the best part of her life living in a random run-down third-world ghetto of a city then that was up to her, but she couldn't expect Elodie to come traipsing out here after her. Not when there was nothing for the children. Nor, indeed, anything for grown-ups. Besides, she returned home a couple of times a year. If that was enough contact with family for Bridie, then that must be all the contact Bridie wanted to have. Elodie certainly couldn't recall any invitation for her to visit. Far be it for her to have forced herself on Bridie.

She tried to think how to explain any of that to the bishop. It didn't seem possible. Not without sounding callous. Not without him having to know so much, every detail of their lives, none of which was his or anyone's business.

'I suppose, yes, that is something I regret.'

'Well, I cannot let you have the master keys.'

'No, but I—'

'But I will give you a letter of authority to present to the person who holds a set for me in Beb. Professor Yacine is at the university. You can gain access to the chapel with my blessing.' He smiled. 'Will you be staying in Beb long?'

'I don't think so, probably just a couple of days. It depends on what I find when I get there.'

'Your husband, your family, they are with you?'

'No,' she shook her head. 'I'm on my own.'

The voices from the sacristy faded. Bishop Bonouvrie had come straight to his office after mass, had yet to remove his vestments. Because he hadn't wanted to keep her waiting? Because he'd wanted to remain dressed in his priestly garb?

'Another thing you could perhaps help with.' She stopped herself, gauging his expression. 'Do you have contact details for any of her parishioners there? I would very much like to talk to people she knew and worked with.'

The bishop tugged the sleeve of his cassock, straightening it where it had ridden up over his wrist. 'You're aware that Sister Sebastian had no congregation?'

'I'm sorry?'

'There was no congregation in Beb. It's been years since there were any Catholics there at all, and while Sister Sebastian did run ecumenical services for a while, I believe, the last Christians of any denomination departed Beb some four years ago.'

'I had no idea.' Elodie stared at him, trying to think if she knew this – whether it was something she'd been told at some point but had failed to take in and remember. She was sure not. If she'd known then her mother would have known too, and from the way Mummy talked she was under the impression that Bridie was the sole minister for a large and disparate group of ex-patriot Christians. 'So what did she actually *do?*'

The bishop raised his eyebrows. 'The building belongs to the diocese, but Sister Sebastian herself was under the authority of her order.'

'I'm sorry, I don't understand.'

'It was helpful to the diocese to have someone living in the chapel, taking care of the building and so on. As to Sister Sebastian's day to day ministry, that was a matter for her director in the Sisters of the Divine Mercy.'

'Is there no one in Beb you could put me in touch with?'

The bishop shook his head. 'Tahar Yacine may be able to help you. He is a good friend to us. He knows your sister well.'

'Did you know her?'

'Of course.' He smiled. 'She came here every month or two. We supplied her with consecrated hosts. And, naturally, she needed her confession heard, also.'

Elodie felt her cheeks flush. Bless me Father, for I have sinned; it is more than twenty years since my last confession.

Bridie: what had she told this man, under the confidence of the sacrament? What secrets had she spilled? What might Bridie have said about her in the process? She looked down at her hands, lying clasped in her lap. Was that the secret of his perspicaciousness, that he already knew everything there was to know? Yet if Bridie had talked at any length about her relationship with her sister, then surely the bishop and Fr Tellier would not have invited Elodie to participate in the mass as they had done.

'You must have seen her quite recently,' she said, looking up to meet his gaze.

'Not for several months.'

'But during the time her order said she was exhibiting signs of a mental breakdown?'

The bishop regarded her carefully, as if weighing something in his mind.

'She made a remarkable journey,' he said, at length. 'A remarkable spiritual journey, that is.'

There was kindness there, in his ageing eyes. Compassion. No condemnation, if indeed he was privy to the truth.

'I'm not sure I know what you mean.'

'When she first came to this country, her experience of God was very punitive. She could never be good enough for Him, no matter how much penance she did, how many good works she tried to cram into her days, how rigidly she adhered to the hours.' He laughed, a gentle, baritone chuckle. 'Gradually, so very slowly, she found it in herself to forgive others. And at precisely the same time she began to find that God could forgive her, too.'

She felt uncomfortable, acutely self-conscious. But she couldn't do what she felt like doing and end the conversation, take her leave, flee this room that now felt stuffy and claustrophobic and awful.

'You're saying you didn't see any signs of a breakdown?'

The bishop shook his head. 'No.'

'Why would her order have said that, then?'

He held his hands up, palms out. 'There are so many different ways we experience God.' His hands fell back on the arms of his chair. 'There are bound, sometimes, to be – misunderstandings.'

☙

Several groups of young West Africans were hanging around in the church when she emerged from the bishop's office. They were formed into groups, chatting, laughing, socialising animatedly. Elodie walked past the statue of St Francis of Assisi, the church's patron, his arms spread, smiling benevolently if stonily from his niche as he surveyed the current flock. She looked for Fr Tellier, thinking that she should say goodbye, but there was no sign of him.

She'd not gone ten yards from the church grounds when an African youth, around twenty she guessed, fell into step beside her.

'Hello, Miss, please, Miss, I've seen you in church.'

'Yes, I came to meet the bishop.' She smiled and came to a stop, unsure whether he might know who she was. 'I'm the sister of Sister Sebastian, the nun who lives out at Beb.'

'I live long long away, two hours it take to walk here, two hours to walk home.' His teeth were bright white, gappy, his hair short and tight curled. He had on a flowery shirt. His neck was thin, scrawny. 'You can spare twenty dinar for a taxi?'

She felt a flash of disbelief; this was the last place she'd have expected to be hit on for money. She started to walk.

'I'm sorry. I put everything I had in the collection.'

He kept level with her. 'Such a long walk in this hot heat, Miss. Just twenty dinar, please, Miss.'

'I'm sorry, I said, I have no more money.' She tightened her grip on her bag strap and quickened her pace, looking over her shoulder to assess the traffic stream. Then again, she wasn't sure about crossing the boulevard and returning to the deserted side streets, not now this man was pestering her.

'Every week I am making this half-a-day walk for my Sunday obligation. Won't you bless me with a taxi fare this one day?'

Faster.

'Please, Miss, ten dinar it will take me a lot of the way to my home.'

He was matching her strides, skipping sidewards so as to look at her directly.

'Look!' She stopped abruptly and turned to meet his eyes. 'I've told you, I don't have any more money. I'm sorry you've got a long walk. I'm sorry it's so hot. I'd love to help you if I could, but I can't. Now, please leave me alone.'

'I can come to your hotel. Where are you staying? You can get money there.'

She made to move off again but stepped abruptly into the road, taking advantage of a narrow gap between the oncoming cars. A horn blast but it seemed to work: by the time she made it to the other side of the wide avenue, the youth was nowhere to be seen. She stayed on the far pavement for a while, trying in vain to see where he'd gone while her back had been turned, feeling she would be better for definitely knowing his whereabouts before retracing her route back to her hotel. She contemplated returning to the church on the pretence of seeking out Fr Tellier, but then decided that was the most likely place he'd gone to, so rapidly had he disappeared. Eventually, with no further sign of him, she made her way back through the maze of residential roads to the sanctuary of her hotel.

There was a note at reception along with her key. An elegant fountain pen inscription to *Dr Elodie O'Shea, By Hand*. She dropped her bag on the floor of her room, levered her feet from her sandals, and flopped on her bed, thumb tearing the envelope. There was a plain cream postcard inside.

Dear Elodie,

It was a pleasure to meet you yesterday. Would you allow me to stand you lunch tomorrow? I had intended to invite you here, but I thought it might be interesting for you to sample one of the local restaurants. I'll pick you up with my driver at 12.30pm unless I hear to the contrary. I hope that fits with your plans. In particular, it would be good to talk prior to your departure to Beb.

Kind regards, Anne (Armstrong)

That was kind. Though it was also transparent. The fact that Anne had mentioned Beb meant her husband must have briefed her. She wasn't sure she could tolerate with politeness any further attempt to dissuade her from going. She let the card fall on the bed beside her. For a moment she savoured the sensation of safely being back in her hotel box, away from confusing side streets and inaccurate maps and priests and bishops and young chancers trying to tap her for cash.

Perhaps she'd over-reacted. Was he just enterprising, a spur of the moment opportunist? The more she thought about it, the more she thought he might well have been the man who'd passed the collection basket on her side of the church. He would have seen the sizeable contribution she'd put in. What could twenty dinar possibly mean to her? Back home it might just buy her a latte and a pastry in a fashionable café. She doubted he'd use it on a taxi. What use might he have put it to? Who might he have returned to, what family, friends: grinning, showing them the huge sum the foreign lady had blessed him with at church that morning. Had she been downright uncharitable, refusing him point-blank? Then again, the folly of opening her bag and extracting her wallet out there in the street right in front of him.

She couldn't think. She couldn't think about any of that. She needed some time; time and some headspace. Uppermost in her mind was a craving to replay her conversation with the bishop, to go over it again in detail. He'd chosen his words so carefully, she could see that now. She had to get her head round the fact that Bridie's life here was not what she'd been led to believe. And she needed to try to work out whose responsibility that was.

She found the mass sheet in her bag when tucking Anne's card away. She must have shoved it there when Fr Tellier came to collect her straight after the service, though she had no recollection of doing so. Mission Sunday. Elodie sat herself on her bed. The sheet had the day's readings, readings Elodie had failed to listen to a word of in church, so disorientated was she by being back at mass again.

A *reading from the prophet Isaiah*

The Lord has been pleased to crush him with

suffering. If he offers his life in atonement, he shall see his heirs, he shall have a long life and through him what the Lord wishes will be done. His soul's anguish over he shall see the light and be content. By his sufferings shall my servant justify many, taking their faults on himself.

This is the word of the Lord.

A reading from the letter to the Hebrews

Since in Jesus, the Son of God, we have the supreme high priest who has gone through to the highest heaven, we must never let go of the faith that we have professed. For it is not as if we had a high priest who was incapable of feeling our weaknesses with us: but we have one who has been tempted in every way that we are, though he is without sin. Let us be confident, then, in approaching the throne of grace, that we shall have mercy from him and find grace when we are in need of help.

This is the word of the Lord.

Elodie put the mass sheet on the bed next to her, closed her eyes and pressed her fingers against her eyelids. It was so long since she'd allowed these voices into her mind. These disembodied prophets and apostles, words echoing down the generations, at once clear and opaque, open to interpretation and extrapolation, the phrases, sentences, verses simultaneously significant and random. This was Bridie's world. Mummy's. This was not the world she inhabited. Her world was girded by knowledge and laws, facts and certainties. Sure, the knowledge was provisional, open to revision. But it worked. It allowed prediction, explanation. It allowed scientists wherever they were in the world to understand one another – these were laws that were unaffected by culture, tradition, gender, age or race. Hers was a world of pattern and form. Of truth and objectivity. A world where even chaos was understood.

She lay back on the bed again, stared at the ceiling, the motionless ceiling fan. Only now did she register that the air conditioning was finally on. A certain time. The room was comfortable, cool at last. She could sleep for a while, take an afternoon nap, catch up on the broken night, switch off her mind and stop thinking – about what Bridie had done; about what she had done. The idea seemed overwhelmingly appealing. What had she become? Once upon a time she'd have relished this opportunity, a chance to get out there and experience things. How often over the years of motherhood, juggling career and kids, struggling with Adam's increasingly erratic moods and the slow-motion destruction of their relationship; how often had she fantasised about escaping from it all, if only briefly? How often had she dreamed of recapturing the delicious freedom of going where she willed, beholden to no one, her every day filled with novelty and stimulation? Adversity, too, yes. But even adversity was invigorating. Made her feel alive.

Alive.

The Lord has been pleased to crush him with suffering.

Bridie. Someone you love disappears. The laws and facts of your world are rent asunder, the foundations – the solid, unshakable pillars on which your life stands – are, in an instant, no longer there. Patterns are distorted, forms are destroyed. Someone who is integral to your story, indelibly in your memory, who frustrates you and comforts you and understands you and baffles you and infuriates you and rejects you and loves you. Someone you love vanishes from your world as

61

swiftly and implacably and irretrievably as the blip on a radar screen when a plane plummets from the sky. You have to know what happened. You have to know why.

Six

THE COACH STOPPED at three in the morning, pulling off the A1 somewhere near Doncaster. She woke as its engine silenced; disembarked along with the rest of them, neck aching from sleeping upright, her nausea – travel, fatigue – aggravated by the strident neon inside the services. Hollow-eyed travellers traipsed the concourse. Off to one side, coins chundered into the winnings tray of a slot machine. Too-loud muzak piped into the public spaces. She went to the loo, doused her face with cold water, noticed with dismay that her skin was already registering its protest, several spots livid on her chin and cheeks. All the shops were closed with the exception of a Wimpy. The thought of burger and chips made her want to heave.

What were they called then? Comfort breaks are a modern invention. In the late Eighties, if they'd called them anything it would have been a pit stop. Whatever it was, it was soon over, and she hauled herself back up the steps of the National Express coach. Still another four hours trapped inside, the vibration of the wheels and the engine permeating everything, jangling the fabric of her being. She vowed next time she would take the train, during the day; would save enough from her leaflet delivery job if her father still wouldn't play ball.

True to her word, Bridie was there at the bus station on St Andrew Square in the metallic light of dawn.

'Hey, Sis!'

They hugged each other, Elodie's shoulder bag swinging round and thudding against Bridie's side as they embraced.

'Welcome to Edinburgh!'

Bridie led her through a succession of streets, carrying her holdall for her: past Waverley Station, across a bridge over the multiple tracks bringing trains from all parts of the country. Elodie was struck by the greyness of the stone, every building sombre and forbidding. It was her first time in Scotland, her first time further north than Warwickshire, in fact. The buses were green and cream, the snatches of conversation from passers-by heavily accented, but they passed a Woolworths, and a Fine Fare, and the taxis were the same black cabs as in London. It was simultaneously strange and familiar. She marvelled at how at home Bridie was, swinging confidently through this city she had known only a couple of months. How different she seemed in this new context, away from the suburban semis, the sprawling commuterland of Bexleyheath. How grown up she looked, all of a sudden.

'So how is it?' she asked.

'Edinburgh? Fantastic. Honestly, El, I can't tell you. There's so much going on. I've got a great bunch of friends. Don't think I've been to bed this side of midnight since I arrived.'

Even despite lugging Elodie's bag, Bridie's step seemed jaunty. Elodie was always half a pace behind, had to make her legs move just that bit faster than felt natural in order to keep up.

'How about the course? How's that going?'

'Guess how many lectures I've got each week?' Bridie was laughing, mischievous. 'Six hours! I can't tell you, the stress of it!'

She was dressed differently, too. Zig-zag print leggings,

an outsize jumper. Only the black lace-up pixie boots were things Elodie recognised. The morning air was chilly but Bridie hadn't worn a coat. Elodie felt staid in her jeans and sweatshirt and quilted jacket.

Bridie's hall was an imposing building off Cowgate. They had to climb several flights of dank stone steps to get to her corridor, the crisp scrapes of their shoes echoing in the stairwell.

'The others won't be up yet,' Bridie told her, unlocking the door to her room. She showed her inside. 'Do you want anything? I'm starving.'

Bridie went to the communal kitchen, while Elodie took stock of her student home. There was a single bed, a long desk built-in along one wall, a sink in one corner with several mugs perched on its ceramic rim. Bridie's stereo and a spider plant sat on top of her trunk. There were the posters of Queen and Alison Moyet that Bridie had brought from her room at home; and a new monochrome print of a rumpled double bed in a light-filled room titled *Amagansett*. Elodie sat at Bridie's desk. Beside a stack of half-a-dozen books was a half-penned essay on something called *Notes from Underground*. And an empty Flake wrapper. The window looked out onto the side of another building, a metal fire escape bolted-on to meet some latter-day safety regulations. Elodie liked it, this study-bedroom; a little cocoon. She felt a pang of jealousy. Bridie had made the break, had left the rules and rigours of their home and school behind her, was out on her own in this shared six-bed flat with its freedom to stay up late and get out of bed whenever she liked. Six hours of lectures a week. Two whole years until Elodie could do likewise. Two whole years that stretched ahead of her like an uncrossable desert.

'There you go.' Bridie returned with tea, and a plate stacked with rounds of buttered toast. She perched herself cross-legged on the bed, gathered her curly brown hair into a loose bun and secured it with a scrunchie. She took a slice of toast.

'So, how's school?'

Elodie rolled her eyes. 'OK. It's a lot of work. I've got homework coming out my ears.'

'Well, you've only got yourself to blame. Richard – he's down the far end – he's doing chemistry. Really heavy time-table. And Vicky's a medic. We never see her.'

'What do you do all day, then, if you don't have anything to go in for?'

'Oh, you know.' Bridie cast a glance round the room. 'I've joined half a dozen societies, and there's always people to hang out with.' She grinned. 'Actually, there's a fair bit of reading, and a load of essays to do. But I'm loving it. Honestly, El, it's nothing like English at school – that was pretty towering, how dull and deathly Miss Bennett and the others managed to make it. I feel like my eyes are finally open here – the worlds and minds you can enter, just by opening the covers of a book.'

Elodie drank some tea. It tasted like hot water.

'And how's home?' Bridie asked.

'Oh. Dad's pretty bad.'

Bridie's eyes narrowed a little.

'Mummy bought my ticket out of the housekeeping.'

Bridie took a bite of toast. Spoke with her mouth full. 'He'll get over it.'

The stink Bridie had unleashed, coming to Edinburgh. Elodie had listened from the late-evening upstairs landing, their mother's calm comments barely audible from behind the closed lounge door, his raised voice, escalating to shouting, penetrating the wood as though nothing were there. There were plenty of places nearer, if she was determined to fritter away three years of her life reading storybooks. And he was the one who was expected to bankroll it. She wouldn't qualify for much of a grant: they were too well-off, or so the government said, *in its infinite wisdom.* She could bloody well live at home, study her poncey degree in London, if she cared one jot about the impact she was having on the rest of them. You'd think he'd have been proud, the first person in the family to go to university.

'He can't stand us being smarter than him,' Bridie said.

It was true. Just the other week he'd been in a complete stew about the neighbour's extension. Elodie had used some O-level trig to prove that the nearest corner came to exactly the prescribed distance from their fence. His threats to report the neighbours to the council would come to nought. All his rage, his frustration, his fury, had come out at her. As though it were her fault.

'How's Mummy?' Bridie asked.

'She's all right. Not great.'

They sat in silence for a few moments. The tea mug was warm in Elodie's palms. Steam rose in tendrils, evaporating into nothingness before it got anywhere near her face.

'El, do you mind if we leave it? I'm sorry you're stuck with it, but it doesn't belong here. You can come as often as you like, any time you need a break – you can come and kip on my floor and switch to a school up here if you want. But the rule is: you leave him down there where he belongs.'

'What about Mummy?'

Bridie sighed. 'Mummy can come and stay, too, if she wants. But she won't. She's a grown woman, El. She can make her own choices.'

They went out later, Bridie showing her Princes Street, the Royal Mile. They had lunch in the canteen in the students' union. She took her to the English faculty, showed her inside one of the empty lecture theatres – rows of tiered wooden seating sweeping in semicircles; desk and lectern and white-board way down at the front, at the foot of a dizzying rake. Elodie was tantalised, the thought that this kind of world could soon be hers: the vending machines, the groups of young students larking and chatting, the noticeboards festooned with photocopied fliers for debates and parties and students' nights in various clubs.

Bridie's flatmates were around by the time they returned. Competing music came from several rooms, clashing in a ca-cophony in the corridor. Some kind of cooking was going on, a girl and a boy – Lizzie and Tim – filling the kitchen with the smell of frying onions and sizzling mince. There was no plan that she could discern; people just drifted and congregated in one of the other rooms, across the hall from Bridie's, sitting on the bed, on chairs, on the floor. Someone donated a beanbag to her. Elodie couldn't keep track of the names, who was who, who lived here and who came from elsewhere. It didn't seem to matter. She got chatting to one or two of them but she felt gauche, pathetic – a schoolgirl with nothing much to say to these sophisticates. Gradually she accepted her role of onlooker, of aspirant novice; listened to the tales of late-night drinking, of sporting endeavour, of cracking jokes that had been played on people whom everyone knew except her.

Tea was ferried in at intervals. As afternoon gave way to evening steaming pots of rice and chilli were deposited in the centre of the room, and doled out on plates by Lizzie. Tim handed round cans of beer to any who wanted. His hair was dark, short, tousled. He had green eyes and a cleft in the centre of his chin. He gave Elodie a can. She thanked him, got a smile in return, and forced herself to drink it even though the taste was bitter and unappealing.

The chilli was hot; her eyes smarted and her nose ran. She had to slip out at one point to find herself some tissues. Bridie was chatting and laughing with some of the others. The Eurythmics were playing. Elodie started to feel a pleasant buzz from the alcohol. Tim was sitting next to Lizzie; she wondered if they were an item. He had a rugby shirt on, wearing it as a casual top. Another girl arrived, was greeted warmly by everyone, turned out to be Vicky, the one who was studying to be a doctor: she'd been in the library all day, revising for her first set of exams. The CD was changed: The Waterboys. Vicky sat on the floor by Tim, her legs curled to one side, a plate of food balanced on her thigh. She was petite, with thick blonde wavy hair and vivid blue eyes. At one point, Elodie saw Tim rest a hand on her shoulder.

Again, without signal, it was time to go out. They walked as a straggling band through the dark Edinburgh streets. Bridie was at her side, trying to fill her in on who was who. Elodie wanted to ask about Tim, but dared not, in case her sister got any inkling that she was feeling in any way attracted to him. First stop was a noisy bar; Bridie ordered herself a vodka and orange, and told her it was OK for her to have one, too, she easily looked eighteen. Tim came to join them. It turned out he was reading English as well, though studying different modules to Bridie; he was into nineteenth century classics, whereas Bridie was heavily into something called modernism. What was Elodie going to do, when she came to go to university? Biochemistry, she told him, either on its own or as part of a life sciences degree. Great, he said. *Elodie's the scientist in the family, aren't you, El?* Tim and Bridie laughed. Elodie laughed, too, though she wasn't sure why.

They went on to a club, entered by a bouncer-protected door, then straight down a narrow stairwell, emerging into a bar area with the dance floor beyond. The pulsing house music, nothing she recognised, filled her instantly with the desire to dance. And dance they did, Bridie and Tim and Lizzie and Vicky and Richard and most of the rest of their friends. Elodie watched at first – the way they played, the semi-serious posturing, but the knowingness that the moves they were making actually looked good – then cautiously she moved to join them. Sweet sixteen. The sound filled her head, the flashing lights starred her eyes. The group opened to allow her in. The absolute thrill of this life. The sickening thought that it was not hers. People were being kind to her because she was Bridie's sister, but when she left at the end of the weekend, none of them would remember her, none of them would give her more than a passing thought. And a guy like Tim – his dancing understated and achingly cool – would not be in the slightest bit interested in her.

⁂

She woke just after nine, her head muzzy. Light was filtering through the thin curtains. The floor felt hard against her hip and shoulder despite the fold-out zed-bed's foam. She rolled on to her back, easing the pressure points. Bridie stirred beneath the heaped-up continental quilt on her bed. Elodie's insides felt utterly flat: the dislocation, the lack of belonging.

Bridie sat up, looking to see if she was awake. She let out a little groan.

'Morning, El.'

'Morning.'

'Sleep well?'

'All right, yes.'

Bridie swung out of bed.

'I'll fix us some toast.'

She padded off to the kitchen in her t-shirt and knickers, leaving Elodie alone. Back in Bexleyheath, their parents would be washed and dressed, breakfast done, dishes cleared away, getting themselves ready to go to nine-thirty mass. Mummy would be smart in a matching skirt and jacket; their father in suit and tie. Everything would be neat. Everything would be respectable. Elodie wondered what a Sunday morning here would look like, in this amazing new life.

The Catholic chaplaincy was pragmatic, it transpired, scheduling its service for ten-thirty in recognition of the Saturday night before. They got there with a couple of minutes to spare. Up at the front, three jeans-clad lads, guitars slung low on long straps, and a drummer with a full kit, were playing an instrumental. It wasn't a church as such; just a seminar room in the earth sciences building taken over for the purposes. An embroidered altar cloth was draped over a couple of trestle tables arranged side by side at the front, crucifix and chalices laid out in readiness. Chairs were arranged in rows, the weekday desks shoved back against the walls. Bridie showed Elodie to a group of vacant seats near the back. She sat herself so there was a space next to her on the aisle side.

'You'll like Fr Eddie,' Bridie whispered to her. 'He's the business.'

The band finished their piece, and struck up a modern song Elodie had never heard before, *Shine Jesus Shine*, a lanky guy in a Roxy Music t-shirt leading the singing through a mic on a stand, the drummer and bassist whipping it along with an uptempo backbone. The priest – Fr Eddie, she presumed; in his thirties, with close-cropped hair and wire-framed glasses – came through the door and processed briskly to the front, standing behind his makeshift altar and beaming at the assembled students. Elodie was surprised, looking around; there must have been more than fifty in the room. Here and there people started clapping in time to the music; others held their hands aloft. She felt a rising embarrassment – there were faces smiling, voices raised loud to meet the volume of the amplifiers. People looked happy, enthused, joyful even.

She'd never heard anything like it in a church before. It was more like a gig than a service. Bridie, to her relief, was neither clapping nor waving her arms, but she was singing lustily, and gave Elodie a big grin when she saw her looking. She broke off to speak in her ear.

'Great, isn't it?'

Elodie nodded, though she felt acutely uncomfortable, these voices and hands raised in uninhibited – what? – *emotion* for a figure she had only ever thought of as distant, dry, dead; hanging on a cross. Already she felt a slight panic, trying to think what she would say when the National Express delivered her to Victoria, and Mummy would be waiting to meet her, eager for news of Bridie, and bound to be wanting to know what her new church was like.

Just then, at the height of the hymn, a late-comer appeared on Bridie's left, easing himself into the space she'd left free. Dishevelled hair. Stubbly face. A sheepish grin. A mouthed

'Sorry' to Bridie, and a friendly nod to her gawky, shy sister from back home. Tim, it seemed – gorgeous, rugged, utterly unattainable Tim – on top of everything else, Tim turned out to be a Catholic, too.

Seven

Dear Mummy

Of course I remember Winnie. I'm sorry to hear she's so unwell – do please send her my best.

I do appreciate what you're saying about the kids. They're quite used to my being away, so I don't think that's the issue. Maddie is at a difficult age, and Adam and she rub each other up the wrong way a lot of the time. I realise it's a difficult situation for you but I really need your help. I know you'll be able to find a way through.

I met with the bishop yesterday, and he was extremely helpful. He's had frequent contact with Bridie over the years, and he cast considerable doubt on what the order have been saying about her mental health. He's given me an introduction to an academic in Beb who also knows her, so I'll be able to learn more on the spot. Talking to the bishop, Bridie was evidently highly valued, though he had some interesting things to say about her work out here, which rather surprised me. What did you understand her role to be in recent years?

The consul's wife is taking me to lunch later today. All is well here, but the prospect of some friendly company from back home is welcome. I'm hopefully setting off for Beb tomorrow.

With love, E

Dear Maddie

The pool is fantastic, not the longest in the world but I've been doing a load of lengths which cools me down and confirms how unfit I am. I'm so impressed at the way you keep at your training. I'm absolutely certain that I wouldn't have done the same at your age. I know you're disappointed with your recent results but, really, darling, you're your own hardest taskmistress! I think you're doing fantastically and I just hope that, somewhere inside, you can feel an inkling of the pride in yourself that I have for you.

Speaking of training, I gather there are some issues with getting you to the early starts. Please try to be flexible, darling, it won't be for long. Nana's doing her best but it's not just you she's got to think about. Even as I write this I know it won't go down well, but please try to help as much as you possibly can at the moment.

Lots of love, Mummy xx

Dear Ollie

Thanks for your email, darling, it did my heart good to read it. Did you type it all yourself?! Mrs Jennings is absolutely right and I hope things settle down with Gavin very soon.

The outfit sounds marvellous! Have a lovely time, and don't make yourself sick by eating too much chocolate.

I'm getting along famously. Not much to report – just boring grown-ups stuff in the main. There's a cat at the hotel who sits on a chair by the reception desk and scrutinises everyone's comings and goings. Generally you don't see many pets out here – I'm not sure I've seen a single person walking a dog since I arrived. Do give Pogo a stroke from me.

I know mornings aren't your favourite time, but please help Nana as much as you possibly can by getting yourself ready without being asked.

Lots of love, Mummy xx

Dear Henning

I really hope you pick this up before you fly. I'm sorry but I'm not going to be at the airport after all – the consul's wife has invited me for lunch and I think I'd better go. She's definitely worth cultivating. She is an old friend of the vice-chancellor at UCL, so we have a connection.

Anyway, it's very straightforward. I'm at Hotel Splendid ('A Splendid Hotel'!), room 31. Don't let the taxi take you anywhere else!

Much love, El xxx

Adam – look, please, I've had Mummy tearing her hair out, and I simply don't need any more grief. Can you not manage one day without there being problems? It's bad enough being out here without having to worry about what's happening at home. I've lost count of the number of times I've covered for you, and all I'm asking for is a bit in return. I know you're upset with me, we can talk about it when I get back, but for the moment would you PLEASE stop all the passive-aggressive stuff. If you can't bring yourself to help then could you at least try to keep out of Mummy's way and let her get on with things as best as she can.

Elodie

Anne put her sunglasses on, tucking the empty case between the condiment pots and a small vase in the centre of the table, its single marigold vivid orange in the sun.

'Beautiful, isn't it?'

The terrace afforded views over the whole city. In the foreground, the ville nouvelle, its ordered grid-work of streets evident from this vantage. There was nothing above a few stories high; none of the skyscrapers and towers of a twenty-first century capital. The tallest structures were the minarets of the numerous mosques scattered throughout the conurbation. At a certain point the tone shifted, the grey-white of concrete giving way to the earthier ochres of the medieval town, where ancient building was jumbled on ancient building in an amorphous mass that sprawled down the slope towards the floor of the valley below. The terracottas and greens of the moorish roof tiles shimmered in the heat haze. The noise of horn blasts and traffic was far distant. Elodie heard birdsong from behind her, and only now realised its absence from the city from which they'd come.

'It's like looking down on history, I always think.' Anne spoke without taking her eyes from the view. 'In its heyday this place was a great confluence of cultures. Land routes from Europe, sub-Saharan Africa, and the Middle East converged here. It used to be incredibly cosmopolitan, peoples from all over coming to settle, either for economic opportunity, or for security. Over there, on the far side, that's the Jewish quarter. They came in their thousands from Andalusia, back in the Middle Ages.'

Elodie followed the direction Anne was pointing in. The

houses on the other side of the valley were taller, more regularly arranged, rendered in a sandier material.

'I didn't realise there was a Jewish population here.'

'There isn't, not now. But they were at the heart of the commercial life of the city for centuries. All the synagogues are long gone, but you can still visit the Jewish cemetery.'

A waiter arrived at their table carrying a sunshade. He handed over menus, and returned with a carafe of water and some bread. Anne said something to him in Arabic, to which he nodded assent. Elodie noticed that he kept his gaze averted, made little eye contact. Anne tore the demi-baguette in two, leaving half in the wooden bowl for Elodie.

'You were posted here earlier in the year, you said.'

'Yes.' Anne looked amused. 'Helsinki before that. There's nothing if not variety.'

'Do you like it?'

'Like might be putting it a little strongly.' Anne poured water into each of their glasses. 'It is interesting, though. Quite a change.'

She passed Elodie a menu. 'I don't know what you fancy, but their soup's rather nice.'

Elodie spent a few moments contemplating the French translations, piecing together descriptions of the dishes from her rusty vocabulary.

'Will you have something, Jack?'

Anne's driver had seated himself at a table a discreet distance from theirs. *I can't leave him in the car, he'd melt.* He was shaded by a palm, but even so it was far too hot for him to be comfortable keeping his jacket on.

'Just a coffee, ma'am, please.'

Elodie didn't feel incredibly hungry anyway. 'Soup sounds

lovely.' She handed the menu back to Anne. 'Has your husband always been a diplomat?'

'Peter? No. He was in the army for twenty-odd years.'

'I thought so,' Elodie said.

Anne laughed. 'Is it that obvious?'

'No, just that my husband comes from a military family. You get to know the signs.'

'Is he in the army? Your husband?'

Elodie shook her head. 'No, much to his father's dismay. Interrupted a seven-generations tradition by being such a pathetic weasel.' She glanced directly at Anne. 'That's what his father would say.'

'We know too many people like that. It's not the life for everyone by any means, if you're not suited to it temperamentally. What does your husband do?'

'He was a lawyer, but he's in the civil service now. Defence procurement. It's the closest he could get, but it never satisfied his father.'

Elodie took her half of the roll, prised off a corner, held it poised to eat. 'Do you work as well?'

'Not these days, not unless you count the business of being a consul's wife, which is more than enough to keep me going. I used to head an educational charity. I paint a bit in my spare time.'

'Do you have children?'

'Two. Boys. They're boarding in Somerset. How about you?'

'The same. Well, same number, girl and a boy. They're not boarding, though.'

Anne nodded. 'Mine love it. Just as well, really. Children need a settled upbringing, don't you think? They wouldn't

79

have a friend in the world if they'd been traipsing round with us the whole time.'

Elodie wondered how it worked, what their relationships were like. What effect these prolonged separations had on the children; and on their parents. Anne seemed a warm enough person; the sort of person who would deal with life's ups and downs without drama.

'They come out to you in the holidays, I imagine?'

'Used to. They still do for a couple of weeks each summer, but they've got lives of their own now in England. Peter's sister's their guardian, she lives in a village just outside Yeovil, so they base themselves there. I gather it's become a congregating point among their friends. I don't think she realised quite what she was letting herself in for.'

The waiter returned and Anne placed the order. Elodie wondered whether she'd always spoken Arabic, or whether it was something she'd picked up since arriving. Whether she'd been equally adept at Finnish before.

'And you're at UCL?' Anne sat back in her chair, glass of water in hand.

'Yes, biological sciences division. I'm a molecular biologist by training.'

'What's your area?'

'The group specialises in insect metamorphosis.' Elodie smiled. 'It's incredibly arcane. We're trying to find a way to interrupt the life cycle of the *Anopheles* mosquito, to stop it ever getting past the pupal stage. If we can do that, we'll potentially have a biological control for malaria.'

'How fantastic. Hats off to you. That must be very exciting.'

Elodie thought of the genome sequencing protocols, the

endless virus vector inoculations, the failure again and again to achieve gene insertion and expression, the adult mosquitos emerging time and again, leaving redundant pupae behind them, into the warm-lit incubation tanks in the fifth floor animal house.

'By and large it's mind-numbing repetition.'

Anne laughed. 'I know what you mean. You could say the same for the life of the British consul's wife.'

Her face stilled. Elodie took a sip of water. The coolness. The condensation on the side of the glass.

'But you find it interesting?'

'Well, bits of it are, I suppose. But the number of dreary functions. Trade delegations; junior ministers from this and that department; everyone wanting to know what HMG might be prepared to do for them. *This* is what I most like about the role—' she waved a hand in Elodie's direction - 'helping people, Brits who've got into a fix of some sort. Not that I'm anything other than appalled at your situation.' She looked momentarily contrite. 'I'm sorry. That came out awfully.'

'No, please,' Elodie said. 'You've been very kind. I knew what you meant.'

Their soups arrived. More of a casserole, Elodie decided, assessing the chunks of chicken, carrot, courgette, onion floating in it. She followed Anne's example, squeezing the slice of lemon perched on the side of the dish into the broth, rinsing her fingers in the little bowl placed in the centre of the table. She took a spoonful of soup. A complicated flavour, not spicy as such, but a fusion of subtle tastes - cumin, tarragon, other notes she couldn't distinguish. She hadn't been entirely convinced about soup in such heat; had merely acquiesced to Anne's recommendation. But this, she could see, was just right.

'When do you travel to Beb?'

Elodie hesitated. 'Potentially as early as tomorrow. I've got a friend arriving this afternoon. It depends on how soon we can get organised.' She held Anne's gaze. 'Your husband wasn't in favour.'

Anne spoke a notch more softly. 'Peter – well, Peter and I – we're very mindful of your situation. The fact is, there are hats and hats, and when he's wearing his consul's hat, he is rather constrained. London is very twitchy, what with everything that's been going on in Iraq and Syria.'

Elodie nodded. 'Of course, I—'

'But we do want to be of whatever help we can.' Anne glanced at Jack, who appeared absorbed in the views over the city. 'Peter says if you do travel to Beb then you should definitely go by public transport – which basically means bus. You'll be safer in a crowd than in an anonymous *grande taxi*. This is the hotel the consulate has used in the past,' she handed Elodie a folded sheaf of paper. 'They've been reliable before, and the consulate has been a good source of business. The proprietor is a chap called Azoulay. Peter knows him through the trade association. If I can get hold of him by phone, I'll put a word in for you.'

'Thank you.' Elodie unfolded the sheaf. The address of the hotel was typed on the first piece of paper. There were several blank sheets behind, each bearing the letterhead of the British Consulate.

'Peter can't give any official backing, of course, but if you encounter any hitches then jotting something down on one of those ought to help smooth your way.'

Elodie looked at her. Her frank blue eyes. 'I don't really know what to say.'

'We'd have to say we'd no idea how you came by them, if ever we were asked.'

'I understand.'

'This is a moderate country,' Anne said. 'Good ties with the UK; very good ties still with France. It's the Berber influence, I think. And the people are generally hospitable to a fault.'

'That's terrifically reassuring,' Elodie said. 'I don't know. It makes Bridie's disappearance seem something more everyday. Something more mundane. I met with her bishop yesterday, and he cast doubt on what her order said about her having had a breakdown and gone walkabout. Having said that, it was quite some time since he last saw her. I don't know what to think anymore. She might be dead – I know that – I know the chances of that go up with every week.'

Anne had finished her soup. She laid her spoon to rest carefully. 'Yes, of course. But, in fact, we had several instances of personal crises with Britons in Finland.' She smiled wryly. 'Too much vodka and not enough daylight. I wouldn't give up hope. Quite a number do turn up, eventually.'

Elodie sat back in her chair. Jack, the driver, was sipping his coffee. Not reading. Not using a device. Not doing anything. People could lose their minds for any number of reasons – loneliness, despair, grief, abuse, drugs, stress, genes. That was the great hope. That in some way Bridie's life had become utterly pointless. That she'd perhaps lost all faith, but the cost of admitting it, the price of acknowledging that everything she'd invested herself in was meaningless, was too great for her to bear. The bishop, even though he'd seemed so set against the idea, had kindled that hope just a little. No congregation, nothing for her to do out here for *four years*. Had it been so hard for her

83

to swallow her pride, to beat a retreat home and do something different with her life, reinvent herself yet again? It was weird, hoping your sister had fallen into dark despair – yet only so much. Enough to see no other way out than to disappear. Not enough to have done anything serious, or permanent. Would she? Would the Bridie she had grown up with kill herself? The thought horrified her, but she didn't think so. That wouldn't be what the Bridie she had always known would do. But then, if she was honest with herself, she had to admit that she no longer knew who Bridie was. Had she become someone different, undetected by Elodie, what with the estrangement between them, the fleeting intersections these past many years. Could Bridie, unnoticed, have become someone completely other? Could she, Elodie, have done the same?

⁂

They passed a construction site on the way back into the city. Wooden scaffolding, the poles and planks warped by humidity, heat, and years. It looked ridiculously rickety. A workman was hand-over-handing a rope, laboriously raising a bucket of mortar to where he was working on the upper deck. She didn't recall seeing the building site on their way to the restaurant. Perhaps she'd missed it; or perhaps they were returning by a different route.

'What time does your friend arrive?'

Elodie glanced across at Anne. 'His plane gets in around now. He's making his own way to the hotel.'

'Has he been here before?'

Elodie nodded. 'A few years ago. He's with the WHO. There aren't many countries he hasn't visited.'

84

'How about you? How long since you were last here?'

'No, I haven't.' Elodie looked out of the window again. There was a young man walking along the pavement, dressed in Western clothes, *Sail Fast* or *Sail East* on the front of his t-shirt, she couldn't quite be sure which as they flashed by. 'It was never something we did. This was Bridie's place.' She glanced back at Anne. 'I was never invited.'

Anne looked thoughtful. 'I'm sorry. I just assumed.'

'Don't worry, please. If I'd wanted to, I could have come. It's just that this was never top of the holiday list. I don't know, it's difficult to explain. Bridie never came and saw my lab either. You don't, do you? Go and see where people work? That's what Beb always felt like to me. I was always so busy at home.'

A sudden image, reeling through her mind. Adam, throwing a newspaper on the floor with pent-up frustration, storming out of the room and slamming the door with frame-juddering force. She couldn't see herself, but she could feel herself – standing quietly in the aftermath, staring at that slammed door, its faux antique brass handle and its thick white gloss, contemplating her options. The days of silent hostility to come. The weariness. The wearingness of it. The children; their family; their home. The almost overpowering resignation: give up, give in, was it really worth it?

'Do you have time to see a bit of the medina?' Anne's voice caused the moment to dissipate. 'If you've never been, you probably ought – it's quite phenomenal.'

Elodie checked her watch. Henning would be a while yet, getting through immigration and reclaim, shrugging off the teeming multitude of potential drivers, making the taxi journey in from the airport. And: if she wasn't there then it simply wouldn't matter to him. He'd sort himself out with a snooze, or a beer, or a dip in the pool, and when she finally turned up he'd be completely fine and would simply want to know how she'd been getting on. There'd be no withdrawal. No stonewalled silence. No protestations of fatigue every evening for days on end. Yes, maybe he'd have been getting a little bit worried, but that would melt away once he knew she was fine. It would be no big deal. No small deal. No deal at all.

'All right,' she told Anne. 'Thank you. Maybe for an hour.'

Jack drove to the edge of the ville nouvelle, parking the car with its diplomatic plates adjacent to the old city wall.

'This is the south gate,' Anne said, fastening her headscarf in place. 'You can't go any further by car.' They got out, and Jack blipped the central locking.

'All right?' Anne said.

The chauffeur nodded.

'Let him go ahead,' Anne told her. 'We'll come a pace or two behind.'

The gateway was framed by a horseshoe arch, decorated with exquisite tiled patterns in blues, yellows, greens. It was imposing: wide enough for a couple of carriages to pass either side with comfort. The massive timber gates were clad in an intricately worked burnished brass, and held back against the two-metre-thick walls by enormous retaining hooks. Jack merged with the stream of Arabs entering the old city; Elodie stuck close to Anne's side. She caught glances from people coming the other way, curiosity or indifference. Preoccupied expressions, or laughter between friends, or talking rapidly into a mobile. She was aware of their otherness – there were no other Western faces in the throng – and they were clearly noticed, but this was ordinary, everyday life and no one seemed in the slightest bit interested. None of the hustlers of the airport. None of the trappings of a tourist zone.

Once through the impressive archway they entered a small square, but it quickly constricted to become a narrow lane, branching in places and seeming to funnel them into ever diminishing space. A wooden lattice-work roof, suspended between the walls either side, shading and dappling the whole street, made it feel even more enclosed.

'Let's go to the madrasa,' Anne called forward. Jack acknowledged by holding up a hand.

There were small shops lining either side of the lane – holes in the walls, really, with little room for anything beyond the shop keeper and a choice few items. Most of the stock was outside, rugs and pots and clothes piled or arrayed on racks. They veered past a stack of wooden crates containing cauliflowers and some sort of green leaf that she didn't recognise, and she almost walked into a whole lamb carcass dangling from a hook on the other side of the alley. A camel head, and several goats' heads, were lined up on the butcher's counter, sightless eyes fixed on the human stream churning past. Flies buzzed around them; a couple of ragamuffin cats sat patiently below. People weaved in and out, brushing her, bumping her. Smells came one on top of the other: tobacco smoke; excrement; sandalwood. Sounds snatched her attention: Arabic, excitable voices, bartering the price of goods. Elodie felt a lurch of claustrophobia; checked that Anne was still at her side.

'Mind out,' Anne said, nodding ahead.

Two pack mules, laden with enormous saddlebags bulging with clothes, loomed out of the crowd, their wrangler urging them on with repeated cries and flicks from a switch. Elodie stepped swiftly aside; sensed the power in the animals' muscles as they surged past.

'Quite something, isn't it?' Anne said.

Elodie nodded, rejoining her.

'I remember, the first time I came. The feeling of being hit. All this teeming life just bowling into you. There are miles of streets and alleyways like this, you'd get utterly lost.'

A couple of boys, running headlong, darted between them.

'Jack knows it pretty well.' Anne took Elodie's arm, as if sensing her sudden internal unsteadiness. 'He's been based out here for years. He's been round every square inch.'

Elodie looked at his back – his shoulders stretching his linen jacket – as he pursued a straight course through the turbulent humanity ahead of them. Initially she'd assumed they were to follow him in imitation of the Arab tradition for walking. Now she wondered if it was more so he could act as battering ram. It was comforting to be in his wake. She had the sudden realisation that, if he'd been stationed out here for all that time, he might have met Bridie; might even have known her. She wondered how she could get a word with him. It seemed to be understood between him and Anne that he was to remain detached from their proceedings. It struck her, too, that he and Anne seemed to have slotted into some kind of routine. She wondered how often they had walked round the medieval vieille ville together; wondered whether Jack accompanied Anne on her every excursion.

'Your husband wasn't able to come?' Anne asked.

'No,' Elodie said. All around them there were voices, chatter, banging, the thin warble of a transistor radio. 'He's holding the fort back home. My mother's helping too. She does a lot with the children.'

'Does she live locally?'

Elodie nodded. 'She moved to be near us when my father died. It's been good for both of us.'

'Was it recent?'

'No, my father died years ago. I was pregnant with my second – he never got to meet him. Mum must have moved within about six months.'

'Here's the madrasa.'

They waited while Jack went to talk to the custodian at a gateway up ahead on the right. He glanced their way a couple of times, a greying man in his fifties in a simple round-necked tunic and pyjamas. Jack beckoned them over.

'We can enter with his blessing.'

Anne smiled at the gatekeeper, who gave a slight bow as they passed, and laid his hand on his chest: 'As-salaam alaykum.'

Anne reciprocated the gesture. 'Wa-alaikum salaam.'

Elodie followed the others through the gate. A sudden transformation. Opening out before her, a substantial court-yard, light but somehow cool here in the shade. How could all this space be hidden behind such an insignificant doorway in a cramped and dingy street? The courtyard was surrounded on all sides by a colonnaded walkway. Every inch of the facades – the stucco, the cedar-wood beams and shutters – was carved with the most exquisite fine patterns.

'What is this place?' Elodie asked.

'The oldest religious school in the city. One's not allowed into the mosques, but this gives a taste of the architecture and craftsmanship. What is it, Jack, about six hundred years old?'

'At least.' Jack was scrutinising the balcony that ran round the first storey, giving views on to the tranquil courtyard below. It was supported at intervals by ornate wooden corbels.

'I love stepping from the hurly burly into this.' Anne wrapped her arms round herself. 'It's like an oasis.'

If she hadn't known what was outside the walls, Elodie would have believed herself to be in the middle of the country. Somehow, they were completely insulated from the sounds of the thronging street. There was instead a calm here; a calm you could practically hear. Elodie focused on the silence. There was a faint susurration, like a never-ending out-breath. Like listening to the sea in one of those shells.

A visual fragment: young Muslims, men exclusively, walking in twos and threes under the colonnades, books held to their chests, their heads bent in murmured conversation.

'It reminds me of Oxford,' Elodie said. 'I had a friend at Magdalen. It's just like the cloisters.'

'Yes, funny isn't it, how certain forms are repeated across time and cultures.' Anne started forward. 'I can't imagine there was much exchange of ideas between architects back then. I don't know, maybe there was.'

They walked together into the brightness of the courtyard; Jack remained in the shade. The sun seemed to be shining with renewed strength, as though the tall walls were a lens, focusing the heat into this rectangular space. There was a small fountain in the centre, sited in the middle of a shallow square pool. A soft, delicate splashing.

'Where are the students?' Elodie said.

'They're on a break,' Anne said. 'The hajj. We wouldn't have been allowed in otherwise.'

'Do you know what it means?' Elodie pointed to the running script carved into the rim of the fountain.

'Verses from the Qur'an, I'd expect. I can't read Arabic.'

They stood for a few moments, watching the water leaping and dancing, sparkling in the sunlight. A chaotic system, Elodie decided; impossible to predict the next spurt or spume even if one knew every parameter of water pressure and turbulence in flow.

'The chap who's flying in,' Anne said. 'Is he a friend of your sister's?'

Elodie hesitated. 'No, Henning's never met her. He's coming to buddy me.'

Anne nodded. 'It can get very lonely, living in another country, away from home. Did your sister find that?'

'I don't think so, no. Not that she ever said.'

'She was here a long time.'

A decade. Actually, longer. Could have come back at any stage. 'She loved it – Beb anyway. It was everything she wanted to do.'

'She was at Oxford, you said?'

'No, Edinburgh. She did English. Got a first. Went into teaching initially.'

'She must be very bright.'

'I know. I know what you're driving at. She could have done anything. Instead she ends up in the back of beyond doing God knows what for God knows whom. It's difficult to see it as anything other than a waste, really.'

Anne reached down and dipped her fingertips in the fountain. 'I'm not sure I'd have believed you if you'd told me, back in my university days, this was where I'd be now.'

'I didn't mean – I'm sorry, that must have sounded crass.'

'It's not anything I haven't thought myself a thousand times. It's funny, really, the twists and turns – how a life unfolds.' She straightened up, looked at Elodie with a crinkle of amusement. 'When I left college I had my sights firmly set on arts administration, the goal being to end up heading some fabulous public body like the ENO or the RSC or the Arts Council or something by the time I was fifty. Instead I kept having to interrupt my career to follow Peter abroad, not to mention having two babies along the way, and by the time I emerged the other side of it someone else was doing what I'd always intended to do, and I had nothing to tell Peter it was my turn to concentrate on when he came out. So here I am.'

Elodie smoothed some flyaway hair from her eyes. 'I've been pretty focused on my career, really. Haven't let anything get in the way.'

'I don't mind, exactly,' Anne said. 'I've had enormously interesting experiences, have lived in parts of the world I'd never have dreamt of going to. I just think it's funny, the way things turn out. Are you doing exactly what you wanted?'

Elodie paused. Her work had always been immensely satisfying, the buffer against the vicissitudes of life outside. Could she let that go? Let go of the one constant?

'I am, really,' she said. 'I love academia. And I have two great kids. There are always some things I'd like to change, but that must be true of everyone.'

Anne nodded, glanced at her watch. 'We'd better get you back.' They turned from the fountain. 'I hope you've enjoyed seeing something of the medina. We've only scratched the surface.'

'It's been wonderful, thank you. And thank you for lunch.'

Jack was waiting for them, leaning against a pillar, his arms folded across his chest. They fell into step behind him.

'And thank you for the information you gave me.' Elodie patted her shoulder bag. 'I really appreciate what you and Peter have done.'

⚛

He was sitting out on the poolside patio, in the shade of a parasol, a tall glass of sparkling water on the table in front of him, a segment of lime among the ice cubes. A paperback open in his hand. Legs stretched out in front of him, crossed at the ankles. She watched him reading; oblivious to her presence. She felt suddenly awkward, a teenager at a disco. It was like this every time they met. Stepping outside of her real life and into this other life that only she knew. Making herself vulnerable, her desires unmistakable simply by virtue of her presence. Something also about the time lapse, the weeks and months of sporadic emails and furtive Skypes that had to sustain them. The void in which idealisation could take hold, the void in which the real Henning would become gradually displaced by the Henning of her imagination. It wasn't that they were so very different. But this Henning, the Henning in front of her, looked paler, his blond hair that bit longer and less kempt. Attractively so. And she had never seen this check shirt, these kingfisher blue shorts, these walking sandals before. How little she really knew him. How much of his life went on away from her gaze.

Watching him seated at the poolside table reminded her. Toronto, the latest international symposium on malaria, four hundred delegates spilling out of the lecture theatre into the vast concourse where lunch was being served. She'd stayed back to ask a question of the last speaker. By the time she emerged the queue was snaking back on itself; by the time she'd loaded her plate and collected her orange juice there were no tables left. She'd stood for a time, scanning the gathering, looking for somewhere to sit. She didn't fancy joining an established group. The awkwardness of plonking herself down, forcing the others to break their conversation and include this newcomer; or else to give her a brief smile and continue their discussions, leaving her lemon-like on the periphery. But there was one possibility, a table with a solitary occupant, eating his lasagne with a fork in one hand, his attention focused on the tablet propped up on its case next to his plate.

Of course she considered his gender. Of course, in those moments of indecision, she registered the attraction. He was lean, fair, somewhere in his mid-forties, his face lightly tanned, with a day or two's worth of blond stubble, his navy linen jacket casual but expensive, giving him an air of insouciant authority. But this was an international scientific conference, they were both delegates, the rules were entirely different. There was nothing to be read into a woman approaching an unattached male and asking to join him for lunch. No doubt he was happily married, or in some form of long-term relationship. She walked across and placed her tray down with a simple 'May I?'

When had they reached the invisible line? He ignored her to begin with, smiling a welcome then apologetically explaining that he wasn't being anti-social but he was chairing a seminar that afternoon and needed to run through his material. She could have eaten in obedient silence. It was glancing at him every now and then, his fingers working the touch screen as he scrolled through whatever document he was reading. She liked his hands, was drawn to them: the way he stroked rather than flicked the screen as he moved the text slowly down.

'What seminar are you doing?'

He looked up. 'Biological Control: The New Era,' he told her.

'Ah, OK,' she said, 'that's interesting. That's the one I'm signed up for.'

'Really?' He extended his hand. 'Henning Dietz, WHO.'

'Elodie O'Shea,' she told him, 'UCL.'

They shook hands. She was acutely aware of his touch. He asked her about her work, expressed delight when he discovered which group she was with, said he was thrilled that she was here. Yes, he'd read some of their papers, it looked a very exciting area, he'd be keen to have her contribute to proceedings this afternoon, what kind of progress were they making? She liked the sound of his voice, measured, with a calming timbre, and a Scandinavian sing-song to it. He seemed to forget all about his last-minute read-through. They spent the rest of lunch discussing the problems she was encountering with gene insertion. Henning promised to put her in touch with a professor in Turin who'd had experience using similar viral vectors in bees.

They hadn't reached the invisible line at lunch. They left the table still colleagues, acquaintances. She found herself distracted by his presence during the seminar, registering the way he moved as he prowled the front of the small lecture theatre, inviting contributions from the floor, facilitating discussion among the assembled scientists. She liked the way he was on it, gesturing with decisive hand movements to call forward comments from different parts of the room. She became ridiculously nervous, waiting for the moment to describe her group's approach. Was she imagining it, or did he glance her way more often than was necessary were he simply keeping an eye out for her raised arm?

They reached the line afterwards, when she hung around till every last delegate waiting to ask private questions had left. Instead of having a question of her own she'd simply told him that she thought it had gone well. He asked where she was staying for the conference, and offered to walk back with her so they could continue their discussions. Arriving at her hotel, he enquired whether she would like to join him for dinner. She could have politely declined and just handed him her card and said she hoped they'd be in touch. That was when they reached the line, and stood, either side of it, contemplating each other across the divide. Each wondering whether the other wanted to step over; whether stepping over was what they themselves wanted to do. And whether, if they took that single step, they would be rebuffed or received.

She accepted the invitation, and they shared a meal, and a bottle of Rioja. Conversation drifted to the personal. She discovered that for him, too, marriage had become not just unsatisfactory but poisonous, something that he had only recently managed finally to break free from. There were so many uncanny parallels between what he told her of Marta and what she recognised with Adam. A shared understanding grew between them, as did the need, the craving, for consolation; to be something wonderful to another human being once again.

The look from the porter on the hotel reception as she collected her key, Henning by her side.

The sense of brazenness as she realised that she didn't care.

Finally, the crossing of the line. And the finding of comfort there.

And it was an irresistible comfort. In the months that followed they'd engineered meetings in London, Geneva, Stockholm, Birmingham, and Dallas. A year of contending with short sojourns of solace with each other, and now this: Bridie gone, a mission of discovery, the offer from Henning to create the pretext to be with her once again.

She stepped out into the pool area, walked quietly to his table.

'May I?'

He looked up, pleasure animating his features. 'El!'

He stood, novel in hand. They half-embraced, kissed cheeks, sat down, looked at each other, smiling, evaluating. So different to how they'd been when last they'd taken leave of each other. So different to how they would be again, soon, she was sure of it. But for now it seemed impossible to slot immediately into anything other than being colleagues, acquaintances, fledgling friends. She could still feel where his stubble had prickled her cheek. It seemed wrong, too intimate.

'Sorry I couldn't meet you,' she said. 'Have you been here long?'

'It's OK,' he said. He folded the corner of a page and closed his book. 'I have got settled in my room. They have brought me a drink. They have assured me that, yes, the nice English lady is resident but, no, her key is here so she must still be out with the woman from the British consulate who came to collect her in a very enviable BMW, but they would be sure to come and let me know the moment she returns, except that they haven't, you have, and that, my dear, is just fine with me.'

His clowning. The lilt in his English.

'It's so good to see you,' she said.

He must have detected something in her eyes. He placed his book on the table. They embraced again, for longer this time, both of them leaning forward in their seats.

'You all right?'

She nodded silently, her hair, his hair, intermingling. The smell of him filled her mind: the aloe splash he used; the musky undertone – not at all unpleasant, but masculine, corporeal; perspiration from travel, from hauling his suitcase and bag in the heat and humidity. She pulled him closer, one arm over his shoulder, the other around his waist. Breathed in. Felt tears dampen the corners of her eyes.

'It's lovely to see you,' she said again.

They broke apart when the man from reception came. She ordered a spritzer. She moved her chair slightly, closer to him, more into the shade.

'How was your flight?'

'It was fine, yes.' He chuckled briefly. 'Do you know what they have now in Geneva airport? A meditation room! That's what they call it. My check-in was right at the far end of the hall; I saw the signs. I think a spiritual space in which to contemplate your maker before embarking on your journey. Most interesting.'

She smiled. 'And did you?'

'I had a look. It was very carefully done. It cannot look like it is for any particular religion, of course, so no artefacts, just chairs and pictures of the mountains. I was expecting it to be empty, but there were a surprising number of people when I was there.'

'And how is life in Geneva?'

'Yes, it's good, actually. There's a great exhibition at the SAKS I wanted to take you to. A really thrilling German painter. Disturbing and provocative and very beautiful. I think you would like it a lot.'

They talked some more, swapping bits of news from the surfaces of their lives. She was aware of her alertness, weighing everything he said for any hint that things might have changed for him, that there might be someone else on the scene, that what there was between them might no longer be on the same footing. She didn't like that thought. Could find nothing to substantiate it, either. He gave snippets from the other research groups in his programme, the problems they were contending with at Stanford with their entomo-pathogenic fungi, the mixed results of the Congolese trial of larvicidal bacteria. These were their common grounds, the places they could go to in safety to get used to each other again. She liked the hollow at the base of his Adam's apple, the few hairs visible at his shirt's open neck. Sometimes when their eyes met she stopped hers flicking away; stayed resting on his pale blue irises, trying to read them. Kindness and liveliness and intelligence; but reserved somehow. Her drink arrived. She sipped it several times in succession, eager for the release that the alcohol would bring when it reached her brain. He was holding back; there was a withholding in his eyes. He asked about her children, how they were getting on? She told him about Maddie's swimming, Ollie's guitar. His two boys were growing up fast, had formed some sort of rock band with friends from college. By convention he would not ask about Adam, where she had got to in her eternal dilemma. That would come later, when they were ready. When they had regained their intimacy.

But something was wrong, she was sure of it now. There was a reservation. There was something he was not saying.

'Henning? What is it?'

He looked at her. He shook his head. A wry smile.

'You are too perceptive. You always have been.'

'Henning, you're scaring me.'

He glanced around.

'Come on,' he said. 'Let's go to my room.'

'They're from Maaloula, in northern Syria. One of the oldest Christian enclaves in the Middle East.' He held them out to her. 'They're not nice.'

She took the photos, A4 blow-ups. The figure was lying face down, limbs untidily sprawled. There were dark blots at various points over the back of her white habit. Elodie was mesmerised by them. They seemed impossibly small, like little spats of mud, like they couldn't really have been responsible for causing any harm at all, let alone death.

'She was called Sister Isidora. It's unclear exactly what happened.' Henning was speaking again. 'Most likely she had been abducted – the location is some forty kilometres outside the town. Possibly she had seen a chance to escape, and they gunned her down. All the entry points are in her back. It wasn't a planned killing, and there's been no attempt to make propaganda out of it. So far.'

She sifted through the pictures, different angles, same body. The veil was spilled to one side, and part of the nun's face was just visible in some of shots.

'Oh, Henning. She looks so old.'

'In her early seventies, apparently. Syrian Christian. They still speak Aramaic in her community.'

There was a cluster of low buildings in the far distance, and a single massive tree just twenty yards from the nun's body. The contrast between the upright stoutness of its trunk, the leaf-laden arcs of its branches, and the lifeless woman crumpled on the ground above where its roots must run. Had she been making towards it, hoping to find cover, protection, somewhere to hide? Elodie couldn't imagine that she could run, at her age; certainly not quickly. A sudden spool: the elderly nun, her features contorted with effort and fear, hands holding her habit above her ankles, stumbling and hurrying across this arid ground, breathing quietly through her nose at first but rapidly giving up and gulping great noisy gasps of air through her slack lipped mouth, nearly at the huge tree that had stood sentinel over this patch of God's earth for decades, when an out-of-focus figure with a chest-long black beard stepped into the background of the scene and raised an automatic rifle to his shoulder.

She looked up at Henning. 'How did you get them?'

'My friend, Philippe, in the special rapporteur's office. He's been keeping an eye out for information for me – for you. They were taken by a special forces unit – at least, that's what he implied. I don't know what nationality – no one's officially on the ground there. And I don't know when exactly, but recently.'

'Are they on the internet?'

'Not yet, though I wouldn't give it long. They could leak from the UN. Or maybe other images or information will come to light. Philippe thinks she must still have been in the hands of the gang who seized her – that they hadn't had a chance to sell her on to the jihadis. If that's the case then they might still try to make something out of the fact of her disappearance, though that would be more valuable if she were a Westerner. Or it may be that the jihadis turned out not to be interested, so the abductors just disposed of an unwanted asset.'

Elodie was transfixed by the photograph. The finality of what was depicted. The loneliness and terror implicit in the moments leading up to the rip of percussive gunshots. By the sudden alteration, the sickening turbulence it created in her situation.

'Has this got implications for Bridie?'

Henning came and sat beside her on the edge of his bed. Put an arm across her shoulders.

'The special rapporteur's office monitors the market very closely. ISIS has prices out for foreign military personnel, diplomats, journalists, but no one is asking for humanitarian workers or religious. I know, there have been aid workers caught up, but either that's been a mistake, or else the jihadis have found it played out too messily with condemnation from Muslim groups in the West. But if this represents something new from al-Qaeda, then I'm afraid possibly, yes. They perceive themselves as marginalised by ISIS. Conceivably, they may see taking religious figures as sufficiently shocking to get themselves back in the headlines. It was a tactic in Algeria in the early nineties, for the GIA.'

She gathered the photos up, neatened the pile, turned them over and placed them face down on his lap. She leaned into him.

It had been the hardly spoken fear ever since they'd learned that Bridie had disappeared. But so much seemed against it. For all the official caution, the Foreign Office had nothing to suggest that what had happened was tied up with the unrest convulsing so much of the Islamic world. This country, like so many in north-west Africa, was more stable, more Western-looking. As each week passed and no new information came to light it seemed increasingly likely that Bridie was one of the ranks of the ordinary: those who had simply gone missing abroad. Now, though.

Henning laid his other hand on her knee. A confusion of thoughts swirled in her mind. Numbness. Disbelief. That this could actually be happening – to Bridie, to her, to them? They were just ordinary people. Nothing they had done could ever have marked them out for this. Fearful images that she could only half acknowledge: Bridie walking, feeling sudden clamps of hands around her upper arms, a hard metal muzzle thrust against her chest, wild eyes above bandana'd faces, urgent commands in a foreign tongue, a pick-up slewing to a dusty halt alongside, doors flying open, bundling her inside.

'Hey. I think we should keep our nerve.' She felt Henning's fingers on her cheek, brushing a tear that had spilled silently. 'What happened to her, to Sister Isidora – tragic as it is – it is probably completely incidental. We're a very long way from Syria, from Iraq, here – geographically and in every other way. Come on, dry your eyes.' He reached for the phone mounted on the wall by the headboard of his bed. 'Let me get you another drink.'

☙

They ate in the hotel, sharing a chicken tajine, though her appetite was blunted. Henning wanted to know everything she'd learned to date: Bishop Bonouvrie, the consul, the circuitous assistance provided by his wife.

'It's good advice,' he said, 'to travel by bus. We will be among normal people, not marking ourselves out. It shows confidence. It is exactly the opposite of what anyone would expect, and that's the exact thing we want to do.'

She had thought he'd be against making the trip to Beb. The photographs, and the chill they'd seeded in her heart, had changed the complexion for her. In her most walled-off spaces she'd given voice to a new temptation – or perhaps an old one that had been there ever since the trip was conceived, only now given a wisp of legitimacy by the news Henning had brought – to stay here, holed up in this hotel with him. To send a stream of fictional emails to her mother with news of obstacles and hindrances and final impossibilities, returning empty handed at the end of the week. As soon as she acknowledged the thought it provoked an inner revulsion at the dark corners of her heart. How could she do that to Bridie? Content that she should remain missing forever, the only people on whom she ought to be able to rely – her family – given her up for lost? Even though it felt hopeless, even though she felt a new current of fear, the thought of Bridie still alive somewhere – perhaps disturbed, perhaps in utter despair – being abandoned in her hour of need. That was beyond contemplation.

Henning's room was along the corridor. They stopped outside her door. He drew her towards him. She felt the warmth of his body against her thighs, her hips, her breasts, their every point of contact. They kissed. She had so longed for this, had so wanted to be in his arms again. She couldn't respond. Too many conflicting emotions. She broke the embrace, took his hand.

'I want to show you something.'

Henning followed her into her room. She drew the drapes

across the French doors, switched on the side light, opened the drawer of her bedside table, and retrieved Bridie's dedication card.

'This was given out at her final vows. It's the saint whose name she took. He annoyed the emperor of the time by converting everyone to Christianity.'

Saint Sebastian's martyrdom. A beautiful youth, naked but for a loin cloth, bound by ropes lashed round a tree. The multiple arrows piercing his flesh, protruding though calf, thigh, flank, neck, each wound unrealistically bloodless, the expression on his face bizarrely serene.

'OK. I see.' Henning sounded thoughtful.

'He survived this first attempt, so legend has it, and some widow nursed him back to health. As soon as he was able, he went out preaching against the emperor, so next time he was clubbed to death and dumped in a latrine. I guess it wouldn't make such a good picture.'

She dropped the card.

'Henning? Hold me?'

They undressed, curled front to back on her bed, naked in the heat. Henning's arm was around her waist. Perspiration formed between them but she paid no heed. She stared at the far wall, noticing for the first time that the paint was bubbled and finely cracked on either side of the balcony doors.

After a while, he spoke. 'They're short-listing next week, you know.'

'Yeah,' she said. 'I know.'

The WHO, stung in the Sixties by the failure of its previous much-trumpeted attempt, newly buoyant with the advances being made in biological control techniques around the world. Poised to announce a new formal goal of malaria eradication by 2040. Putting together a team to coordinate the global research and implementation effort, a team Henning was in charge of head-hunting for.

'They've confirmed the package. School fees will be covered.'

Could she really do it? All the grief and turmoil? Even though he viewed her with such antipathy, Adam would erupt, she knew he would – the sheer rawness of his fury if he were to be abandoned. The implosion of her children's worlds. Yet, if she could get them through it. In the end it would be a fantastic opportunity for Maddie – they could get her in somewhere with brilliant swimming facilities. It could open all sorts of doors. Ollie would find it harder at first, but he would adapt, she was sure he would. There'd be enough time for him to settle in before starting his GCSEs. They'd be able to see Adam for half-terms and exeats, spend the long holidays in Geneva with her. What about the dog, though? That would break Ollie's heart. And Mummy, who'd moved to be near them: stuck on her own in a house down the road from her prickly son-in-law, the rest of her extended family flown? What about her work, her colleagues, her friends: Seal and the rest of the UCL crowd?

'You only need put in an application,' Henning said. 'They assure me it will be a formality.'

She reached behind herself, stroked the outside of his hip, his thigh, felt him stir against her.

'Can we leave it?' she said. 'I can't think right now.'

She felt him tense with her rebuff, though barely percep-tibly. She half-expected a gap to open between them, a few millimetres of air coming where skin had lain against skin. But Henning stayed close, remained in contact.

'OK. Sure,' he said.

She closed her eyes and leaned her weight more completely against him. This was what she wanted, true intimacy, the presence of another with no expectation, no rejection, just acceptance and comfort and permission to be.

Eight

S HE WAS DANCING with her best friends – Natalie, Peter, Sheena, Iona, Matthew – a loose circle of them in front of the DJ's rig. Shoes and trainers on the wooden floor of the church hall. Sporting make-up now she was finally allowed to wear it (officially). The music was too poppy – Dexy's Midnight Runners, Gloria Gaynor, Michael Jackson – but this was Malc, a man of indeterminate middle years, proud owner of twin decks with a cross-fader, with big sideburns and a penchant for an Embassy No. 1 while leaving a 12 inch playing, who did all the church dos and youth club discos and who'd done Bridie's 18th, and who naturally would do Elodie's as well.

Rockers Revenge came on, *Walking on Sunshine*, getting on a bit but still a half-decent track that might get played at a proper club. She was working up a good routine, copying some steps of Natalie's, when Pete stepped across and shouted in her ear.

'Your sister's here.'

She looked over. Bridie was standing in the doorway, scanning the hall, Tim at her side. Elodie took leave from her friends.

'Hey, happy birthday!' Bridie said, hugging her. 'You look fantastic!'

'Thanks.' Elodie smiled, spreading her arms out and looking down at her dress.

'Yeah, you look great,' Tim said. 'Happy birthday.'

They trooped to Elodie's table, where her presents and cards were stacked in an untidy pile. Bridie and Tim divested themselves of their jackets. Tim offered to go upstairs to the social club and fetch them all some drinks.

'Have you been home?' Elodie asked, once he'd gone.

Bridie grimaced. 'The M1 was chocka – we came straight here. They not around?'

'They're coming down later. You know what it's like – too noisy to hear yourself think, let alone have a proper conversation.'

The sisters laughed.

'You having a good time?'

Elodie nodded.

'Where's Ross?'

Elodie shook her head.

'Oh, El! What happened?'

Stupid tears, at her birthday do. Bridie's arm round her shoulder. 'He dumped me, on Wednesday. Didn't think we were going anywhere, not with us going to different universities.' She wiped near her eye with the heel of her hand. 'Is it smudged?'

Bridie inspected. 'You're all right.' She gave her back a little rub. 'What a bastard. He could've waited till after today.'

Elodie nodded. 'Pete and Matt are furious. They won't speak to him.'

Tim arrived bearing a circular tray, a pint for him, two rum and cokes for the sisters.

'There you go,' he said, setting them down. 'All legal, decent, and honest – at last!'

The music was loud, and, much as it would have pained

them to admit it, their father was right, it did make conversation difficult, certainly between three. Tim sat quietly, nursing his lager, while Elodie and Bridie drew close and bent their heads together.

'So, listen, hon: sod Ross. I never liked him anyway. Up his own arse. Just wait till you start at Imperial. You'll have guys falling over themselves.' Bridie glanced across at Tim, who was looking out at the dance floor. 'It worked out for me, and you're far better looking!'

She was being kind, Elodie knew that. The sight of Tim sitting there; Bridie's Tim.

'You're definitely set on London?'

'Yeah,' she said. 'I confirmed it last week.'

Opening the envelope up in her bedroom, her hand actually shaking such that she struggled to get the piece of paper unfolded. Then there they were: Chemistry A1, Biology A2, Physics A. Straight As! She stared at the results sheet, drinking in the sensation: AAA, one after the other in a neat little column. Three tiny letters that meant she couldn't have done any better. And a distinction and a merit in her Special papers, too. Mummy had actually cried when she went downstairs and passed her the slip without saying a word. There was flurry over the next couple of days. Mr Marshall, the headmaster, phoned from the school with the extraordinary news that her chemistry marks had been the highest nationally for the Cambridge Local Examinations Syndicate. Her chemistry teacher, Mr de Silva, rang shortly afterwards to urge her to take a year off and reapply to Oxbridge: *With those results, Elodie, dear, you will walk in*. Mummy said she must do what she wanted. Dad said she would have to get a job if she did because she wasn't going to sit around on her backside for an entire year. And she did briefly flirt with the idea – the golden stone quads, a scout for her room, the chance to be free – but really, within a day or two, realised firmly that it wasn't what she wanted. Imperial had been what she'd wanted, back when her predicted grades had been an A and two Bs. And it still was.

'You really should get yourself a place in halls, you know.' Bridie was speaking again.

'No, it's fine, I don't want to.'

'There's nothing to be scared about, El, you'd manage fine – I wasn't even homesick once. It'd be so much easier to meet people, to go out, join in with the crack. I don't know how you'll manage that, having to come back here every evening.'

'It'll be fine,' Elodie said. 'It's not like Edinburgh. They don't have enough places anyway. Loads of people live out in London. I just don't see the point of getting a room in a poxy flat in Hounslow or somewhere just so I can say I've left home.'

Bridie had been against her studying from home from the outset, said the whole point of university was to gain independence. She hadn't wanted her to apply to London in the first place, even back in the A and two Bs days, said she should draw a line at least a hundred and fifty miles away and only apply to places north of it.

'Dad didn't want me to go either,' Bridie said.

'It's not him. I wouldn't stay for him. I just don't fancy it. Can we leave it?'

Bridie shrugged. 'Your birthday.' She pushed her chair back. 'Just going to the loo.'

Tim moved into Bridie's seat once she'd gone.

'So,' he shouted, 'did you get anything nice?'

'I got a Walkman from the parents, and a fountain pen, a really nice one, a Sheaffer. Money from the rellies.' She nodded at her pile on the table. 'I'll open that lot tomorrow.'

'We've got something for you in the car,' Tim said.

'Thanks.'

They sat in silence for a moment, listening to the music. D-Train, *You're The One For Me*. Still a bit dated, but Malc was looking up.

'You not fancy a dance?'

Tim nodded to the dance floor. Her crew were still there, up near the front. The rest of the space had filled up nicely, bodies everywhere – most of the upper sixth had been invited, plus a bunch of friends from the youth group.

'Come on, then,' she said, and they made their way to join the others.

Tim was a good dancer, nothing showy, but a maddening air of confidence and some really slick little moves that he hardly seemed aware he was doing. Nat came across to her, shimmying stupidly, her arms stretched out.

'Woohoo! Happy birthday, Ellie!'

They were all a bit boozed up. It was the year of eighteenths, though they'd been drinking at the Crook Log since they were in lower sixth. Hers was the very last birthday in the gang – the baby of the year; if she'd been born just a couple of weeks later then she'd've started school a whole year later.

Nat hugged her, arms around her neck. Spoke into her ear. 'Who's your new boyfriend, then!'

Elodie drew away, felt herself blush. They all knew who Tim was, had seen him a number of times when Bridie had been down in the holidays. She didn't dignify the tease with a reply, just carried on dancing. Natalie strutted back across the circle to Pete's side. Elodie felt horribly self-conscious, avoided looking at Tim, gazing fixedly at Malc - grooving to his tunes, single headphone held to his ear - until Bridie came back to join them.

Tim had Bridie's room, so Bridie had a lilo on Elodie's floor. Elodie's ears were ringing in the silence. The ceiling was coloured a faint orange by the street lamp across the road. She tried to gauge Bridie's breathing.

'You still awake?'

The sound of a body turning.

'Yeah.'

'When are you going back?'

'Tomorrow, straight after lunch. We're working on Monday.'

Bridie had a summer job on reception in the ultrasound department of the Edinburgh Royal Infirmary. Tim was temping at HMV on Princes Street. They were saving to go travelling the following year, after graduation. Since moving out of hall at the end of her first year, Bridie had lived full-time in Edinburgh, returning for visits when time allowed.

'Ross wanted me to, you know, do it. With him.'

The sound of a body turning some more.

'I wouldn't. I said no.'

'Is that why he dumped you?' Bridie asked.

'He said everyone else was doing it, and he wasn't going to stick around if I wouldn't.'

'Christ, El, what a jerk. You're better off without him.'

She'd been with him the whole sixth form, as long as Bridie

had been with Tim. Nearly as long. She could remember Bridie asking her on the phone, just a few weeks after she'd come back from her first visit to Edinburgh, if she remembered meeting a guy called Tim when she'd come to stay? Sure I remember him, she'd said, trying to keep her voice casual. Her heart had kick-started in her chest: had he been asking after her? Had Bridie been tasked with brokering another visit, a chance for Tim to get to know her better? A second later and she was crushed. Bridie had started going out with him. That's great news, she'd said, her voice bright. Did Bridie remember a boy called Ross Dunlop, really tall bloke who played cricket for the school, and whose dad had been a rugby international for Ireland? No? Well, anyway, that was who she was going out with herself. It wasn't strictly true, not then anyway. But within a week, after a couple of tightly folded notes, it was.

'Bridie?'

'Yeah.'

'Have you and Tim? You know.'

A giggle. 'Not really. Not all the way, anyway. We want to wait till we get married.'

'You're getting *married*?'

'No! Not yet, not for a while, anyway. We've talked about it, I guess. But we think we should do the travelling thing, then get ourselves jobs and things, and then think about set-tling down.'

Bridie and Tim. Settling down.

'Where would you live?'

'I don't know. Edinburgh, maybe – we both love it there. Or Tim's folks' place is really nice. It's expensive, though, Sussex.'

'You wouldn't come back here?'

'Bexleyheath? Not in a month of Sundays.'

Elodie lay there. Bridie, flying free. With Tim, rugged good-looking Tim from an English Catholic family who loved her so much he was happy to wait till they got married.

'How far *have* you gone, then? You and Tim?'

Another giggle. 'Oh, you know, touching and stuff. Heavy petting, that sort of thing. It's nice. Really nice. But we're that much older.'

Then: 'El? You won't tell Mummy, will you?'

'About you and Tim heavy petting!'

'Any of it. Don't mention that we're going to get married. I want to tell her myself, when we're ready.'

'Sure. Of course. Cross my heart.'

A rustle of the sleeping bag, Bridie turning over.

'Night, El. And happy birthday.'

'Thanks. Night. And I'm happy for you.'

'Thanks.'

A few minutes silence. Still the ringing in her ears. Tinnitus. From Malc.

'Bridie?'

'Mm?'

'Sometimes in the middle of the night, if I wake up and I'm trying to get back to sleep, I can hear Mummy downstairs, crying.'

Movement. Bridie sitting up on the lilo, a spectral shape in the orange glow.

'I went down once, the first time. She was really crying, Bride, really weeping. I said what's the matter? She wouldn't say for a bit, then she said: Sometimes I wish I'd never married your father.'

Bridie let out a long breath. 'Shit. Poor you.'

'Poor her. She's really miserable, Bride.'

'I know. But there's nothing we can do.'

'I think he might have hurt her again.'

There'd been just the one time that they knew of, before Bridie had left home. He'd been apoplectic with rage, some row about Granny and something she was meant to have said to him, Mummy doing her best to get him to see reason, to see that she hadn't meant anything by it. Bridie and her, retreated to their rooms, regrouped on the upstairs landing. At one point, at the height of a tirade, a sudden thud of someone landing against a piece of furniture, or a wall, then the sound of several bits of crockery falling. There'd been gaps in the display on the dresser the following day.

'You really must move out. She's only staying because of you. Get yourself a place in hall, El, even a room in a poxy flat in Hounslow. Please.'

'She'll never go. Where would she go to? She hasn't even got a job.'

'She can get herself a job. She can go anywhere.'

'You know she won't. She can't.'

There was only one family they knew that had broken up. The Carraghers. Their son, Mark, had been in her class in primary school, but he hadn't passed his eleven plus, had gone to Bexley Tech instead. The dad had moved away, a step-dad had moved in, but the mum wasn't allowed to go to mass anymore. Or at least, not to communion. Everyone said that's why they'd stopped going to church, Mrs Carragher and Mark and the other boy whose name she couldn't remember. It was too humiliating for her, to sit through the service but be barred from taking the host.

'I don't know what to do.'

'You can't *do* anything, El. Just live your own life and let them get on with theirs. Listen, I'm sorry and all that, but I've had it with him and I've kind of had it with her, too – always excusing him and saying it's cos he's not well and he doesn't mean it – and I'm only really here cos it's your eighteenth, and I love you very much but I've got to get some sleep cos we've got to drive the whole way back tomorrow and I'm absolutely knackered. I'm sorry, I don't mean to be angry with you and I know it's your birthday and everything, but the whole thing does my head in and I can't be doing with it any more. OK?'

Elodie pressed her lips hard together.

And listened to the ringing in her ears.

Nine

Dear Mummy

That was exactly the right thing to do, and I know Kenny's mother would back you up entirely, so don't worry on that score. He can be a little so-and-so sometimes.

I'm sure Ollie will be all right watching the film. Just check on the back, near where they have the certificate and the running time etc. It'll have a sentence giving an idea about the potentially tricky content. As long as it doesn't say anything stronger than 'mild peril' then I'm sure it'll be OK.

And I'm sorry about Adam and Maddie. I know how much it upsets you. All I can do is email him and appeal to his better nature – though I've not been able to get in touch with that side of him for a long time. You of all people know he doesn't mean it, not really, not deep down.

I'm leaving for Beb just now. The consulate has been very helpful, and are sending one of their people with me – a chap called Jack, who works there as a driver, but who is, I think, a bit more than that. I've got a letter of introduction from the bishop so I'll be able to get access to Bridie's place.

I'm reliably informed that I'm about to head into the back of beyond, so probably best to assume you'll hear nothing from me for the next two or three days. Having said that, I hope to track down Bridie's internet café when

I'm there, so I may be able to get an update to you. But don't worry if you don't hear. I'll be all right.

Mummy, do you remember that time when I was at Imperial and I flew out to San Francisco to visit Bridie and Tim, and I got into a rare old state at the airport and left you that long answer-machine message with my last wishes and testament in case the plane came down! I felt bloody silly when I got back safe and sound, but I was glad I'd done what I did because we none of us know what's going to happen to us from one minute to the next, do we? Anyway, I'm not going to get all maudlin on you here, but just to say again that I really admire, and am grateful for, all you did for me (and for Bridie) over the years. I don't suppose I'll ever know quite how hard it was for you, though I do have some inkling. But, anyway, thank you. And, if by any bad luck I were to have an accident or something out here, and I didn't come back home, I've got letters that I wrote for Maddie and Ollie for when they're older. They're in the bottom right drawer of grandpa's old desk, in that concertina file (in the 'W' section). Will you get them out and keep them safe, and make sure the children get them when you think they're the right age. Please do that yourself; don't give them to Adam to look after. Thank you.

I'm being ridiculous! Or at least ultra-cautious. It's being so far from home, I think. Nothing is going to happen – just like the plane made it safely to San Francisco and back – but I just wanted to make sure you knew.

Anyway, I've got to go and get my stuff sorted. Much love for now,

Elodie xx

Dear Maddie

I'm taking the 'no news is good news' line, and imagining you've been too busy with everything to find a moment to pen an email to your mother – that's absolutely fine, darling. This is just to let you know that I'm going to Aunty Bridie's now, and I'll be out of touch for a few days, so if you do email then don't think I'm ignoring you if you don't get a reply.

I'm feeling quite ready to come home just as soon as I've been to Beb and sorted out what I can to help Aunty Bridie. I'll look forward to catching up on all your news then.

Missing you and love you very much.

Mummy xx

Dear Ollie

Nana told me what happened, darling, and I'm very sorry to hear it. Kenny has some difficult things going on in his life at the moment, and very often when people are hurting about one thing they end up taking it out on someone else. Anyone, really – whoever happens to be around, regardless of whether they've done anything to deserve it or not. That's not to excuse his behaviour, but it can help to try to understand what's going on for other people. Anyway, Nana tells me you're all right, and I'm very glad to hear it. You're a brave soldier.

Nana also told me you took Pogo to the park all by yourself! which is an incredibly grown-up thing to do. How did it go? Was he well-behaved? You're very good with him, darling.

I'm catching the bus to Aunty Bridie's in a minute.

Beb is a very poor city, and there aren't many people with internet, so I'll email you again when I get back to the hotel here. Yesterday I went to the very old part of the city and saw a butcher's shop with a camel's head! Yuk!

Lots of love, darling.

Mummy xx

Adam

I'm heading off to Beb. I've got quite a lot to contend with out here, and I'm grateful that you're helping Mummy, but I think it would be best if you just let her deal with Maddie, if at all possible. She's at that age when she probably responds best to a woman's perspective. It's hard, if you've had a long day and you've had a couple of glasses of wine, to find the patience. I'm not saying it's your fault – it takes two to tango – but it does take two, and if you were just to leave it be then she wouldn't have anyone to kick against.

Dear Mummy

Just to say, I decided against emailing Adam, I can't see it going any other way than badly. Maddie will make herself scarce if it's getting out of hand – she not infrequently goes over the road to Jacinta's, and I really don't mind if she stays over there, in fact. If you keep your head down, too, then he'll blow himself out without having anyone to thrash against. For some reason, Ollie manages not to get himself in the firing line, thank God.

Anyway, I really must go.

Much love, E

She felt strangely vulnerable, checking out of Hotel Splendid. It had been a decompression chamber, a sanctuary, a space in this country in which she could be normal, where she didn't have to cover herself, where she could wear a swimsuit, drink alcohol if she wanted, not think about how her behaviour would appear to others. A home from home. They'd decided to lodge their suitcases there, to travel light to Beb just with hand luggage – they'd only be gone a couple of days, and it gave her some small comfort to think that they'd be back by the weekend. Somehow, leaving the cases was a talisman, a way of making sure that would come true.

Descending the stairs with Henning, she saw the American woman was already poolside again, rubbing suntan lotion into her arms while her children played with an inflatable turtle in the water. Elodie wondered if they would be there all morning – all day, even. How long could these girls entertain themselves while their mother lost herself in yet another paperback? She realised that she'd never seen sight nor sound of a husband, a father. She remembered her assumption, that they were here to visit him. She'd jumped to conclusions. They could just as easily be running away from a badly dysfunctional home, an abusive one even, some tenuous past connection bringing the woman here to this unlikely location – the last place anyone would think of looking for them – where anonymity was easy and dollars went a long way. Elodie felt a twinge of regret, wishing she'd found an excuse to strike up a conversation with the other woman during the course of her stay, to discover her story, her reason for being there, and to have explained herself in turn. Perhaps then Elodie would have meant something to her. She might have noticed Elodie leaving, and waved and sent her daughters across to say goodbye, calling out good luck wishes for Elodie in her quest.

As it was, she and Henning traversed the central court-yard, and made their way through to the lobby, without their passing registering. Just another couple of strangers on their way.

'Here.' Henning reached out for her bag.

They were at the entrance doors. Three steps down and they'd be on the street.

'I can manage.'

'I know you can,' Henning said. 'They'll assume we're married. You must allow me to carry your luggage.'

She relinquished her grip. Glanced in the glass of the doors to check her pashmina was arranged appropriately.

Henning went to the edge of the pavement, looking down the street for an oncoming *petit taxi*. He looked particularly handsome in his stone-coloured chinos and a white collarless shirt. *Not even I can wear shorts*, he'd laughed at her upstairs, when she was bemoaning the sexist clothing codes. And it was true. When she thought about it, she'd only ever seen men in long trousers since arriving. It seemed they had their constraints, too.

He spent the journey to the bus station briefing her.

'No one should speak to you directly, they will always talk through me. If anyone says anything to you, make no eye contact, but look at me instead. We can sit together on the bus because it's long-distance – only the local ones are segregated. No public displays of affection, though, so for the next few hours you're going to have to keep your hands to yourself.'

She gave him a punch on the outside of his thigh, where the taxi driver was unable to see.

'When we get to the other end, we're going to walk to the hotel your consul recommended. It's only about a half-kilometre. Stay just behind me and look at my back at all times. I won't look at you at all, so if there is any problem you must call my name once, loudly. It perhaps seems a bit elaborate, but the important thing is to convey complete confidence. OK?'

She nodded. He'd made her jettison Anne's headed notepaper on the grounds that diplomatic personnel were the last thing they needed to be taken for. He'd brought WHO documentation for her instead, complete with a photoID lanyard from the Geneva headquarters that had cost him a certain amount of string-pulling and favour-calling. Both of them were travelling under their doctorate titles. He'd given her a quick run-down on schistosomiasis, the endemic parasitic scourge of this region, and some skeleton details of a trial the WHO was planning of an alternative to the current drug treatment. As it happens, he'd laughed, Beb is right in the middle of an area of high resistance to praziquantel. It's the perfect cover story, if ever we find we need one.

'Henning?' she said. 'Are we going to be OK?'

'This is the bus station,' he said, the taxi pulling over at the side of the road. He looked at her, his hand on the door handle. 'This country still has appalling poverty, and with it appalling hygiene, in the provincial areas. Out of abduction and bacterial dysentery, I'd say there is far greater danger from the latter. I wouldn't be coming otherwise.'

The bus had a skylight in the roof, the perspex cracked and partly missing, a flattened cardboard box taped across it to block the hole. Elodie was fascinated by the conductor – at least, that's what she called him in her mind. He was stationed in a barred booth midway along the body of the bus, and anyone who boarded would come to his cubicle to pay their fare. Change was evidently an issue: countless times he would scrawl an IOU on the back of someone's ticket. She was amazed at his mastery of his world. When enough other passengers had paid in low denomination coins he would whistle or incline his head, summoning one of his many creditors from where they'd found a seat. He seemed to remember exactly what was due to each of them without consulting the figure he'd written earlier. And he managed to square accounts with everyone prior to their reaching their point of disembarkation.

Henning hadn't needed an IOU. He'd paid with exactly the right money. He'd changed several notes at the hotel before they'd left.

Most of the women on board were traditionally dressed in hijab or burka; one mother had a baby on her front, swaddled in a papoose. But a few wore contemporary Western clothing. One young woman, dark complexion, thick black hair apparent at the edges of her headscarf, wore a long-sleeved t-shirt with *Blonde Inside* written on its front. The sight reassured Elodie, suggesting that even heading away from the capital, a measure of diversity was acceptable, a visual confirmation that this was indeed a liberal culture where extremism would struggle to gain a foothold.

It was only the men who talked, though. A group of lean, muscular youths had gathered near the back of the bus, and though their Arabic meant nothing to her, their body language spoke of high-spirits and latent energy. An older man stayed swaying next to the conductor's booth, chatting animatedly to him between stops: she wondered if he might be his father, or an uncle. She was careful not to make eye contact with anyone, but she was also reassured by the absence of interest. No one gave Henning or her anything other than a passing glance. She began to feel more at ease. It was so absolutely normal; everyday life continuing around them, unperturbed by their presence. She'd been stupid to allow herself to be spooked by the pictures Henning had brought.

Even so, Henning had been insistent that they do nothing to provoke any interest or offence. So in common with the rest of her sisterhood, she sat wordless, watching the world unfold outside the windows, being rocked as the bus barrelled along the single carriageway. Here and there she saw an isolated factory. A man loading a donkey cart, children playing nearby. At one point she glimpsed a herd of goats fanning out over a scrubby rubbish tip site, goatherd walking slowly in their midst. Olive grove after olive grove; rickety wooden sentry posts erected at intervals alongside the vast crop fields, but she never saw anyone occupying them. Huge aloe vera plants were growing around the edges of the groves, their succulent blue-grey-green curvilinear leaves beautiful against the ruddy earthen landscape. She wondered if they conferred some ecological advantage to the olive trees, perhaps harbouring a natural predator that would keep pest populations in check.

Hour gave way to hour. Her legs began to feel intolerably restless; her buttocks sore from the continuous pressure. She was sticky and hot and utterly bored. Henning was impassive on the seat next to her, seemingly fascinated by the semi-desert through which they now travelled. She wished she'd established if it would be permissible to read. When would this journey end? She was wrestling with a mounting desire to move, to speak, to do anything. How could people stand to simply sit for so interminably long? She kept giving herself another five minutes, then another five. Just as she was thinking she would simply have to defy Henning's instructions and do *something*, they were suddenly in the lushness of a river valley, verdant after the sparseness and struggle of the land through which they'd passed. And there were the first signs of habitation again: a partly completed equestrian property, multiple stabling blocks in varying stages of construction. Finally, they began to motor past jumbles of square, flat-roofed houses, here and there a second storey appended in rough red blockwork. And clusters of shops. Then taller commercial buildings, apartment blocks. Up and down the bus, passengers started to get to their feet. They had arrived in Beb.

The streets round the bus station were thronged. It took a little time to work the stiffness out of her legs, which seemed to have forgotten the art of walking. She felt exposed, kept her eyes on Henning's back the whole time, glad, for once, of the conventions that demanded she retreat into herself and disengage from the world. Every loud noise - every shouted word, a distant siren, the high-pitched protestations of a woman arguing loudly to her left - she mentally flinched, expecting any moment to detect sudden movement, to feel hands upon her, to see Henning bundled down. It was an enormous relief when Hotel Akouas came into sight, marked out by the blue-railed balconies running around each storey, and the national flag hanging limply above the unprepossessing entrance portico. Henning had led them straight there, seemingly without consulting a map as far as she could see.

She was glad she'd not told him of her own miserable efforts navigating to the Catholic church in the capital.

The lobby was cool and calm after the swelter of the street. The floor was stone tiled, with a couple of enormous earthenware pots containing some dwarf variety of palm, rattan chairs arranged around them. The palm leaves were yellowing, she noticed, as though sickening for sunlight. The hotelier was perched on a high stool behind the counter. Within a few seconds of the doors closing behind them he'd jumped down, coming towards them with arms outstretched.

'Bienvenue! Welcome! My name is Azoulay!'

His beard rolled down over his white tunic almost as far as his waist. His eyes, sunk deep beneath heavy brows, were nevertheless animated, friendly.

'You are from the British embassy, yes? You have come to seek the English nun?'

'I'm sorry?' Henning had come to a halt, was seemingly thrown.

'Madame Armstrong telephoned. I have been expecting you.'

'Of course!' Elodie stepped past Henning, abandoning local convention as she realised what had happened. She smiled. 'She did mention she would try to call. We're very glad to be here.'

'Please, come.' The hotelier made a funnelling movement with his hands, as though passing a rugby ball towards the reception desk. 'We will complete your registration, then I will show you to your rooms.'

Elodie gave Henning a look, trying to say: it's OK. He shook his head, barely perceptibly – puzzled, annoyed, maybe both.

They filled in their papers, M. Azoulay keeping up a constant chatter that made it hard to concentrate.

'You will be very comfortable here, your every need will be attended to. It is some time until the evening meal. Can I offer you something to drink or eat now, perhaps, after your long journey? You have travelled by bus! The economic conditions are worse perhaps than I had understood!'

Henning's passport, stark in its brick-redness, was the only thing that caused any pause in Azoulay's output. But if he were going to ask how a Swiss national came to be associated with the British consulate, he clearly decided better of it. He remarked instead on the lightness of their luggage, insisting that he carry their bags up the stairs for them, maintaining his incessant commentary all the way. Elodie was content to let him babble, the words washing over her, feeling awful that she'd forgotten Anne's offer to prepare their way, worrying what Henning would be thinking, after being so emphatic that they shouldn't be associated with the diplomatic service.

Finally they reached her room, and the hotelier put their bags down in the corridor. Elodie thought for a moment that he was searching his pocket for the key, but when he withdrew his hand he was holding a dog-eared photograph.

'My son,' M. Azoulay said, turning the picture towards them, falling silent for the first time. He seemed expectant, as though they would look at the photo and somehow recognise its subject.

The gangly youth in front of the brownstone building was a stranger to her. Elodie looked at him for a polite few seconds, noting his Western clothing, his toothy smile, the slight hunch to his shoulders that suggested he wasn't entirely at ease.

'He looks a fine young man,' Henning said.

'That is his university in America," Azoulay told them. 'Boston. MIT.'

'Fantastic,' Henning said.

Elodie wondered if they were supposed to produce pictures of their own offspring; whether this was part of some social ritual she knew nothing about.

'There will be no one to take over the hotel when I am gone now,' M. Azoulay said, the falsely bright tone vanished from his voice. 'But I am glad. Chemical engineering, that is a good future for him. Please.' He opened the door to Elodie's room, and stooped briefly to place her bag inside. 'I wish you well with your search, madame. I wish you every success.'

Elodie thanked him, then shut herself inside. A couple of minutes later, Henning let himself in, closing the door behind him and leaning against it with a sigh.

'OK, that was a surprise.'

'I'm so sorry. It was the consul's wife. I completely forgot.'

'Never mind, there's nothing we can do about it.' He closed his eyes briefly. 'He was nervous, though, wasn't he? All that talking.'

'Do you think there's a problem?'

He was silent for a moment.

'She recommended him highly. Anne, I mean.'

'I'm sure it'll be fine. I'm just feeling paranoid, that's all. It makes everything seem suspicious.' He stepped away from the door, came across and gave her a hug. 'Let's sort our rooms out. Are you coming to mine, or am I coming to yours?'

Ten

I T WAS LIKE driving through a movie set: the billboards, the clapboard houses, the cable cars, the great roadways sweeping down vertiginously steep gradients, undulating in places where the hillside briefly flattened before plunging on again. How many films and TV shows had she seen all this in? *Bullitt*, *Dirty Harry*, *Starsky & Hutch*, cars chasing each other down these iconic streets, roaring into the air like ski jumpers, wheels spinning, engines racing, before crunching down on to the tarmac again with spurts of scorched-rubber smoke, the chase resumed. Even the yellow cabs felt artificial, as though placed there specifically to lend authenticity to the San Francisco experience.

'Pretty neat, isn't it?' Tim said.

'Incredible,' Elodie agreed.

He was sitting up front, next to the driver. He'd twisted round to look at her. She guessed he must have felt the same when he and Bridie first arrived.

'We've lined a few things up to keep you going.' Bridie was next to her. Kept rubbing her hand, her arm, excited to see her sister again. 'The only way to beat the jet lag is to stay up as long as you possibly can. You'll be absolutely hanging by the time we let you go to bed. But you'll thank us in the morning!'

They dropped her stuff off at the apartment, gave her some time to freshen up – an amazing walk-in shower that dumped a torrent of water over her tired body from a massive rose suspended from the ceiling – then marched her straight into town. Walk. Don't walk. The fire hydrants, squat and gold with stubby outlets and dangling chains. The roads were hulked by great Fords, and Mustangs, and Dodges.

They ate burgers and drank beers in a bar at the top of Coit Tower with views out over the city and the Pacific beyond. She could see Golden Gate bridge, small boats trailing silver wakes, gulls wheeling high in the air yet below their level. The sea fog loitered beyond the bay as though sizing up the moment to make landfall again.

'Your hair looks great,' Bridie told her.

'Thanks.' She touched the nape of her neck self-consciously. She'd got herself a new cut – a short bob, which the stylist had layered in some clever way so as to give a bit of volume to her otherwise flyaway hair. Part of the rehabilitation after Richard. Part of the getting herself back on her feet again. She was still getting used to it, the feeling of her neck being exposed, of not being able to wear a pony tail or tuck her hair up in a bun.

Bridie looked different, as well, tanned from months on the road – India, Nepal, Thailand, Hong Kong, New Zealand, now west coast of America – leaner, too, as though some puppy fat had been shed for good along the way. Her clothing was cool: baggy baseball top, woven cotton wristbands, jeans that had done several thousand miles. She sat next to Tim, the two of them sagged together in the capacious sofa across the low table from her, drinking Budweisers straight from the bottle, their eyes polished by their succession of adventures. They were living it, fulfilling the dream, experiencing parts of the world Elodie could only imagine. She felt intensely weary all of a sudden, the alcohol hitting home. Bridie and

Tim kept up a continuous banter, regaling her with tales from their travels: the run-in with gem smugglers in Rajasthan, Tim being hit on by cruising gays in a park in Delhi, the 'living goddess' they'd seen being paraded through the streets of Kathmandu, the fabulous beach parties and all-night raves in Goa and Koh Pha Ngan. Later, seeing she was seriously flagging – she must have been awake for close-on twenty-four hours – they took her dancing at a club on 16th and Mission, but it was a waste of money because she was too dog tired to get into it.

The apartment belonged to some uncle of Tim's who was out of town for a few months. The living area was huge, open-plan; oak floors and designer furniture. The stereo system piped sound around the entire flat, even into the bathrooms. Tim said the artworks were valuable originals, though she'd never heard of any of the painters and sculptors. She turned down a last drink; Bridie showed her her room – kingsize bed with a welcoming side-light already glowing.

'Night, Sis,' she said, giving her a hug. 'Nothing to get up for in the morning, so just relax.'

'OK, thank you,' Elodie told her.

'And, listen, I'm really glad you came. I didn't think you would. It's ace having you here.'

She did her teeth in the en suite, then, not bothering to change out of her clothes, she flopped into bed. The sheets were of cool Egyptian cotton, the duvet cover crisp, the feather pillows cosseting. Her mind was buzzing with fatigue and impressions and emotions. The end of the road with Richard, a summer suddenly in disarray, then one of those erratic in-ternational calls from Bridie. The extraction of the promise to book a flight to San Fransisco without delay. The gathering of gifts from Mummy and Dad, a standby seat on United Airlines, and she was here.

❧

Bridie was curled up in a huge blue armchair with massive sides and a tall back cushion, reading a novel, when Elodie surfaced in the morning. She didn't hear her at first, coming barefoot into the living room. Something about seeing her like that for the first time in ages, engrossed in her reading, unaware that she was being observed – such a typical pose – gave Elodie a sudden insight. That's what she'd done, that was how she'd got through the teenage years at home: by escaping into fictional worlds. She hesitated for a moment, struck by the force of the empathic connection. Then she called a morning greeting, breaking the spell.

Tim had gone out to a music store across town. Bridie fixed her some coffee, some real stuff that she ground from the beans then brewed in a tall glass cafetière. The smell was rich, enticing.

'So, sounds like you guys have been having a brilliant time,' Elodie said, sitting down with her mug.

'Yeah.' Bridie eased herself back in the blue chair. It looked like an artwork itself. 'It's hard to believe it's nearly over. It's been the best.'

'When are you home?'

'Late September. We're holing up here for another few weeks, then down to Peru probably. But my PGCE starts in October, and Tim's got to find a job.' She groaned. 'I don't want to go back, though.'

Elodie nodded. There was a brief hiatus.

'So what happened?' Bridie asked.

'Oh, you know.' Elodie looked down at the coffee mug in her hands. 'Said he needed some time on his own. That the thought of going round Europe with me was too oppressive. That he wanted to be free again.'

'That's shit.'

'It hasn't been great for a while, not really. He was probably the one with the guts enough to finish it.'

He was OK, Richard: drummed in a band, was into unusual foreign films. But he was too serious; there wasn't much laughter. And he didn't really get her. They were on the same course, but to him it was just what he did to justify having three years experimenting with life in London. For her, it was her world. She loved the intricacies of molecular biology, the secrets it revealed about how life actually worked. The mind-blowing complexity of even a single cell – how specific ligands, binding to their receptors, would trigger cascades of events within the cytoplasm, the nucleus; affecting function, structure, cellular growth and differentiation. Knowledge of just one such pathway, painstakingly defined through years of collective research, was the equivalent of understanding one particular instrument playing one solitary note – a violin, say, sounding a mellifluous middle C. The orchestration of the life of one cell was akin to a hundred-piece orchestra rendering a fully rehearsed symphony, innumerable players and parts combining with perfect synchrony into a beautiful and coherent whole. Scale that up to the realm of the organism – a creature comprised of billions of cells, all singing their symphonies, each symphony the equivalent of a single note in a dizzyingly ineffable meta-work, and you had some inkling of the extraordinary world into which science was beginning to see. Her research project for her forthcoming final year was to concern a chemical called ubiquitin – a protein found in virtually all living things, its structure remarkably conserved across diverse species, suggesting a pivotal role in some vital cellular process. Yet no one knew the first thing about its function. She could spend her life studying in this field, and only ever scratch the surface.

One day, perhaps, she would meet someone similarly committed, similarly interested in burrowing into the workings of life. She wanted to travel like Bridie, wanted a soulmate like Bridie had found in Tim, someone to explore both the wide world around them, and the molecular world within. Richard might have been the former, but he was never going to be the latter. It was a good thing they had come to an end.

She went and fetched some things from her bag.

'Mummy sent you these.' She handed across the seven-pack of cotton briefs from M&S. 'Said your others must be threadbare by now.

'And this is from Dad.' She passed Bridie the little box, watched her open it. Elodie knew already what was inside, a St Christopher on a silver chain.

'A bit bloody late,' Bridie said. 'We're nearly home now.'

'Come on, Bride. He is trying.'

Bridie closed the lid, the medal still inside. 'Yeah, well.'

'He's a lot better these days.'

'Is he?' Bridie looked at her. 'How, exactly?'

'He had an operation done, something on his knee. He had some kind of experience when he was coming round from the anaesthetic. Some kind of an epiphany.'

'What, a sudden realisation of what a complete arsehole he's been our entire lives?'

Elodie sighed. 'Something to do with his mother. He was completely rejected by her. Pretty much grew up being hated for ever having lived. It's affected him, scarred him pretty badly.'

'No shit. I know how he feels.'

Neither Elodie nor Bridie had any memory of their father's parents, both of whom had died when they were very young. The one photograph Elodie had seen depicted a stiffly formal couple, her grandfather quite short, with an air of puppyish eagerness to please; her grandmother big-boned, and arms-folded, and a heavy face set in a bleak frown.

'He's having some kind of group therapy, every Wednesday evening. It's making quite a difference.'

Bridie made a dismissive noise.

'Honestly, some days he and Mummy almost look in love.'

'Please, El, you're making me feel sick.' She dropped the knickers and the jewellery box on the floor beside her chair. 'Good luck to them - really - I hope they're really happy together. But let's not pretend he hasn't been a complete and utter nightmare since as long as we can remember.'

Her father, beside himself with rage. Raising above his head the stool Elodie had made in woodwork at school, smashing it down on the floor just a couple of feet from where she was cowering, splintering the joints she'd chiselled with such effort. Shattering its integrity. Breaking it completely, irreparably.

'I'm trying to forgive him.'

'Yeah,' said Bridie. 'Good for you. Let me know how that goes, won't you?'

'OK, listen, I'm sorry.' Elodie got to her feet. 'Sorry I brought it up. I'm just the delivery girl, OK? You do your own thank you cards.'

She walked through to the kitchen, started opening cup-boards: glasses and mugs; oils and spices. Bridie came and stood in the doorway.

'I'm sorry. I shouldn't have said that.'

Elodie turned to her, nodded.

'There's nothing much for breakfast,' Bridie said. 'You'll have to forgive me that as well.'

They ambled down to a nearby store to pick up bagels. Bridie bought her a genuine Hershey bar for afterwards. They took their food to the park, watched some American lads playing a scratch game of baseball while they ate.

As the days passed they settled into a rhythm of sorts. Tim was replenishing cash reserves doing silver service waiting in a fish restaurant on Ghirardelli Square. He had dual nation-ality by virtue of having been born in the States during one of his mother's visits to émigré relatives, so he had no need of a green card. His English accent was going down a storm with the diners, and he was pulling in a fortune in tips. Days when he was working, Bridie and Elodie mooched round the city, window-shopping or sunbathing in the park, or hung out at the apartment reading. Bridie was working her way through Armistead Maupin's *Tales of the City* and insisted Elodie read at least one while she was here in San Francisco. Days when Tim was off they went adventuring – a boat trip out to Alcatraz, exploring Haight-Ashbury, soaking up the sights around the marina, flying Tim's uncle's stunt kite down at the beach. Evenings they would drink beer and cook food and listen to music. Night times Elodie would tuck up in her oversize bed, trying to read, while Bridie and Tim took themselves off to the apartment's other bedroom. Through the wall, she could make out the sounds of their lovemaking: the movements, the creaks, the occasional laughter, seeming to go on and on. She felt achingly lonely. She'd lost her virginity with Richard but sex had proved disappointing. They were only ever able to do it at his place in Earls Court with its subdivided rooms and its thin walls when his sports fanatic flatmates – Neil, Nigel, and Tim2 – were elsewhere. Never at hers, under her parents' roof. Richard had little staying power, invariably climaxing while she was still warming to the sensation of his being inside her. She had never experienced an orgasm with him; had felt cripplingly unable to explain the things he could do to make her feel good.

She knew it was wrong. She would lie there in that San Francisco bed and listen to the sounds of her sister being made love to by Tim, and she would think about him as he was on the beach, in those long Bermuda shorts, bare chested, bare footed, trim musculature working as he guided and stunted the kite, the off-shore wind messing up his hair. Her sister's boyfriend. She shouldn't be thinking of her own sister's boyfriend that way. But, to her shame, she did. Could see him in a movie clip: lying alongside her, the mat of hair on his chest tapering to a line down the front of his flat stomach, smiling at her, leaning down to kiss her, their tongues meeting hesitantly then more boldly, feeling the electric touch of his fingers over her breasts, her belly, between her legs. When she came she forced herself to do so silently, for fear she would be unmasked.

It became painful. The three of them, larking about, chucking a frisbee around in the park, having to be careful not to allow her gaze to linger too long on him, not to throw to him more often than she did to Bridie, not to laugh too long at his antics, not to dwell too admiringly on the effortless way he could pluck the disc from the air and launch it unerringly again with a casual flick of his wrist, constantly worried that her sister – who knew her better than anyone in the world – would otherwise sense her betrayal.

The first Sunday they milled around the apartment in the morning, drinking coffee and reading newspapers that Tim had been out to buy from the store. The unspoken thing finally spoken: *We've not been to mass, really, not while we've been travelling. But you go if you want to go, there's a church a few blocks away, I can walk you round.* She didn't. She no longer went herself, at least she hadn't on any of the Sundays she used to stay in up London with Richard. She still accompanied her parents whenever she was at home. Wasn't brave enough to face what she knew would come – the anger of her father; the crumpling of her mother – if she announced that she no longer saw the point; if, indeed, she ever had.

The second and final Sunday they went to Candlestick Park: the San Fransisco Giants taking on the LA Dodgers in the local derby. They ate hot dogs oozing with mustard and tomato sauce. And buckets of popcorn. *Home Run!* animations on the giant display screen made them laugh. They joined in the Mexican waves with a knowing irony. The carnival atmosphere was unlike anything in a British sporting fixture. They got caught up in it, the three of them, hollering and cheering their team's successes as though they'd lived there all their lives, clasping each other in mock despair when the Dodgers pulled ahead. After the third innings, Tim disappeared to the loo, returning with a grey Giants baseball cap which he plonked on Elodie's head, and gave her a big grin.

'There you go, El. Souvenir of your stay.'

He was working when she had to leave for the airport.

They said their goodbyes at the apartment before he left, Tim kissing her on the cheek, resting his hand briefly against her elbow.

'It's been great,' he said, 'you joining us here. I know it wasn't the best of circumstances for you. But I feel we've got to know each other better.'

She felt herself blush at his reference to Richard, at the way she could still feel the points of Tim's touch long after he'd broken contact with her skin.

Bridie came with her in the cab. At the airport, she buddied her through check-in, celebrated with her the unexpected upgrade to club class, then sat and shared a final coffee before she went through to boarding.

'You have a great rest of trip,' Elodie said. She felt hollowed out inside.

'Thanks. You, too.' Bridie's smile was bright, innocent. 'Have a great rest of summer.'

They hugged, a long embrace, their bodies pressed unself-consciously together.

'You won't say anything to Mummy, will you?' Bridie said, speaking close to her ear. 'About how things are? Between me and Tim? And church and everything?'

Elodie shook her head, stood back and looked at her. Bridie. Her beautiful, flowing-haired sister: her sun-flushed face, her limpid green eyes, the elegance of her cheeks.

Elodie brought a hand up, traced a cross with her thumb over her chest, right where her heart was.

'Don't worry,' she said. 'Your secrets are safe with me.'

Eleven

THE *PETIT TAXI* took them funnelling through labyrinthine streets. Much of the journey was spent crawling along, stopping and starting, the superheated air shimmering with the exhaust fumes of the cars ahead, the incessant horn blasts sounding less angry or frustrated than resigned and bored. Pedestrians and cyclists and motor scooters overhauled them, weaving in and out of the coagulated traffic. There didn't seem to be any of the straight wide boulevards of the capital. No space in which to move with freedom.

'I always thought of this place as some kind of small-town backwater,' Elodie said, watching out of the window.

'Third largest city in the country,' Henning said. He was resting his elbow on the door on his side of the cab; his other hand was holding hers. "Population around four hundred thousand. It's the gas. Beb's ten times the size it was just a few decades ago. Phenomenal rate of growth.'

Their palms were becoming wet with perspiration, but she didn't want to let his go. 'You're amazing; you do know that, don't you?'

He looked at her quizzically.

'The stuff you know.'

He shrugged. 'You get into the habit of briefing yourself. It never pays to arrive somewhere with no idea where you're going.'

There seemed to be endless amounts of litter, plastic bags

and discarded wrappers lying on the pavements, in the gutters, from time to time animated by gusts of hot breeze, stirred into little eddies. The residue of consumption.

'The way Bridie talked, you'd've thought it was poverty-stricken.'

'It is. Massive fields of natural gas, but hardly any of the wealth stays round here – that's the story everywhere in Africa. Most people will have less than five dollars a day. It's not exactly a fortune.'

'All these cars, though.' Elodie was amazed at the number of them, mostly identical little boxy hatchbacks in black or white or grey, their tail badges bearing an Arabic insignia.

'What's your phrase? Cheap as chips? What we pay for a car in the West reflects the huge cost of production – the raw materials are next to nothing. All global manufacturers have third world plants where the labour is cheap. These are Renaults, you know, turned out by a subsidiary in Algeria.' Henning laughed. 'And you wouldn't believe how cheap petrol is!'

She gave his hand a squeeze. "I couldn't have done this on my own.'

'Sure you could.' His eyebrows pulled low over his eyes when he was serious. 'But I'm glad to be here with you.'

She moved across so she could lean against him. She liked the feel of their bodies touching. She liked the solidity of his shoulder. She liked the solidity of his character, too; nothing seemed to perturb him. Last night, same as the night before, all she'd wanted was to be held. Worry, dislocation, guilt; she couldn't seem to get to that place where desire lived. But she'd felt bad for him, aware that their previous assignations had been oases at which they'd both drunk thirstily. It wasn't the sex as such – though, God knows, it felt good to be alive in that way again. It was the being wanted – Henning being unable to resist her, wanting to bring her pleasure; and that made her want him almost uncontrollably, made her want to gift him a similar ecstasy. When they'd laid plans for this trip, for him to take a few days leave and join her here – for them to seize this golden opportunity of her being away from home – she'd revelled in the anticipation. Fantasised about being with him in an anonymous hotel, basking in sweltering heat and each other's nakedness. But that was in London – where her day-to-day life had never contained Bridie, where the fact of her sister's disappearance seemed bizarrely unreal. In London it was all still abstract; everywhere she looked life still seemed to be exactly as normal. Any second the phone could have rung and there'd have been Bridie: apologising for causing them so much worry, explaining that she'd simply decided to make a pilgrimage to a monastery in the Atlas mountains, or had needed some headspace out at the coast, or had been treated by an old university friend to a month travelling round Andalusia, and she hadn't thought to let anyone know because she hadn't thought anyone would notice her having gone, so sporadic were her usual communications and so infrequent were her visits home, and she was really sorry to have caused so much fuss, and she promised never to do anything like it again.

Elodie brought her hand up and curled it gently round Henning's upper arm, sliding her fingers in snug against the side of his chest. The cotton of his shirt was damp. She liked that, liked that he was living, breathing, perspiring, and here with her. Last night in bed in the new hotel, dismayed at the basic room, feeling wretched at her lack of libido – and maybe, yes, just a niggle of anxiety that he might start to question why he had come all this way at such personal cost; whether she was truly worth it – she had reached this same hand down and started to caress him. And she could feel that he was already semi-aroused; that he was wanting her. Yet he'd put his hand on hers, stopped her. Moved himself back a little so he was able to look in her eyes. *If you aren't feeling like it, then we don't have to.* And she'd confessed her loss of desire, and her worry that he would lose interest. And he had pulled her close so that she could feel his voice in his chest and he told her that sex was just one form of intimacy, and it was only something they should share if they were both in the mood, and that if all she really needed right now was to be held then that is all he would do, and that holding each other was another form of intimacy every bit as connected as making love. If not quite such exquisite good fun.

And she loved the way he leavened it with a joke.

Adam. In the years of slow-motion car-crash – when they still shared a bed, and she was trying so hard to save the marriage, to keep the family alive – every now and then, through all the coldness and misinterpretation and rejection, she had craved some semblance of physical intimacy. There was the thought that maybe it would act as a point of warmth, might begin a thaw. And he would turn his back, belittling her advance. *You'd better go frig yourself, then.*

'This must be it,' Henning said.

Out of the cab window, the sign above the gateway, L'École Nationale Supérieure de Beb.

✦

The guy on the reception desk told them the office they were looking for was to be found in the Faculté des Sciences Humaines, a drab block that wouldn't have been out of place in sixties Thamesmead. Third floor. Halfway along the corridor on the left. There didn't appear to be any secretary, just a name plate on the door: Professor Tahar Yacine. Elodie knocked. They waited. Elodie knocked again. They waited some more. She tried the handle. It was locked.

'Who is this guy?'

'The bishop gave me his details. I don''t know the connection, exactly, but he holds the keys to Bridie's chapel.'

Henning tried knocking. Still implacable silence.

'Perhaps he's taking a class.'

'Or it's a holiday.' Elodie had a sudden memory of the madrasa, Anne telling her the students were absent because of some festival. Though maybe it was over now: they'd seen plenty of young people milling around the campus as they'd came across.

Henning was looking up and down the corridor, as though the absent academic might suddenly appear from a stairwell or something. 'Shall we ask the guy on the front desk?'

The thought of retracing their steps. Perhaps to be told that the professor was away on leave, or on a lecture tour, or some calamity had befallen him that would present yet another obstacle in the path of her understanding.

'You'd've thought he'd have mentioned it when we asked for directions,' she said. 'If he knew he wasn't going to be here.'

'I don't know.' Henning sounded for all the world as though this were simply an academic problem: a question of methodology, or study logistics, or research finance. Henning sounded as though this wasn't the greatest hitch she'd hit to date. Why had she listened to the bishop? Why hadn't she insisted that he equip her with copies of the keys before she left for Beb? She'd been so ludicrously deferent, just because he was a figure of authority in a church that had once framed her growing up. A letter of introduction and an airy assurance that all would be well – that was no kind of plan. Shot through with the potential for mishap. And she'd *known* that at the time. Yet she hadn't been able to say anything. What was that about? Why was she remotely afraid of offending him, someone she'd never even met before and very likely wouldn't meet again?

'You stay here, in case he turns up.' Henning sounded decided. 'I'll go back to reception and see what I can find out.'

She watched him as he walked away down the corridor. His broad back. His easy movement. He was an attractive man, in better shape than most others of his age. He was a runner – 10Ks, the occasional half-marathon – she liked that in him, that he was fit, that he still took care of himself. *I haven't always*, he'd laughed when she told him this. *I got to ninety kilos in the bad old days. I was consoling myself with fine food and fine wine. It's like my waistline was an index of my unhappiness.*

There was a window overlooking the campus. She looked out. Spartan concrete buildings, functional and inelegant, none of the architectural flair with which a modern British university would be constructed. None of the landscaped grounds, or commissioned sculpture. This place had been thrown up at minimum cost. She wondered what it would be like to work here. She loved her own institution, felt a quiet pride at her affiliation. Crammed into tight spaces in the heart of London, the old buildings redolent of centuries of academic endeavour, the new additions full of soaring modern confidence. Stopes, Lister, Crick, Maynard Smith – so many scientific greats among the ranks of alumni. Jeremy Bentham's auto-icon sitting in its wooden display case in South Cloisters. You couldn't walk through the lobbies and public spaces and not be touched by a sense of awe at the advancement and learning that had been conducted there. Which imbued her own work with an additional frisson; an ambition that the control of one of mankind's greatest scourges, malaria, may one day be added to the litany of UCL's achievements.

Yet any institution was only the sum of its people. There was no history here, no beauty either, but the campus on which she gazed was teeming with life, students spilling from buildings at what was evidently the end of lectures for the morning. The corridor on which she stood began to fill with the sound of voices, footfalls. She felt a sudden yearning to be back where she belonged, back in her office, her lab, back in front of a lecture theatre full of another wave of undergraduates. The absorption in experimentation, the comradeship of colleagues, the debates and brainstorms as they sought to overcome problems. Would she, could she, leave these behind? Up sticks to Geneva? Move from a world of knowledge – the accretion of it, the propagation of it – into the kind of world Henning occupied: policy, catalysis, coordination? Even if she could make the jump professionally, what of Maddie and Ollie? The price of her rebirth would be the death of their family – though it was dead already, in all but name. But it would be the loss forever of the relationships they currently enjoyed. There would be new ones, built in Switzerland – skiing in the winter, lake swimming in the summer, thermal baths and exquisite chocolate and European culture. Henning, they would surely warm to him; maybe form friendships with his boys, meet other new kids and become fluent in French without even realising they were doing so. Within a year or two they would feel at home; that would be true for Ollie, certainly; perhaps Maddie was too old, would cling in any way she could to old roots. But even if Elodie stayed put things were never going to remain the same, and it was foolish to deny herself the chance of a new beginning on the mistaken grounds of an aspic-frozen past that no longer existed, if it ever had. Even if that thought simultaneously seized her with grief.

'It's OK!' Henning called from along the corridor. She turned to meet him. The purposiveness of his stride. 'Looks like he was taking a seminar. If we wait here he should be back soon.'

She scanned the faces coming along the corridor. The female students were without exception conservatively dressed – none of the jeans or long-sleeved tops she'd seen many young women wearing in the capital. And though this was a mixed university, the students themselves seemed to adhere to a self-segregation: the gaggles of undergraduates that passed were comprised of one sex or the other. Young eyes, still shaping their perceptions of the world, rested on her briefly as people passed, blankly curious. She was struck by the self-containment of the women, conducting themselves demurely. In a comparable corridor at UCL the walls would have been echoing with chatter and banter and laughter and complaint.

She wondered if this might be Professor Yacine long before he reached them: a tall man in his early fifties, clean-shaven, thick black hair flowing from a centre parting, dressed in a plain grey tunic, a pile of papers under his arm, with a confidence in his step and an alertness in his eyes. She was right; as he neared them he touched his hand to his chest and bowed his head briefly.

'As-salaam alaykum. Are you waiting for me?'

The question was addressed to Henning but Elodie stepped forward, her hand outstretched.

'Professor Yacine?'

He nodded, taking her hand in a single firm shake.

'My name is Elodie O'Shea, I'm Sister Sebastian's sister. This is my friend, Henning Dietz. I've got a letter from Bishop Bonouvrie.'

'Ah, don't worry, please.' Yacine produced a key from his pocket. 'Come inside. The bishop called me. You are wanting the keys, yes?'

He led them into his office, showed them to the two chairs in front of his desk.

'Please, have a seat. You are very welcome. Would you like some mint tea?'

Elodie started to shake her head but Henning said that would be lovely, if it wasn't too much trouble.

'I'm having some anyway,' the professor smiled. 'What do you say? I'm parched? I haven't stopped talking all morning.'

He left them in his office; Elodie felt a moment of unreality. She was finally here. About to speak to someone who knew Bridie and the life she had come to live.

'It's always better to accept hospitality.' Henning got to his feet, and crossed to the wall where several framed diplomas were hanging. 'Where would you British be without your pots of tea? What's his field, do you think?'

Elodie could see that the certificates were in Arabic. There was an English language journal open on the desk. Upside down she could read the title of the paper: *The Hinterlands of the Qur'an: The Edges of the Eternal and the Temporal in Early Hanbalite Thought with Analogs to Catholic Theology.*

'Some sort of theologian, I guess. That would make sense.'

Yacine reappeared, holding the door open with his shoulder while manoeuvring a large tray through the doorway. He set it down on his desk. A tall, elegant teapot with three cups on saucers.

'I have nothing to offer to eat, I'm afraid,' he said.

'Don't worry, please,' Elodie said.

Yacine seated himself in his own chair, smiling at Henning as he too returned to the desk.

'I presume there has been no word from your sister?' Yacine asked.

Elodie shook her head. 'How well did you know her?'

'We worked closely together. I have come to think of her as a good friend as well as a valued colleague. What has happened, it is very distressing.'

'Please tell me as much as you know,' Elodie said. 'It's been so hard finding out any information."

Yacine reached for the teapot, began to pour. The smell of mint came much more strongly. Elodie could see bits of leaves swirling in the tea, their initial flurry slowing and stilling as they began to settle to the bottom of each cup.

'I am ashamed of my own countrymen,' Yacine said. 'Your sister was a true friend to us. True friends should be shown true friendship, not driven out like a modern-day leper.'

'What do you mean?' Elodie sat forward in her chair. 'What happened?'

Yacine passed Elodie then Henning their drinks, and pushed the sugar bowl to the edge of the tray.

'The students here,' he said. 'English is such a vital skill. It doesn't matter what they're studying – engineering, medicine, law – they are all hungry to learn it. It's the international language: with it, the world is opened up; without it they are severely disadvantaged. Arabic, Berber, French, all fine if they want to stay home.' Elodie noticed that he put three heaped spoonfuls of sugar in his own cup. 'I am the exception – I studied abroad for some years, but I returned. For most, once they have good English, and a marketable qualification alongside it, few of them choose to remain. Canada, America, Australia, Britain: the opportunities for a good life are many. And who can blame them?' He took his spoon and started to stir, mint leaves and dissolving crystals animated in the miniature whirlpool he'd created. 'It is easier to blame those who are seen to have led them astray.'

'Professor,' Henning said. 'Elodie has been told – by the order her sister belonged to – that her mental health had been deteriorating, that she had suffered some sort of breakdown.'

'Well, that is one way of putting it.' Yacine rested his spoon on its saucer with a ceramic chink. 'I suppose my perspective is to look at what caused this, this breakdown, in the first place.'

'You said driven out,' Elodie said. 'Who drove her out? And what has Bridie to do with students learning English and going abroad?'

'I'm sorry?' Yacine said.

'Sister Sebastian,' Elodie said. 'Bridie is her real name.'

'Bridie.' Yacine paused, as though trying to square the memory of the missionary nun he had evidently come to know with this stranger's name. 'You do know that for many years your sister has been running English language classes for our students? In fact, not just for students; for anyone, although I don't believe many of my fellow citizens took advantage.'

'Her order didn't say anything about that.'

Yacine took a sip of tea. 'They did not approve. Not in the slightest. Sister Sebastian was in conflict with them over it for a long time.'

'Didn't approve?'

'They demanded that she stop – on several occasions, I believe. Your sister simply ignored them.'

Elodie sat for a moment, digesting the information. Mummy had never mentioned Bridie doing English language tuition; never gave any impression that she was doing anything other than ministry work. And to ignore the orders of her superiors. Having taken a vow of obedience. In that, at least, she could see something of her sister, something of the old Bridie. But not the Bridie she had turned into; not the Bridie who had determined to become a nun in the first place. It struck her as both plausible and implausible. She was unsure why she should accept this Muslim academic's version over that of Bridie's superiors in the convent at Reims.

'If Bridie's order disagreed with what she was doing here, surely they would just have pulled her out? Closed the mission and sent her elsewhere?'

Yacine shrugged. 'The chapel is in Bishop Bonouvrie's gift. His belief is that the most effective mission is to serve – to meet the needs of the people one is living among. Sister Sebastian saw this great hunger to learn English, and knew it was a need she could meet. She had no desire to proselytise – she wanted to meet people where they were, rather than expect them to come to where she was. She said to me more than once that she would prefer to show a thousand people how Jesus served others than to convert one person to the Christian faith. My understanding is that her superiors held the opposite belief. That they felt this was an abandonment of her mission. What is the phrase? That she had become a native?'

Yacine had finished his mint tea. He placed his cup back in its saucer. Elodie's was virtually untouched. She took another sip; it had cooled perceptibly in the time she'd been listening.

'Professor. You said Sister Sebastian had been driven out,' Henning spoke. 'This was by people here in Beb, or her order, or who? It would be really useful to know exactly what happened.'

'I'm sorry,' Yacine looked at his watch. 'I have a faculty meeting very soon. I know these things are important, but it is very complex. Can I invite you to my home this evening – I will be honoured to give you a meal. We will have much more time.'

He opened a drawer in his desk, handed Henning a card.

'My apartment is on campus. Would you come at around seven? There is a phone in case of difficulty.'

'Thank you. That is very kind.' Henning started to get to his feet.

'Professor,' Elodie said. 'The keys to the chapel. I would love to go there.'

'Yes, yes, of course.' Yacine delved into another drawer, and brought out a set of heavy iron keys. 'Please, you can return these this evening when you come.'

☙

The route took them through a marketplace, traders sitting on low stools or cross-legged on the ground, surrounded by piles of vegetables and fruit, displays of pots and brassware. A fish-monger was methodically chopping the heads and tails from a batch of little fish. She could feel the stallholders' momentary interest – some called out to them – but she ignored them, pressing on in Henning's wake. The sun was high overhead, scorching her. People milled everywhere, getting in her way. Voices jumbled in her ears, together with the plaintive bleating of goats. One moment she was aware of the whiff of body odour, the next struck by the smell of frying meat, only for that to be supplanted by a pungent aromatic spice. A cloud of flies rose from a pile of fresh dung. They passed a butcher's stall, a dozen chickens cooped in a makeshift pen. As they approached, a customer was pointing out a bird; the butcher grasped it and held it to his chest and cut its neck with a single slice of his knife.

The square narrowed down to a lane and suddenly the crowds were behind them. Here and there men, leaning cas-ually against door jambs, observed their coming and going in silence. Elodie felt on edge; she wished they'd taken a taxi. The image of that Syrian nun – she couldn't even remember her name – hurrying forward, gulping great gasps of air, then an indistinct figure stepping into view in the far distance, raising a weapon to his shoulder.

'Just round the next corner,' Henning called out.

The chapel was supposed to be on a small square, accord-ing to the map Professor Yacine had scrawled for them in his office. It was more a dilation of the lane, a solitary old tree in its centre around which the roadway bifurcated. Yacine had drawn a crude rectangle through which he'd scored a cross. The building to which he referred was in front of them: a plain whitewashed facade with a single archway; a small dome, surmounted by a crucifix. 'Chapelle du Sacré-Coeur' was painted in fading script to the side of the entrance.

The porch sheltered a heavy wooden door. Elodie inserted the key then grasped the metal ring and turned. Inside she heard the lock shift. The door gave a few inches. She glanced at Henning, who nodded. She pushed, swinging the door open, and stepped inside.

After the glare outside she could initially see very little, the few high windows letting in only modest pencils of light. But within seconds her eyes adjusted, the gloom receding. The pews wouldn't have looked out of place in a village church in England: dark wood, carved details at their ends. But their arrangement immediately struck her. Most were lining the perimeter of the chapel, their backs to the walls. Those left in the body of the church had been spaced out widely, leaving large aisles between them. If anyone had been here they would have been hard-pressed to find anywhere to sit. Every bench of every pew was crammed with books. There must have been many hundreds of volumes, perhaps even thousands, squashed side by side, spines facing out, as though a great congregation of literature had gathered silently to worship. Elodie stood for several moments, trying to take it in. It made no sense. No sense at all.

She could feel Henning's eyes on her, but didn't know what to say. She crossed to the nearest pew. There was a label stuck with brittle yellowing sellotape to the end of the bench: Fiction G - M. Each book spine was labelled with a neat rectangle of paper, on which some kind of three-digit classification had been written in pen. She walked slowly along, scanning the titles and authors, most meaning nothing to her but occasional ones familiar: Graham Greene, James Joyce,

Ian McEwan. Most volumes were paperback; here and there a larger hardback poked its head and shoulders above the ranks.

She turned to Henning, who had come to her side.

'This place is like a library,' she said.

He cast glances left and right. 'I don't know about like. This place *is* a library.'

They meandered together up and down a few of the aisles, Henning hanging back in front of one of the other fiction pews, looking for a favourite author, Elodie going on, noting the other section titles: Philosophy and Psychology, Art, Linguistics, History, Drama, Religion, Social Sciences.

'Where the hell did all they all come from?' Elodie said.

'England, certainly – they're all in English,' Henning said, waving a title he'd been tracking down. 'She's got Paulo Coelho in translation. Did she have a big collection, your sister?'

'She always was a bookworm. But these can't all be hers. No one could possibly read this much in an entire lifetime.'

They came to another bench where Science started. Elodie slowed down, browsing the volumes on display, hopeful she would be able to make better sense of something nearer to her own field. The mix was eclectic and without apparent order: textbooks on the properties of radio waves, a primer in quantum mechanics, methodological problems in geodetic survey. Here and there, though, she noticed titles that were familiar from her own undergraduate days – an old volume of Ganong's *Review of Medical Physiology*, its orange cover dog-eared; and a superannuated edition of Alberts' *Molecular Biology of the Cell*. There were several popular science books: Stephen Jay Gould was well-represented, as was Richard Dawkins. Next to a copy of *The Blind Watchmaker* her eye was caught by a hardback, its faded brown board cover snagging something in her mind. She reached down and eased it out from the snug embrace of its neighbours: *The Limits of Science* by Pierre Rousseau.

'That's Bridie's,' she told Henning. As much to convince herself of the unerringness of her memory as anything, she opened the front cover. The familiar blue-ink handwriting on the flyleaf inside: Bridie O'Shea.

'She gave it me to read, years ago. Must have been when I was doing my PhD. I think she thought it would say something about the limitations of science as a system of knowledge – you'd think so, from the title – but actually it was just a partisan polemic about how great French scientists have been over the centuries. She was so eager to hear what I thought, and when I told her, she was really puzzled. She hadn't actually read it herself! I gave her one of Peter Medawar's books instead.'

She stood there, in the chapel thousands of miles away that had become her sister's world, staring at her handwriting. *Bridie O'Shea*. Neat, sloping letters, attractive tails to the B and the S. Bridie O'Shea: sitting at the white formica desk in her room, carefully folding back the front cover of the latest book she had saved up to buy, her Parker pen inscribing her name on the inside so that nothing of hers would ever go astray. Bridie O'Shea: nominating the Bible gifted her by the Jesuit missionaries, her pen tracing those same letters just inches from Fr Gerry's own inscription: *You have a vocation.* Bridie O'Shea: signing that identical signature on a consent form in a clinic in Edinburgh. Elodie felt suddenly cold – a neurasthenic chill – despite the heat. Something about Bridie's name, written in her own hand. She felt an overwhelming need of her, to be able to hug her and hear her 'Hey, Sis' in her ear. To know she was safe. To receive her forgiveness for what she had done.

'This Medawar book?'

Henning was extracting another volume from a little further along the pew. He held it out to her. *The Limits of Science* by Peter Medawar.

She nodded. Opened the cover, a faint nausea at what she already knew she would find written there.

Elodie Mary O'Shea

'Oh, God,' she said.

She pulled out the Ganong, and the Alberts. The same name in each. Written in less confident script – the letters rounder, more girlish – when she'd been an uncertain fresher at Imperial.

'These are my old textbooks, from when I was an undergrad,' she told Henning. 'I'd no idea. How do they get to be here?'

'Did you give them to her?'

She shook her head. She couldn't remember anything like that. Could Mummy have passed them on? But she didn't think she'd left them at home. Perhaps she had. Dumped them there one time when she went off travelling. Maybe she'd never retrieved them – they were no use to her any more, basic textbooks, not at the level she'd reached, and not in an era when any half-remembered fact could be checked with the click of a mouse. The more she thought about it, the more that seemed the only explanation. She was pretty sure all her undergrad lecture notes were boxed up in her mother's loft. She remembered her moaning about it when she came to move house, Elodie laughing and saying it's all right I'll have them back if you're tight for space, only she didn't think she ever did, they must still be in store at Mummy's new place.

'I'll have to ask Mummy. She might have done.'

'Are you all right?'

'I'm fine,' she said. 'Actually, I feel awful. I don't know. I just feel awful.'

Henning came and put his arm round her. 'You didn't know anything about this, did you?' he said. 'This library. She never told you.'

She felt incredibly shaky, like she'd done something very wrong and had been found out and was waiting to face the music. She needed to sit down because her legs were trembly but there was nowhere to sit because there were all these fucking books everywhere.

'I need some water,' she said.

The altar was bare. The wall behind it was semicircular, decorated with a mural of the transfiguration, the paint peeling in places, bare plaster showing through. There was no tabernacle. There was a door to the side, which if this was like every other church of her youth would lead to the sacristy where she might find some sanctuary and a seat and possibly a sink and a glass and something she could drink.

The sacristy did indeed have those things, plus a table and three chairs, a small gas camping stove, some pans and crockery stacked on shelves, a tiny fridge, and a grey corduroy beanbag slumped against one wall. Elodie found a couple of glasses and filled them with water from the tap, beyond caring whether it was drinkable or not.

They sat at the table, each of them quiet for a time, Elodie taking in the spartan surroundings, like a student bedsit or a squat or something.

'This was where she lived?' Henning asked, as though reading her mind.

'She had a flat attached to the church,' Elodie said. 'At least, that's what I was always told.'

There was a crucifix on the table, the body of Jesus hanging – in life or in death, it was impossible to tell which. And next to it, a calendar. One of those ones that folds into a triangle so it stands upright by itself, and each month you flip the newly redundant page over the back. The picture was of a red setter, its coat burnished by a late afternoon sun, poised on a hillside overlooking a rolling landscape. Heathery browns and purples. Dartmoor or Exmoor or somewhere. The calendar was called English Dogs and Their Countryside; she remembered the title. It had been bought from WHSmith. Ollie had chosen it – with her prompting – to give to his Aunty Bridie the previous Christmas, reflecting his enthusiasm for all things canine. It was still showing July. Three months ago.

The flotsam bobbing gently on the surface of the water.

There were other artefacts she noticed now, perched in between piles of plates and bowls on the shelves. Two small photo frames. One contained a picture of toddler Maddie cradling new-born Ollie. She remembered sending it; Bridie had never replied, but she hadn't really expected her to. One more dash against the wall between them. The other photo was of her and Bridie taken on some river boat on the Thames, an out-of-focus Westminster Bridge in the background. Bridie and her. So much younger. She couldn't remember the occasion, but it would have been when she was at Imperial, and Bridie had come down for a weekend. It would have been Tim behind the lens.

Further along from the photographs, she could see a

ceramic Highland cow perched near the edge of the shelf, russet coat and widespread horns, a hark-back to Bridie's Scotland days. A bit of driftwood, painted with a miniature scene of a Cornish harbour, a souvenir from a time Bridie had gone round the south-west in a borrowed VW camper van. Had that been with Tim? That must have been with Tim.

'This is too much,' she said. 'All her stuff. I can't bear it.'

Bridie. Here. Slipping into despair. Going slowly mad. Living in this cramped dingy shithole with no purpose to her life and no way back from the brink. Surrounded by books, and a million miles from anyone who had ever loved her. How had it come to this?

She felt Henning's hand close over hers. 'What do you want to do? We can head back to the hotel.'

'Hang on.'

She got to her feet. She had to see the full extent.

The connecting door led to what must once have been the church office. A narrow bed. Bridie's maroon trunk, several stacks of books on its lid. A toilet in the corner. A toilet in the corner of her bedroom.

She whirled around, rejoined Henning in the other room, filled with an abrupt restlessness. Opened the fridge, saw the mould-encased foodstuffs still inside. Closed the door harder than needed, slamming it shut on the evidence of her sister's life, her sister's descent, her sister's disappearance, and her own guilt.

'Come on,' she said. 'I have to go.'

'Do you want to take anything?' Henning said, getting to his feet. 'Anything for your mother, for yourself, in case.' He looked down. 'Well.'

She didn't know where to start. Couldn't make any decision

other than that she had to get out of here. Maybe she'd come back. Maybe she wouldn't. All she knew was that right now she had to go.

Twelve

S HE HAD A luxurious day ahead. There were a few jobs jotted on the back of an envelope – phone plumber about the shower, run hoover round the flat, a bit of decluttering before the estate agent comes on Monday – but none of them would take much time, and if she found the writing-up was going great guns then she could put off any or all of them until another time. The thesis was really coming together: she'd seen Rosie Glenn, her supervisor, the day before, and had emerged from the meeting encouraged. Rosie had told her she was lucky: not everyone got such positive results at the end of three years' research. How much more difficult it would have been to craft a dissertation out of a bunch of failed experiments; still possible, but it was infinitely preferable to have a story with a satisfying ending.

It hadn't always looked like she would get one. The first two years of her PhD had been dogged by technical difficulties, but finally she had mastered the mutagenesis protocols, and the corpora allata extraction from her *Anopheles*. Did serendipity play a part? Yes, if she was honest. The brute laws of probability should have seen her repeating endless cycles, churning through thousands of batches of larvae, many of them rendered unviable by her radiation, before hitting upon a promising variant. But on only her fourteenth run she had it. She would never forget the thrill, going into the lab after the bank holiday weekend, checking box after box to find innumerable adult mosquitos flying or perched, their discarded pupal cases littering the incubators. And then, to her amazement, peering through the perspex of that one incubator and seeing the fat final-instar larvae still squiggling round in the water tray. Not an adult mosquito in sight.

It had been known since the sixties that if exposed to artificial juvenile hormone, mosquito larvae could be prevented from undergoing metamorphosis.

Thirty-five genes had subsequently been identified as involved in the production of juvenile hormone in *Anopheles*.

Her scattergun mutagenesis had altered one of them critically, so it was no longer susceptible to the crucial off-switch that would liberate the final-instar larva from its earth-bound sluggishness. These larvae, inching along in the incubator in front of her, had no way of halting their juvenile hormone production. They would never grow wings. These larvae would never know what it was to fly.

Twelve months in which to exploit the burgeoning technique of polymerase chain reaction to isolate the gene she'd mutated. Day after day of restriction enzymes and Western blots to work out the critical change. A race against time to identify what Rosie Glenn said could be the key to her future career. And she really should reconsider her plans to take another year-out after gaining her doctorate, Rosie told her. It was all very well the idea of swanning off travelling again, but in the time she'd be away from the coalface, other researchers in other labs might have seized the mantle. Rosie had taken her as far as she could; Elodie needed to come under the supervision of an out-and-out geneticist. Rosie had already spoken with Penny Newton, an old friend of hers at

UCL – there was a post-doc with her name on it, if only she would say the word.

It wasn't a difficult decision. She'd never really settled in Manchester, had no ties here. There were acquaintances rather than friends; a couple of short-lived flings that had come to nothing. London felt like home. And this was the breakthrough that some scientists spend their entire careers striving for in vain, landed slap bang in her lap at the tender age of twenty-five. Travel could wait. She'd be an absolute fool to let this opportunity pass.

All that remained was to put the finishing touches to her thesis, and get it off to the binders before the move. She brewed herself a coffee, fired up her computer, and settled down to continue the writing-up, the day stretching deliciously ahead. She'd not been at it long when the phone rang. She was tempted to let the answer-machine take it, but the thought that it might be the estate agent prompted her to pick up.

'Hello, Elodie?'

She didn't recognise the voice at first. He sounded different. Subdued.

'Yes?'

'It's Tim.'

'Tim! Sorry, I was miles away.' She laughed, but there was no humour in it. Tim had never phoned her, not once in all the years. 'Is everything all right?'

'Listen, El, can you come up? Today? Bridie's asking for you.'

'What is it? What's happened?'

'Nothing. I mean, everything's OK. But Bridie's in hospital – she had to have an operation. She's wanting you to come up.'

'Of course, of course I'll come. Wait. Let me think. Tim: what is it? What's happened?'

'I can't explain on the phone. I'll meet you at the station. Just let me know what time you're getting in.'

'Tim, you're scaring me.'

'I'm sorry, El, everything's OK, but Bridie needs you. Can you come?'

'Of *course*. I'm just trying to get my head round this. Does Mummy know?'

'No. Listen. *Please* don't say anything to your folks. Bridie just wants you to come. Can you do that?'

'Yes, OK. Give me a minute. I'll find out the train times and call you back. OK?'

※

He was standing at the end of her platform at Waverley Station, in a long charcoal-grey woollen overcoat that he must have bought for working at Standard Life, but today it was slung over jeans and a dark green roll-neck jumper. Even pre-occupied as she was about Bridie, the same shameful thoughts came fleetingly to mind. How good he looked, a day or two's worth of stubble on his face, and this mix of the casual and the formal.

They embraced, kissed each other's cheeks, stood back. There was none of his usual ready smile.

'Good to see you,' he said. He didn't seem able to hold her eye. 'Thanks for coming.'

He turned and started to walk. His coat flapping round his scissoring legs. She trotted a few steps to catch up with him.

'So what's happened?' she said.

'She had to have an operation,' he said. 'It wasn't supposed to be a big deal. But something went wrong – some recognised complication, apparently, so they need to keep her in for a few days to make sure she recovers OK.'

'What operation? What's wrong with her?'

'I think Bridie wants to tell you herself.'

He wouldn't be drawn. Throughout the taxi ride to the Infirmary they talked of inconsequentialities – her PhD, his job, her forthcoming move, his rugby and the complete lack of time in which to continue to pursue it. When they reached the hospital he went with her to the doors to Bridie's ward, but held back from coming inside.

'It's not really visiting hours,' he explained. 'But they said it'd be OK for you to come.'

'Aren't you staying?' she asked.

He ran a hand over his jaw. 'I'll head home, now you're here. Haven't had a shower in two days.' He stepped forward, planted another kiss on her cheek. The scratch of his stubble. The smell of his unwashed body. 'You're welcome to come back after. I don't know if you're planning on staying?'

She hitched her bag on her shoulder. 'I bought some stuff. I'll stay tonight at least. Longer, if she wants me to.'

'OK. See you, then.'

'Yeah. See you back there.'

There was no friendly name; no Robin Ward, or Charlotte Ward, or Cherry Ward. Just Ward G2 – Gynaecology. She pushed the swing door; unfamiliar smells disconcerted her – astringent, antiseptic aromas. She walked in, hearing the clanking of metal, the insistent tone of a call-bell, the banter of domestics doing the afternoon tea round. She approached the desk, behind which a couple of nurses were sitting chatting.

'Hi, I'm here to see my sister, Bridie O'Shea?'

'Uh huh, of course.' The younger nurse, a freckled redhead, got to her feet. Smoothed the front of her uniform. Elodie didn't like the way her face had stilled, had assumed the mask of concern that she must think befitting. 'She's in the side room.'

Bridie was in bed, a drip-stand trailing a tube down to one of her arms. Elodie was transfixed for a moment by the deep red colour of the fluid. Blood.

'Elodie?' Bridie had turned at the sound of the door opening. Her face was shockingly pale. Her beautiful hair tangled and lustreless. Her eyes reddened from crying.

'Hey, Sis,' Elodie stepped swiftly across, stooping so as to gather her in her arms. 'Hey.' She felt her own eyes welling, a tightening in her throat. Seeing Bridie like this. She felt her sister's body begin to shake, great muffled sobs into the shoulder of her jacket.

'Hey, what's happened? What's wrong?' She stroked the back of her head. 'You poor thing.'

It took ages for Bridie to be able to stop crying. Elodie fetched her the box of Kleenex, sat patiently while Bridie blew her nose repeatedly and kept trying to dry her eyes, only for a fresh wave of grief to sweep over her.

'I'm sorry,' she managed to keep saying, trying to smile, though her face kept crumpling.

'Don't you worry. You let it all out.' Elodie had seated herself on the side of the bed, her hand resting on Bridie's hip.

Eventually the tears subsided, leaving Bridie becalmed at last. She exhaled through parted lips, her forehead furrowing.

'Oh, El. It's such a mess.'

Elodie looked at her, inviting her to continue.

'I've lost everything.'

'Hey,' Elodie took hold of her hand, gave it a squeeze. 'Tim wouldn't tell me. What the hell's happened?'

Bridie shook her head slowly, side to side to side. 'I got pregnant, El. I was going to have a baby.'

'Oh, Bride.'

'It wasn't great. We hadn't planned it. I lost all my maternity entitlement when I changed schools.'

'It's all right.'

'But there it was, we were going to have a baby. We'd just started getting our heads round it when I started bleeding and I was having these awful pains, and the doctor said I was miscarrying, and it was supposed to sort itself out but it didn't and I just kept bleeding, and I kept having all this horrible pain, so in the end they said I'd have to come in for a D and C, and that would get everything settled down, and—'

'Hey, it's all right.' She moved further up the bed, gave Bridie another hug. Held her for a minute or two before letting go and sitting back again.

'Oh, God.' Bridie wiped her nose with the back of her hand. 'What a mess. It was just routine, that's what they told me. They do them all the time.'

'So what happened? Tim said there was a complication.'

Bridie looked directly at her, her eyes unwavering, holding Elodie's gaze so intently she began to feel self-conscious.

'El. My womb. They put an instrument straight through it, caused massive bleeding. They tried to stitch it up – said they did everything they could, even got the consultant in – but they couldn't stop the bleeding.'

Elodie couldn't make her brain work. She had to run the words back through again in her mind to try to make sense of them. A sudden vision: masked, gowned surgeons clustered beneath a dazzling circular light, bloodied gloves, wild eyes, frantic instructions, nurses running in and out, cold steel instruments lying everywhere on the green drapes that concealed her sister's insensate body.

'So that's why you've got to have the transfusion?' Elodie glanced at the bag, dripping its life blood drop by drop into her sister's vein.

'El, they had to do a hysterectomy.'

'What?'

'They had to remove my womb.'

'How could they remove your womb?'

'They had to, to save my life. I was bleeding to death.'

'Oh, Bridie. *Bridie*.'

They sat in silence, Elodie staring at her sister, her sister who had nearly died, her sister who had always had everything, her sister who would never now give birth. She couldn't compute it. Kept wanting to ask: does that mean you won't be able to have children? Only that would be utterly stupid, because she knew precisely that was what it meant. She just couldn't believe it.

'How could it happen?'

'One in ten thousand,' Bridie said. 'It happens to one in ten thousand women, that's what they told me. Tim always used to say I was a girl in a million.'

There were more tears, but not many. Bridie seemed wrung out, a deflation overtaking her and replacing the rawness of her grief. Elodie felt exhausted, like she needed to lie down and curl up and sleep. She didn't know what to say. Nothing she could possibly think of sounded right. *At least you're still alive. Thank heaven they saved you.* What do you say to someone who has lost something so profound, so vital? And to change the subject, to try to talk of anything else – that seemed impossible, too. Her gaze drifted once again to the drip tube, its dark redness, the clean white bandage around the back of Bridie's hand where the line entered her body. The fingers resting on the woven cotton blanket.

'Bridie, where's your ring?'

Bridie lifted her fingers briefly, as if to look. 'Tim's got it, for safe keeping. While I'm in here.'

The joy of the engagement. The wedding planned for the Spring. Tim finally appointed on to the management scheme at Standard Life. Bridie, twenty-seven, in the prime of life, with her new job in a much better school at Boroughmuir. The high-ceilinged Morningside flat with its other bedrooms ready to be painted pink or blue and filled with a family. Everything utterly unravelled with the slip of a surgeon's curette.

'Won't you be able to sue?' Even as she said it, Elodie regretted the question, its crass tactlessness. What good would money be?

Bridie shook her head. 'They even warned me – it was on the consent form. But you never think something like that could happen to you. Not something so unlikely, so horrific. I couldn't have done anything else, anyway, I had to have the op. I just thought they were going through the motions, that they had to warn me about every possible thing.'

They sat in silence for a while. Bridie closed her eyes and Elodie thought she was dozing, but after a few minutes she opened them again.

'You haven't told Mummy, have you? That I'm in hospital?'

Elodie shook her head. 'Tim said not to. She has to know, though, Bride, doesn't she?'

'No.' Bridie sounded vehement. 'You mustn't say. Cross your heart.'

Elodie looked at her. Wanted to ask what she was so afraid of. But she thought she knew. The cohabitation had gone down like a lead balloon – the condemnatory omission of a welcome-to-your-new-home card, the insistence on staying at a B&B during the one weekend visit to Edinburgh since Bridie and Tim had bought the flat. It was Dad who was behind it – Elodie had witnessed his incandescence at first hand during her own visits home. Elodie had no idea what Mummy actually thought herself – whether she was also opposed, or whether, left to her own devices, she might have accepted the situation as just the way the world was now. May even have come round to the idea – a chance to try living day by day with someone, getting to know their warts and all, before irrevocably binding yourself to them. But Mummy's own opinions were, as ever, unfathomable, sunk far beneath the depths of their father's belligerent domination. It was only Bridie who had never allowed herself to be dominated. She had never again said the word to him, not since the day of the LiveAid concert, but her every action, decision; every development in her life said loud and clear: fuck you. And Bridie was every bit as scathing of Mummy's inability to state, or even to know, her own mind. Her dogged subservience to the doctrine of wifely submission.

Nothing. Nothing could be allowed to give their parents any succour. To create even the tiniest of cracks in Bridie's carapace – a shell formed of self-determination, and tempered by the heat of Bridie's own stubborn righteousness.

Elodie reached out again, and gave her sister one more embrace. Her mind felt numb. She needed some time on her own to think through what had happened. 'I'm so sorry,

Bridie, I don't know what to say. I'm devastated for you. You need some rest. I'm going to head back to yours and freshen up. I'll come back later on with Tim.'

☙

She didn't know the city that well, but with all her trips here she had a fair idea of its geography. She set off in the direction of her sister's flat, finding an odd comfort in the clipped, predictable rhythm of her shoes on the grey paving. It was like their lives were some ornate window, the glass painted with some ostensibly beautiful scene, then a single lump of rock coming from nowhere had crashed straight through with unspeakable violence, sending fragments and shards falling and scattering in chaotic abandon.

The times she'd given in to jealousy. The times when her own life – its latest relationship fizzled to nothingness; grubbing around on a research grant; only managing to afford a poky Mancunian bedsit by virtue of a chunk of her parents' savings and their signatures as guarantors on the mortgage – had seemed incomparably poor. Bridie: with her life's love, their dual incomes and settled jobs, their Morningside home. She wanted to take every last one of those envious impulses and shove them back into some dark maw, if only it could undo what had been done to her sister. At the same time, though, even amidst all this regret, still the stubborn, horrible streak: that her sister had conceived, had even been in a position to know the beginnings of a new life inside her. She despised herself for her jealousy, and despised herself doubly for not being able to feel complete and absolute remorse now it was called for.

She walked beneath the Morningside clock, showing twenty past four. Sat for a while on the bench there, watching the traffic streaming left and right. After a time she made her way onwards, all the way up to Holy Corner, before turning right down Chamberlain Road. Tim's voice crackled out of the intercom when she pressed the button. The door release buzzed. She pushed open the heavy door and trudged her way up the several flights of the shared stairwell.

'How was she?' Tim asked, once he'd let her in.

'Oh, you know.'

'You all right?'

Elodie nodded. Felt the tears come. Tim's hug was awkward, his arms stiff, a slight gap between their bodies. He broke away.

'Come on, let me get you a cup of tea.'

He made them both some cheese on toast, grating the cheddar and mixing in some Worcester sauce like she remembered him doing back when he and Bridie were students, and she used to come for weekends of respite from the tension of home. That caused a sharp pang, something about how simple life had been then. They ate sitting at the breakfast bar in the kitchen. She didn't feel hungry, but forced herself mechanically to chew a few mouthfuls. She didn't know what to say to him, either, and his usual easy chit-chat had dried. Eventually, he spoke, looking down at his plate.

'So what did she tell you, then?'

'Everything,' she said. 'I know you guys were expecting a baby, and that you lost it, and now she's lost her womb. I can't begin to tell you.'

'I'm really glad you came,' he said. 'She needed you. I'm finding it pretty tough myself.'

She looked at him. The muscle flickering at the angle of his jaw. Tried to understand his comment. Of course he would be. The worry that she was going to die, the relief that her life had been saved, the repercussions from the steps that had been necessary to keep her alive. But nothing compared to what Bridie was having to come to terms with.

'Do you know how long she's going to be in?'

'A couple more days, at least,' he said. He kept looking at her, then breaking his eyes away. 'She lost a lot of blood – is going to need another five pints before they'll let her go. What blood group are you?'

'I don't know,' she said.

'She's some rare group, there's not much in the blood bank, and they have to do them really slowly in case she reacts or something. The things we don't know about ourselves.'

'Tim. What's happened. It's awful. It's going to take some time.' She put a hand on his forearm. 'But you guys are strong. You'll come through it. I know you will.'

'Yeah, thanks.' He gave her a weak smile. 'Right now it feels fucking shit.'

Thirteen

Dear Mummy

Thank you for sorting that out with Marilyn – she's been very loyal and I simply couldn't manage without her, so I'd be loathe for anything to upset the arrangement. That's Adam's way of hitting back at me for coming here. Pathetic, really.

I've found an internet café – probably the very one Bridie used, and it feels really weird sitting here emailing you from perhaps the exact same computer (there's only three, and I had to wait quite a while till one was free). I've been to her church, which was weirder still – really quite upsetting, actually, to see what her life here was like, to see the remnants of it just sitting there with Bridie ripped out of the middle of it.

There's good and bad news, I'm afraid. The chap who holds the keys – he's a professor at the local university college, did I tell you that? – knew Bridie very well, and it does sound like she's been suffering from deteriorating mental health for some time. He couldn't say much because he had a meeting, but he hinted at problems with some of the locals and it may be that tipped her over the edge. I'll find out more this evening – he's very kindly invited us to dinner. Even though he didn't have any positive news, it's such a relief to actually meet someone who knew her and her life here. All the stuff with her

Order and the FCO – even me being in the capital here – was just so much groping round in the dark. I was right to come to Beb – it's like I've finally found the black box recorder in this Professor Yacine. Even the little I've discovered so far makes me realise how little we actually knew of what Bridie was doing here, and what her day-to-day life was like. I'm hoping at the very least that we'll be in a better position to understand.

I'd better sign off – I've only got limited time and I need to get emails off to the kids plus a few other things. Thank you for all you're doing.

Lots of love, Elodie

Dear Maddie

Just a quickie, darling – I've managed to find an internet café so I can dash this off to you. Nana says you've been staying over at Jacinta's so I hope you've been having a good time. I'm guessing you're really busy, but I'm just wanting to check that the 'radio silence' doesn't mean you're upset. You might be feeling angry with me for being away at the moment. That would all be very understandable, and you must feel free to tell me your feelings if so. But perhaps you're just run off your feet with everything.

I'm now in Beb, trying to work out how to help Aunty Bridie. It seems she hasn't been very well, and I'm not sure what to do for the best at the moment. Do you remember Selina's mummy had those problems a couple of years ago? Aunty Bridie is going through a similar thing.

I hope your training is going great guns, and that Mr Marsden is pleased with your progress. I'm not sure exactly when I'll be back, but I promise I'll be there well *in time for the county try-outs. On the subject of swimming, where do those Terrible Twins go to school – is it Millfield?*

Anyway, my love, keep well, and I love you very much.
Mummy xx

Dear Ollie

Thanks for your email, darling – I'm at Aunty Bridie's internet café so I managed to pick it up. Pogo was a very naughty boy, and it sounds to me like you did a great job managing a very difficult situation. Try to remember to take his treat-pot with you – he's much more likely to do what you tell him if he realises there's some food at stake!

I'm fine with you downloading the game, but you do need to check with Daddy as well (if you haven't already) because it's his iPad.

The computer here has a slightly different keyboard layout – the one you use is called QWERTY (look at the letters on the top left) and this one is AZERTY. I think it's a French thing (this country used to be run by France). It makes it very tricky to type properly especially because the W and the Z have swapped places, so I don't knoz zhat I'm typing half the time, and the comma is where the M should beM which leads to all sorts of punctuation problems!

I'm not going to be here much longer. I've made it to Aunty Bridie's. She isn't very well, and I'm just going to sort out some help for her before I come home.

Love you very muchM
,ummy x

Adam

I'm really cross with you. What the hell were you thinking of, telling Marilyn she wasn't needed? OK, there's much less for her to do with Mummy there at the moment, but she relies on regular money and you can't just tell her to take a couple of weeks off unpaid like that. You know she's the lynchpin in the whole arrangement, and if you'd pissed her off then the whole thing would have fallen apart. Thank God Mummy paid her. Please do the decent thing and refund Mummy the money. If not, I'll do it as soon as I get back.

For your information, it does look as though Bridie has suffered some sort of mental breakdown, and me being on the spot is proving absolutely vital to trying to work out what's gone on and if there's any way to find/help her. You playing stupid games is not helping.

Elodie

Dear Mummy

I've just seen the news on the computer, about that poor nun in Syria. Absolutely dreadful. I know that's going to make you worry but please don't. There's no suggestion that anything like that has happened to Bridie.

Much love, El

༄

She had similar things on the walls of her study at home. She'd framed the cover of *Insect Metamorphosis*, the OUP publication for which she'd been invited to write the chapter on *Anopheles*. Reprints of abstracts of all the papers – eleven of them to date – on which she'd been lead author. A scaled-down laminated copy of her poster from the previous year's Madrid Congress on viral vectors in gene therapy. She could have displayed them in her office at UCL, but it would have felt immodest. She didn't want to show off. She had a quiet pride in her achievements, that was all, and to have those visible testaments to her work gathered round her in her own private space created an unfailing inspiration-on-demand if ever she needed encouragement to continue beavering late into the evening on whatever was her current project.

To judge by his own collection, Professor Yacine was, if anything, more prolific. Some were in Arabic, but there were several posters and prints she could read. Lectures at the 5th, 7th and 10th Doha Conferences on Interfaith Dialogue, a keynote address at the 34th World Religions Conference, covers of books of which he was cited as either sole or joint author: *God and Man: The Monotheistic Faiths. Three Paths, One God. Belief in Books: Reading the Torah, the Gospel, and the Qur'an.*

'I hope you like pomegranate.'

Yacine's voice came from behind them. Elodie turned to see him entering the room, three glasses of red juice bunched in his hands.

'Thank you, professor,' Henning said, taking a drink.

'Tahar, please.'

They recapped their own first names, and Elodie took her glass.

'You must think me rather proud,' Tahar said, glancing at the prints on the wall behind them.

'Not at all,' Elodie said. 'I was just thinking how I do exactly the same with my own publications.'

'You are an academic also?'

'Molecular biologist,' Elodie said. 'At University College, London.'

Tahar nodded, then looked questioningly at Henning.

'No!' Henning laughed. 'I'm with the WHO, though Elodie and I do work in the same field – she makes the discoveries, my job is to translate them into practical programmes.'

'Programmes?'

'We work on malaria,' Elodie explained. 'Trying to find a biological method to control the disease.'

'I see,' Tahar said, indicating the upholstered chairs ranged round the low wooden table. They sat, Elodie and Henning on one side, Tahar on the other. 'Malaria, of course, is not a problem at this latitude. What do you mean by biological control?'

'There are various parasites and predators that attack the mosquito that spreads malaria,' Henning explained. 'Since the failure of chemical control – there's so much resistance to insecticides, and not enough new molecules coming through – much effort is going into ways to deploy the mosquito's natural foes to wipe it out. Without mosquitos, the protozoan that causes malaria would have no way of getting into the human population.'

'I see. And this would interrupt its life cycle – is that the correct term?'

'Exactly,' Elodie said. 'You just need to break the chain in one place and the whole thing grinds to a halt. Hundreds of millions of lives saved each year.'

Tahar took a sip of his drink. 'And your work? This is with these predators?'

'I come at it from a slightly different angle.' Elodie felt

impatient to turn the conversation round to Bridie, but she was unsure how to do so without appearing rude. 'My group is involved with the hormonal control of mosquito metamorphosis. We've adapted a virus to carry mutated copies of the juvenile hormone gene. The alteration means the genes aren't susceptible to the usual off-switch. If we can get the virus to introduce those genes into the mosquito's DNA then there'll be too much hormone produced. That will arrest development at the larval stage, preventing them from entering metamorphosis, so they'll never mature into the adult insect. It's life cycles again, only we're trying to interrupt the mosquito's so we can get at the malaria parasite in turn.' She gave a laugh. 'That's the theory, anyway. I wouldn't say we've quite got there yet.'

Tahar shook his head. 'I find it astonishing, the level at which we humans are able to manipulate the processes of life. It makes my own work look altogether insignificant.'

'You're a theologian, is that right?' Henning said.

'Yes. I'm interested in the evolution of faith – the different ways mankind has been attempting to relate to God throughout history.' Tahar made a self-deprecating wave with his hand. 'Nothing compared with saving millions of lives a year.'

'You see religion as part of evolution?' Elodie said. She caught Henning's glance out of the corner of her eye. Looked back more fixedly at the professor.

'More that faith itself is evolving,' Tahar said.

Elodie took a sip from her glass. The sweet burst of fruit on her palate. 'In what way, exactly?'

Tahar laughed. 'Well, like your evolution in biology, it is happening at the pace of a snail, but if you look over the sweep of history you can see a gradual convergence of the world's major faiths. The process has reached an exciting phase. I wouldn't use the term religion, incidentally. Faith is the belief in a creator God, and how we relate to Him. Religion is what we humans do to appropriate it for our own purposes.'

'You really think there's a convergence going on?' Elodie was aware of Henning at her side, his diplomat's skills; aware that he would be willing her to drop it. Part of her wanted to drop it, too, but Tahar's idea had piqued her interest, if only because it was so demonstrably wrong. Sr Isidora, that Syrian nun – the pictures were on the web now, Henning had seen them at the internet café – hurrying forward, gulping great gasps of air, a blurred, faceless figure stepping into view in the distance, raising a weapon to his shoulder. 'I'd have thought there was the exact opposite. All this stuff in the Middle East, Afghanistan – the West versus Islam.'

'Well, that mostly concerns the things all wars are about: power, territory, resources, greed. But I agree, the fighters flocking to the Islamist cause appear to be motivated by religion, so it does look like conflict rather than convergence.' Tahar ran a hand through his hair, drawing Elodie's attention to its thick blackness. 'The version of Islam being preached by their leaders is a corruption. It has as much to do with true Islam as the crusades and the inquisition had to do with Christianity.'

'But jihad,' she said. 'That's intrinsic to Islam, isn't it? Waging war on other religions?'

'It's true we are called to protect ourselves if the *umma* – the Muslim community – is attacked militarily. That is not so very different from your concept of a just war, is it not? But the Qur'an teaches explicitly that there must be no coercion in matters of faith. It tells us we must believe in the revelations of all the great prophets – Jesus among them – and that religious pluralism is the will of God.'

He took a sip of his drink. 'All religions have their fundamentalists, and fundamentalists will be at their most – what is the word: vituperative? – when their beliefs are threatened. The global interfaith movement is very challenging to them, of course it is provoking reaction. What we're witnessing is the convulsion out of which a new order will eventually emerge. Your biological evolution is far from bloodless, too, after all, isn't it?'

'You're involved with this interfaith movement?' Henning's question cut across the comment Elodie was forming in her mind, about how biological evolution results in the death of the weak and the survival of the fittest; that it is a brutal, competitive, pitiless process. She felt a flash of irritation with Henning for taking the conversation into different territory, and ever further from Bridie.

'For more than twenty years, yes,' Tahar said. 'It has become the focus of my work. I see myself as contributing to the scholarly foundations of the movement.'

'And it's, what? The major faiths trying to come together – something like the Baha'i?'

Elodie cast a glance at Henning, surprised yet again by his seeming ability to know something about everything. 'What are the Baha'i?'

'Baha'i is a sect of Islam, is that right, Tahar?'

'Not a sect as such,' Tahar said, 'though it did arise out of Islam. The Baha'i believe in the unity of all religions. But the interfaith movement is different to this – it is more concerned with understanding and tolerance between faiths, recognising that we are all following paths towards the same destination.

It goes beyond religion. We have many members who are humanists, and rationalists, and spiritualists. It's about healing the rifts within religions – Sunnis and Shias, Catholics and Protestants – and bridging the gulfs between different religions and with other worldviews. It's about finding the common ground, the truth of what it means to live a good life.'

'No disrespect,' Elodie said, 'but this is the first I've heard of such a movement. I know about ecumenicalism within Christianity, but I've never come across the idea that the major religions are coming together.'

Tahar smiled gently. 'If you will forgive me, I suspect that says more about what is considered important by your country's media. Perhaps even about the stories you like to tell yourselves – that God is dead, yes? That Islam is a dangerous creed?

'Have you even heard of the Common Word letter?' He searched their eyes. 'Over the past decade, hundreds of leading Muslim scholars have come together to invite Christians and Jews to join cause with Islam around the two great commandments common to all our religions: to love God above all, and to love the neighbour as yourself. The initiative has met with an unprecedented outpouring of warmth from leaders of Judaism and Christianity – your own Archbishop of Canterbury, and the Pope no less. The momentum is building every year – we have had landmark conferences hosted by King Abdullah of the Sauds, and King Carlos of Spain. Because it doesn't involve killing anyone, or blowing up a bomb, it is not considered newsworthy. All the same, it is there and it is real, and every bomb detonated and every bullet discharged in the name of hatred and extremism adds to the strength of our cause. We are attracting people of goodwill throughout the world.' He fixed Elodie with a stare, his dark brown eyes frank. 'Your sister included.'

She felt a sudden skip in her chest. 'Bridie was interested in this interfaith idea?'

Tahar nodded. 'I would say it became her greatest love, even beyond the library and her English tuition.'

Elodie drained the last of her pomegranate juice, rested the glass back down on the carved wooden table. Her mouth felt dry, in spite of the drink. Finally, something concrete; an end to speculation.

'Tahar, you had some things to tell us about what Bridie had been going through here. Things that were connected with her mental breakdown. I had no idea she was running a library – I couldn't believe it when I saw what had happened to her church. Now you're telling me my sister abandoned Catholicism in favour of some new world religion? I feel like not only has my sister disappeared, but I no longer know who my sister was.'

'Of course, I understand.' Tahar got to his feet. 'Come through, please. We can talk about these things as we eat.'

Tahar showed them to the other reception room and seated them at the dining table, returning with a large dish which he placed on a skillet in the middle. Steam rose from a mound of couscous shot through with diced lamb and colourful vegetables. Elodie was suddenly aware how hungry she was, watching thankfully as the professor heaped several serving spoons' worth of food on to her plate. The aromas of fried onions, peppers, tomatoes seemed to fill her senses. She waited until the other plates were filled, then picked up her fork.

'Would you like to say a grace?' Tahar said.

'Oh. No, I tend not to,' Elodie said. She felt acutely awkward; looked to Henning for rescue.

'Please,' Henning said. 'Would you lead us?'

Tahar smiled briefly and dropped his gaze. 'Bismillahi wa 'ala barakatillah.'

'Thank you,' Henning said. 'How does it translate?'

'In the name of Allah and with Allah's blessing do we eat. It reminds us of our complete dependence on God for all we need and all we have.' Tahar nodded at their plates. 'Please, bon appétit.'

The food was delicious, subtly spiced; the couscous a delightful crumbly texture. There was stuffed bread to accompany it, reminding Elodie of a peshwari nan with its sweet counterpoint of almond. She wondered if the professor had cooked it himself, or whether there was a wife or a servant behind the scenes.

'Perhaps I feel guilty,' Tahar said. 'Without my influence, perhaps your sister's life would have taken a different course.'

'What do you mean?'

'Sister Sebastian was a member of our regional interfaith dialogue group - Bishop Bonouvrie made the initial introductions. When the last Christians left Beb she was at a loss, wanting to find a role that would allow her to continue her life here. The library was, I suppose, something that grew out of that need. She started to tutor some of the students, and that led to her lending them her own books. When she saw how useful that was, she wanted to get them more. She said her friends back in Britain had shelf upon shelf of books just gathering dust. She made some requests, and soon the parcels began to arrive.'

Elodie tried to finish her mouthful. It was suddenly too

dry, seemed to lodge in her throat before she managed finally to get it to go down. 'So the books in her church, they were sent by friends back in England?'

Tahar tore off a piece of bread. 'To begin with. But it became – viral – is that the phrase? – friends of friends, even some total strangers, sending gifts of books they no longer wanted. It was like a jewel mine to the students. A wonderful source of diverse texts. They are still arriving – some come most weeks.'

'Surely you have a library at the university?' Elodie said.

'Yes, but we have so few books written in English. And English is what our students so desperately want. You may not appreciate it, but your language is the language in which the world conducts its affairs.'

'And Bridie teaching them English, this caused problems?'

'The fundamentalist backlash I spoke of, we are not immune to it in Beb,' Tahar said. 'Your sister's superiors were extremely distrustful of what she was doing, and she met a similar reaction from the conservative imans here. Cultural imperialism, exposure to Western decadence. Underlying it, the fear that our youth would escape our control. For some years our government has pursued a policy of eventual self-sufficiency. There has been a massive expansion of higher education – my own college is a product – in order to train a generation of graduates to take on every role in our society. But there is a tension between what our country, our culture requires, and what individuals want for themselves. New ideas, new ways of seeing the world: they excite and entice those eager to carve their own path, and simultaneously provoke the most severe reactions among those who believe they possess the only truth.'

Elodie rested her fork down. Her appetite, so keen just minutes ago, had shrivelled to nothing. 'What form did these reactions take?'

Tahar gave a sigh. 'Delegations from some of the mosques to begin with, instructing Sister Sebastian to desist. We discussed it at length. She didn't need me to tell her what was the right thing to do. Things became more confrontational. She was very brave; she refused to be intimidated.'

'Intimidated?' Henning, too, had stopped eating.

'There were incidents,' Tahar said. 'Nothing to speak of to begin with, just the occasional slogan daubed on the walls of her church, which were easily painted over. Then there was a morning when she opened up the library to find someone had thrown blood over the door. That was more disturbing. The students organised a watch after that, where there would always be someone with her throughout the day. They were determined to support her and her library.'

'I saw her room, her flat,' Elodie said. 'She left in a hurry. There was still food in the fridge.'

'I very much regret the actions of some of my countrymen.' Tahar sat back in his chair, regarding her seriously. 'It was impossible to watch over her constantly. There was an attack on the church in the middle of the night – a mob of some size, who attempted to break down the door, which held, God be praised. Your sister was on her own inside. The experience must have terrified her. After that we organised for her to spend nights here, and at the homes of other colleagues from the university, and other sympathisers in the city, moving her every few days. It was not an easy time.'

Elodie could feel the pulse in her neck. 'So what happened? What caused her to leave? *Did* she leave?'

'Yes, of course, no harm came to her, I assure you.' Tahar looked uncomfortable, only meeting her gaze for the briefest of moments. 'I don't think it was a single thing, perhaps the accumulated strain. I am talking about these events in summary – but they took place over many months, gradually escalating. I don't think any of us understood the pressure she was under. Beb was her *home*, you understand? She loved the students, the people here. She did not want to leave, but at the same time I think she could no longer see how she could stay.'

'Professor.' Elodie held his gaze, refused to let him look away. 'Do you know where my sister has gone?'

A faint ringing in her ears. The feeling of breath being difficult to draw in.

'I am very sorry. She left the apartment of a colleague one morning, apparently intending to open the library as usual. It was a changeover day – she was due to come here the following night – so there was nothing remarkable about her taking her things with her. All I was ever able to discover was that, instead of going to the library, she went to the bus station. She hasn't been heard from since.'

Like every road in this country there were no street lights. The route back to the hotel had a number of stunted trees along its pavements. In the pitch black of night, the taxi's full-beam picked them out: their trunks had been whitewashed to head-height, rendering them like watchful ghosts. Henning's hand found hers, his fingers enveloping the fist she hadn't been aware she was making.

'She never asked you to send any books, did she?'

Elodie shook her head silently. She wanted to be back home. She didn't know where her home was anymore. Not with Adam. Not with Mummy. Not with Henning. Yet. Ever?

'It feels like a massive rebuke,' she told him. 'Like she was rejecting me along with everything else.'

'Did she not just want to keep things secret? If she'd asked you then she'd have to have told you about the library, and then she'd have to have told you everything else: that she had no mission any more, that she'd become a glorified English teacher instead.'

'She used to *be* an English teacher. There's no shame in that.'

'Maybe it felt like a backwards step. Maybe it felt like she'd failed or something.'

'No, just leave it. Please. You don't understand.'

Henning was silent for a few moments. 'Do you? Understand?'

Elodie tucked her bottom lip between her teeth, bit down on the flesh till it hurt.

'I think so, yes.'

As they flashed round a bend in the road the headlights briefly picked out a group of men, one of them kneeling on the ground, his hands on his head, the others gathered round him in a loose circle, a couple of them gesticulating, frozen in the act of shouting. There were guns. She barely had time to register the scene before they were past. She felt Henning tighten his grip on her hand.

'What was that about?'

'I've no idea,' he said. 'But none of our business.'

'Do you think he was all right? It looked like they were going to hurt him.'

'We don't know that.'

'Don't you think we should call the police?'

'Elodie. What you saw. That could have been the police.'

She gazed ahead, eyes barely registering the scrolling scene. Bridie last seen boarding a bus. In England, there would have been extensive enquiries, leaflet campaigns, her trail picked up at every subsequent terminus, interviews conducted with drivers, passengers, ticket vendors, piecing together the journey Bridie had made. Should she do what she had originally intended, make an appointment to see the local inspector supposedly charged with investigating Bridie's disappearance? The man who had told the British consulate there was absolutely nothing to go on. What she would say to him? How on earth could she tackle the subject without creating conflict? She would be better advised to return to the capital; tell Peter Armstrong about Tahar Yacine's account, let him take it up with the authorities, try to get someone - anyone - to take a proper interest in Bridie's fate. Or would Peter - fiddling with that accursed pen of his - just tell her that she didn't understand the political sensitivities?

'What did you make of Tahar?' Henning asked.

'I don't know. He seemed nice.' She waited, but Henning didn't say anything. 'Why?'

'I'm not sure. I don't think he was telling us everything.'

'How do you mean?'

'The whole interfaith group, the library. He was as much a part of it as your sister was. If she was meeting such opposition, don't you think he'd have been targeted, too?'

'Perhaps he was. Perhaps he didn't feel the need to tell us.'

'But Bridie was lodging with him sometimes, along with

the other academics. It's like they knew she'd be safe with them. Like theirs were safe houses.'

Her eyes felt gritty, tired. The dazzle of oncoming headlights. The thrum of the taxi on the road.

'I don't know,' she said. 'People always scapegoat the foreigner don't they, the person they don't understand? You see that again and again back home, with immigrants and asylum-seekers, how everything that's wrong with the country is their fault, and how if they just got the hell back home then everything would be all right.'

'OK, maybe,' Henning said. 'I still don't get why she left in such a hurry. I just got the feeling there was something he wasn't telling us.'

The taxi started to slow, the indicator light flashing from the dashboard, the driver jabbing the meter to bring up the final fare. Elodie delved into her bag with her free hand, trying to locate her wallet. Felt her fingers brush against cool hard metal.

'Shit,' she said.

'What's wrong?'

'The keys.' She let out a heavy breath. 'I forgot to give him the keys to the church.'

'Never mind,' Henning gave her hand a squeeze. 'We'll get them back to him tomorrow.'

It was the last thing she needed. The initial clarity Tahar had brought was quickly ramifying into further confusion and difficulty. Henning paid the driver, and they disembarked on to the pavement outside their hotel. They stood, the taxi's red tail lights pulling away from them. Henning laughed, pulling his hand out of the trouser pocket where he'd deposited the change. Showed her the hotel key lying in his palm.

'If it makes you feel any better, I forgot to give this to reception when we went out.' He slipped an arm round her waist. 'Come on, let's get inside. I could do with a shower and something to drink.'

Fourteen

THEY FLEW FROM Gatwick, landing in Berne at two in the afternoon. Elodie had the tent in her rucksack, Bridie had the sleeping bags and roll mats. The British July had been characteristically variable, but in Switzerland it was sweltering. They stripped down to shorts and vests in the airport loos, then shouldered their packs and set off to trawl the ranks of bus stops outside the terminal building.

'Where are we headed?' Bridie asked, pausing in front of a departures notice board.

'Nice try,' Elodie said. 'Don't worry, it'll be easy to spot.'

It was. A great crowd of people down at the far end of the bus station, most of them in their teens and twenties, everyone lugging camping gear and ruckies, the occasional guitar slung by its strap over someone's back, hiking boots and shorts and bandanas and shades and baseball caps and giant foam hands and outlandish hats and t-shirts emblazoned with every kind of logo from festivals and bands and designer labels. Buses were rolling up every few minutes, embarking another fifty or sixty people, then setting off again leaving a fug of diesel fumes in their wake.

'OK, so I get that we're going to a festival,' Bridie said. 'And thank you very much. Really. But why not Reading or Leeds or somewhere like that? Why Switzerland?'

The way she said it. Like she couldn't imagine anything good happening in such a staid, conservative country.

'That's part of the surprise,' Elodie told her, laughing when Bridie poked her tongue out in response.

The bus took them climbing up a winding road, switching back on itself every few hundred yards, all the while gaining altitude. Elodie's ears popped several times during the ascent. Out of the window, way below now, she could see the miniaturised city of Berne carpeting the land. Eventually, the road began to level out, and they caught their first glimpses of the site, sprawled across the flattened summit: two massive stages, audience fields stretching out in front, several marquees housing smaller venues, the great arc of tents pitched in the sleeping zone that tracked all the way around the perimeter.

'It's called the Gurtenfestival,' Elodie said. 'It's been going nearly as long as Glastonbury. Generally gets better weather, though. I love that they hold it on top of a mountain.'

They got themselves pitched, stowed their gear, and went and found themselves drinks in the Bamboo Bar. For the rest of the Friday evening they traipsed, arm in arm, round the main and the fringe venues, sampling breath-taking jazz and Euro pop groups and wistful folk bands and any number of circus acts and street theatre performances. Elodie had commandeered the programme they'd been given when they'd checked in, refusing to let Bridie see it, telling her she was going to be entertainments officer for the weekend. But she kept expecting to see a flier or a poster that would give the game away, would let slip that Bridie's favourite band – the band she'd introduced Elodie to, and that Elodie loved in turn – were headlining. There was none.

It was pathetic, really, watching Bridie trying to be grateful. Elodie knew that the decimation of her life would take a long time to heal. Knew that this weekend would be but a drop in the ocean. She also knew that if she'd told Bridie she wanted to take her away from it all, to go to a festival together and just forget everything for three precious days, dance and sing and get thoroughly mashed, that Bridie would have said no, she didn't feel like it, she couldn't face it, it was the last thing she could think of doing.

So she'd kept schtum. Told her they were going away for a surprise long weekend, and that all she needed was her passport, camping gear, summer togs, and the sunniest smile she could muster.

She resolved not to mention Tim at all. If Bridie wanted to talk, fine. But if she didn't then even finer. That was the whole point of getting away.

Saturday, Bridie seemed to wake despondent, no appetite for breakfast, leaving her burger half-eaten at lunch, failing to engage in banter with some ridiculous lads from Folkestone they met in the queue for the bar. The afternoon line-up on the main stage included Skunk Anansie, and a massive blast by UB40, and they seemed to lift her mood. But, even so, Elodie could tell her dancing was half-hearted, and when everyone in the crowd was singing along to I Got You Babe, Bridie excused herself and disappeared off to the portaloos for a long time. Elodie wondered if she should tell her, wondered if it would lift her spirits if she knew what was to come, but she kept her counsel, all the way till seven o'clock.

Roadies: guitars deposited, leads taped down, scurrying off the stage.

Then figures from left and right, one sliding in behind the drum kit, another hoisting the bass aloft. Sister Bliss, close-cropped blonde hair, dressed all in white, taking up station behind her stack of synths. Maxi Jazz in grey slacks and unbuttoned shirt, raising an arm in acknowledgement of the crowd, a huge cheer going up as he emerged from the wings.

'*This* is why we're here!' she shouted in Bridie's ear.

Bridie just nodded at her. Elodie could see moisture rimming her eyes. She wrapped her arms around her and hugged her. 'It's going to be all right, Bride. It's going to be fine.'

They opened with *Salva Mea*, Bliss's entrancing voice floating over a plaintive synth intro that she kept going for ages, teasing the crowd before finally ripping into the techno-inspired dance riff. Then gliding seamlessly into a thumping version of *Insomnia* that they must have improvised on for a quarter of an hour. At some point Bridie seemed to make a decision, throwing her arms up, shimmying and swaying her body with its now-healed scars, her eyes closed as she drew inside the music and let herself go. Elodie was bubbling over: she *loved* this sound, the amazing amalgam of trance house techno soul; she *loved* that her sister, in the midst of her grief, could be, however temporarily, consoled.

Synthesiser chords, spine tingling glissandos from the bar chimes, tantalising percussive riffs on the bongos. The kind of ethereal build-up Faithless excelled in. Then Maxi's voice, his Brixton drawl booming from the speakers, speaking not rapping, like a preacher from the pulpit. New lyrics, new sounds, a new song from their upcoming album:

This is my church
This is where I heal my hurt
It's a natural grace
Of watching young life shape
It's in minor keys
Solutions and remedies

Enemies becoming friends
When bitterness ends
This is my church
For tonight
God is a DJ

And the driving bass kicked in, and Sister Bliss was thumping her keys like they were drums, and the banks of lights were pulsing with a hundred thousand lumens, and the whole place exploded into a single mass of jumping dancing humanity. Elodie had her arm around Bridie, felt the coursing thrill that came only from live music, music loud enough to lift her and envelop her and consume her. Music that was no longer simply sound, but had become substance. And, yes, Bridie was dancing, too – smiling, actually grinning – one hand held high, watching the stage on which played *their* band, the mass of her beautiful hair bewitched by the rhythm of her body. She looked across at that moment, caught Elodie's eye, mouthed a 'thank you' that, had it been actual words, would have been completely drowned in the noise that surrounded them.

❧

The hard ground was barely softened by the roll mats. All around them was laughter and chatter and distant drunken singing in foreign tongues. They lay on their backs, looking up at the vague shape of the flysheet just a couple of feet above their faces, the air in the tent gradually warming and becoming humid with their respiration. Elodie's ears were ringing.

'So how's London?' Bridie's voice seemed disembodied in the dark.

'Good, thanks. It's good to be back.'

'And your post-doc, how's that going?'

'Good, thanks, yeah. It's early days, but it's a great department. Penny Newton, my supervisor, is lovely. So, yes, I'm really happy.'

'Still working on those poor mozzies?'

'Not the same ones, obviously. But, yes, still working on them.'

'Doing what now?'

It seemed so technical, and such a world away from this Swiss mountaintop. 'The gene I mutated in Manchester? We're trying to find a way to get it into mosquito cells.'

'Isn't it in there already?'

'Sure. But it actually stops them maturing, so they never reach reproductive age, so there's no way of getting the altered gene to spread through the population. The idea is to find a virus that's highly infectious to mosquitos, and see if we can use that to introduce the gene, so we can knock out whole generations at a stroke.'

'Oh, OK,' Bridie's tone was difficult to read. 'That sounds quite scary.'

'If you're a mosquito. Not if you happen to be a human being living in a malarial area.'

They lay in silence, Elodie turning over the innumerable difficulties that lay ahead – identifying a suitable viral pathogen, perfecting its *in vitro* replication, all the headaches around gene insertion and vector transmission, and whether they would ever manage to get the exogenous juvenile hormone gene over-expressed *in vivo* in *Anopheles*. Ten, fifteen years work, there, Penny had told her; the post-doc is just the start. Rosie Glenn had been right: this was proving to be the key to her whole career. Maxi Jazz's line came back to her: *watching young life shape*. Hers was taking on exciting form, at least in work terms. There was the nagging absence of a relationship, though. Twenty-six next month. Nothing ever seemed to pan out. Though with what had happened to Bridie.

'I'm giving up teaching.'

'Sorry?" Elodie had been lost in her thoughts.

'I'm not going back, after the summer. I'm jacking it in.'

'I thought you loved it.'

'I did. I do.' She hesitated. 'It's just too painful.'

Elodie thought about it. Working with kids, day in, day out.

'You don't think it'll get better? With time?'

Silence.

'What're you going to do, then?' Elodie asked.

Another long pause.

'I've been going back to church. St Elizabeth's,' Bridie said.

'You left all that behind.'

'I did. But everything that's happened. It makes sense to me now.'

'What makes sense?'

'I was such a fool, El. I thought all that stuff about how to live life properly was a load of bollocks, designed to keep us all in our places. A means of social control. I didn't think it applied any more, not in this day and age, not to me, not with all the freedoms and choices we get to make.'

Elodie turned over, tried to make out her sister's profile in the gloom. 'What happened to you, Bridie, that was just chance. Really really rotten awful luck, and I'd give anything for it not to have happened, but it was just a dreadful, random thing.'

'If we hadn't been having sex then I wouldn't have got

pregnant and if I hadn't got pregnant then I wouldn't have miscarried and if I hadn't miscarried then I wouldn't have needed the D&C. And if—'

'I know, I know.' Elodie reached a hand out, laid it on Bridie's arm. 'But that could have happened whatever. Just because you were living together—'. She shook her head. 'I don't want to sound harsh, but what if you'd got married already, and the same thing had happened then?'

'I don't think it would have.'

'Oh, come on,' Elodie felt irritation rise, had consciously to suppress her reaction. 'Disasters happen to people no matter how they choose to live. You could've been a virgin bride and still ended up in the same dreadful situation. Honestly, Bridie, I bet if you did a study and looked at all the people who've suffered the same catastrophe as you – and I don't want to hurt your feelings – but you'd not find they were all somehow deemed sinners by the Catholic church.'

'You're not listening to me.' Bridie shifted her weight in her sleeping bag, the material slithering. 'I'm not talking about hypotheticals, experiments, studies. I'm talking about me, what happened to *me*. My experience. What's happened to my *life*.'

'OK, I'm sorry, I was out of line.' She sighed. 'But, really, Bride, I hate to see you beat yourself up like this. It wasn't your *fault*. You just feel like it was because of all the guilt crap we absorbed over the years. There's people all over the world having pre-marital sex, one night stands, all kinds of stuff the church wouldn't approve of, and none of them gets to suffer the kind of complication you did.'

She thought of her own love life, the half-dozen partners she'd had, some more serious than others. If anyone were to have been asking for it. And yet, she was fine. Where was the justice in that? Once again, there was the great yawning appreciation of the magnitude of Bridie's loss. How her life could never be the same. She felt sick for her. Scared of what this experience might do to her.

She could make out Bridie's interlinked hands, coming to rest on her forehead, her thumbs pressed against her temples, her elbows jutting into the air.

'Not my fault, maybe, but my responsibility. It's all there, in the church's teaching, how to avoid screwing up your life big-style.'

She should drop it, leave it there. Now wasn't the time. In all probability there never would be a time. She wasn't sure who she was arguing with any more.

'I'm sorry, Bridie, but you're wrong. What happened to you would've happened anyway, whether you were cohabiting or married or whatever.'

Shrieks of laughter from a nearby tent. The quiet strumming of a guitar off in the distance.

'Yeah, but if we had been married then maybe Tim would have stuck by me.'

Elodie lay there, turning that thought round in her mind. She felt incredibly angry with him, leaving Bridie high and dry like that. It'd been *his* baby she'd miscarried, his baby that had set the whole tragedy in train. If he was here now, she wouldn't like to think what she'd do. He'd stayed in the situation for a number of months but things had grown difficult between them, Bridie had told her, the fun seemed to have gone out of their life together, they were bickering and arguing and storming off all the time. Then the fatal blow: he no longer loved her, he realised, he'd made a mistake, he wanted to call the whole thing off.

It was hard not to hear the words he hadn't spoken: that he wanted kids, and that was something Bridie could no longer give him.

Three months ago. Bridie's life, already fatally flawed, had been smashed to smithereens. There'd been the flat to sell, the stuff to divide up, the broken dreams to sweep into a pile and gather in the dustpan and dispose of in the bin.

Their parents, ignorant of anything but the break-up. Mummy: heartbroken for her. Their father: she made her own bed; don't say I didn't warn her.

'I'm sorry, Bridie,' Elodie said, softening her tone as best she could, 'but Tim showed his true colours. I don't think it would have made any difference were you to have tied the knot or not. I still think he would have gone.'

The silence became painful. She kept waiting, straining her ears to hear if Bridie were quietly crying, but there was no sound. She couldn't have fallen asleep. Was she just lying there, seething at Elodie for having spoken home truths? Elodie cursed herself: nice one, El; this was supposed to be a fantastic break for her, a chance for Bridie to leave all the shit and mess behind however briefly. And you have to go and trash it by not being able to keep your tongue still in your head.

'I'm sorry,' she said. 'I'm really sorry.'

'It's OK, I forgive you. You're probably right. He probably would have gone anyway.' A massive sigh.

'What are you going to do, then,' Elodie asked, 'if you're giving up teaching?'

'What happened, happened for a reason,' Bridie said. 'I believe I've been given the clearest possible message that I was never supposed to be a mother. I've taken that lesson

– it's been bloody hard – but it's up to me to do something positive with my life, something constructive out of all the destruction.'

Elodie waited in silence, rebelling in her heart against these notions of messages and lessons, but keeping her lips tightly sealed, determined to do nothing more than listen.

'I've had some preliminary meetings with this religious order, the Sisters of the Divine Mercy. They're based in France. The PP invited them to come and speak at St Elizabeth's. I'm drawn to them, El – their whole purpose is mission, getting out into the most difficult parts of the world to bear witness. I know you won't get this, but I've prayed about it a lot, and I think it's what I'm being called to do.'

'You're going to do mission work with a bunch of French nuns? That sounds good. Where might you go?'

'I'm not just going to work with them, El, I'm going to join them. I'm going to become a nun.'

∗

She was relieved to learn there was a noviciate programme; Bridie would spend two years living in community in the Ardennes before committing herself. Elodie was sure she was acting out of grief, and false guilt – punishing herself because she felt she deserved to be punished. But time would heal, she was sure of it. Perhaps a retreat to a convent in a completely different country would be part of that process. Two years was a sensible timescale – she felt like congratulating those French nuns on the wisdom of it. Even the most grievous pain would lessen and dull over such a period. There was plenty of time for Bridie to rediscover herself, get her life back on track, before she'd be due to take her solemn vow.

So she played along, was encouraging even, throughout the rest of that Gurtenfestival weekend. In a way it was something they could come together over. Was Bridie surprised, relieved – amazed, even – to find her agnostic sister, her Faithless friend, so enthusiastic about her new direction, her new purpose? She guessed she must have been. It wasn't till afterwards, when they'd taken leave of each other, returning to their respective ends of the country – Elodie to resume her post-doc; Bridie to continue the painful process of winding up her blighted life – that she realised that, to Bridie's new way of thinking, Elodie's unexpected reaction could, conceivably, have been interpreted as a confirmatory sign. If so, then how much more so Mummy's response – delight at this Godly turn – even the grudging affirmation of their father, seeing in her decision an appropriate atonement for sin.

Fifteen

SHE ALWAYS PUT Maddie on the left, Ollie on the right. It was automatic, like writing: first-born at the beginning of the line, second-born coming after. Henning was in the shower. She could hear the water streaming, the splashes echoing off the tiles. She didn't want to alarm him unnecessarily, even though her insides felt suddenly liquefied. She kept staring at the photos of her children on the bedside cupboard, trying to remember putting them up, willing herself to realise she'd made a simple mistake and had done things differently this one time.

Her passport and travel documents were where they should be, tucked in the zipper pocket in the side of her bag. Her laptop was still lying on the bed where she'd left it. At least, she often left it on the bed, but the more she thought about it, the more she couldn't remember having used it since they arrived in Beb. So it ought, by rights, still to be tucked away.

She clicked it on.

Windows, booting itself.

'Henning,' she called, opening the door to the en suite.

He turned to her, suds sluicing down his broad chest.

'I think someone's been in the room.'

He silenced the shower, dried himself swiftly, tying the towel round his waist like a sarong. Crouched down to check his holdall. Quickly ascertained that all his money and papers were as they should be.

'I'm sure of it,' she told him. 'The children's photos are the wrong way round, and I always leave my computer hibernated, but it's just booted from scratch.'

'It couldn't have done some automatic update?' He sounded concerned, even though he was looking for the rational explanation.

'I don't think it does them, not unless it's connected. I haven't had wifi since Hotel Splendid.'

He went to inspect the door, but there was no damage round the lock. The windows were closed and shuttered from the inside, just as they'd left them that afternoon, guarding the room as best as possible against the heat of the day.

'Hold on.' He went back to his bag, opening the side pocket. Delved a hand inside. Groped around for a moment then withdrew it.

'Fuck.'

'What?'

'The lanyards. Our WHO ID. They're gone.'

She had never seen him like this. He was always so calm and measured. He moved as he spoke, shedding his towel and pulling on his clothes from earlier.

'Better get your stuff together. Quickly.'

'What's going on?' she asked.

'We have to get out of here right away. Just get your passport and money, we're leaving everything else.'

'What do you mean?'

'Someone has been here, and they've left everything of value. I really don't like that. That feels to me like they might come back at any moment.' He looked at her, fingers skipping from button to button down his shirt front. 'I really don't think it would be a good idea for us to be here if they do.'

He rang down to reception, asking them to arrange another taxi.

'We're going to visit an acquaintance,' he told her.

'It's gone ten.'

He shrugged. 'It's the best we can do. Someone in the hotel must be involved – there's no sign of forced entry.'

She stowed her valuables in her bag, put her laptop in, too. She went to fetch the children's photos.

'Leave them,' Henning said.

She turned to him in silent appeal.

'We need them to think we'll be coming back,' he said. 'We can't get a bus till morning. We can't afford to have them start looking for us.'

They went down to reception, the wide staircase allowing enough of a view to ensure the lower flights were empty.

'Just act completely natural,' Henning said, as they neared the lobby.

He handed the key in. Elodie hung back: it wasn't Monsieur Azoulay. A young guy, early twenties, face shrapnelled by dark acne scars. She didn't recognise him, didn't think they'd seen him since they'd arrived, but in truth she hadn't paid much attention, letting Henning sort everything as would be culturally expected.

'You are going out?' the receptionist asked. It sounded like friendly interest, but how could you tell?

'Old colleagues, at the university,' Henning said. 'They weren't free till now.'

She wasn't sure he should have added that. He was usually so capable, so on-it. That sounded like too much information.

'Will you be late?'

'I don't know. Probably. Will that be a problem?'

'Pas de problem, m'sieur. The night porter will be on duty throughout the night. Ring the bell for entry.'

'Thank you,' Henning said. 'Good night.'

They climbed in the taxi, Henning instructing the driver to take them to the university quarter. Within seconds of setting off, bright headlights appeared behind, casting looming shadows of their heads on the taxi's ceiling. Elodie stared fixedly ahead, aware out of the corner of her eye that Henning was doing the same. She gripped his hand tightly. Minute after minute, and still the car was on their tail. It was close, she could tell that from the fierceness of the glare, it felt like it was practically on their bumper. It could mean nothing, or it could mean everything. Her neck began to ache. Every oncoming vehicle that flashed past, headlights dazzling, was like a threatened blow – Elodie could see it in her mind's eye, a 4x4 suddenly slewing into their path, forcing the taxi into an emergency stop; the car behind halting abruptly just inches away to block any reverse; masked men spilling out into the road, automatic rifles in hand, wrenching open the taxi's passenger doors, the air filled with incomprehensible shouted commands. She could feel the pulse in her neck, could hear it in her ear. Why the hell had she come here? Dragged Henning into all this, too? She glanced at him, his profile light and shadow, staring ahead, thinking: what? Regret, too?

Red lights. The wait interminable. The taxi driver's fingers were drumming on the top of his wheel. She could still hear the engine note from the vehicle behind. Her ears strained for the first sound of a door slamming shut.

They should turn right here. She looked at the driver's fingers, tap tap tapping. He had his indicator on. But there was absolutely nothing to stop him suddenly driving straight ahead, taking them to God knows where against their will.

Green. The taxi swung into a right turn, down towards the university.

The headlights behind did not follow.

'Thank God,' Elodie breathed.

Henning turned to her. Gave her a silent smile. Shook his head ruefully.

The taxi dropped them near the university entrance. Henning paid the driver, and they watched till he was out of sight.

'OK, let's go,' he said.

'Do you think Tahar will mind, us turning up like this?'

'We're not going there,' Henning said. 'We can't trust a soul.'

'Where, then?' she said. They couldn't walk the streets all night.

'You've got the key,' Henning told her. 'We'll stay at your sister's library.'

He had perfect recall for the route they'd taken earlier. There was good moonlight; she recognised the market place, empty of stalls now, here and there the red glow from braziers around which clusters of men were gathered. They strode on, Elodie keeping her eyes ahead, feeling more confident now they were away from the hotel, away from anywhere anyone might expect them to be. Up ahead she saw the tree in the middle of the road, behind it the murky shape of Bridie's chapel. Inside the darkened porch, Henning used the flashlight on his phone to locate the lock. Elodie slid the key home and turned it, opening the door to their sanctuary.

The church had retained the heat of the day, and Elodie

immediately felt its warmth. Henning bolted the door from the inside so they were secure. If there were lights for the main body of the chapel, they couldn't find the switch. Henning's torchlight was swallowed by the space. They made their way carefully, following the pool of near-distance illumination, past the pews with their silent ranks of novels and knowledge that Bridie had assembled in this place. The other side of the sacristy door they did find a light-switch, and their eyes flinched in the sudden brightness from the bare overhead bulb.

'We'd better not have it on too long, in case we draw attention,' Henning said, 'but it should be OK for a while.'

He retrieved a couple of thick, chipped glasses from Bridie's shelves, and ran some water from the tap. They sat at her table, with its crucifix and its English dogs calendar, and slaked mouths dried by adrenaline. She looked at the mementoes, the photos: back among Bridie's things, when she hadn't thought she ever would be.

'Do you think we'll be OK?' she asked.

'I think so,' Henning said. 'By the time anyone realises we're not coming back to the hotel we may even be on the bus out – but at the very worst it will be well into the night, and if they do start to look for us, *and* if they track down the taxi, they'll start at the university. There's no reason to think we'd be here.'

'Are you sure someone is targeting us?' It seemed bizarrely other-worldly, habituated as she was to life in London with its securities and certainties.

'I'm not sure of anything,' Henning confessed, 'except that whoever was in our room wasn't interested in stealing our things. That means they must be more interested in us, in who we are. I don't know, El. If they'd gone to get a price, to see what it would be worth to come back and take us at gunpoint. I don't know. I'd prefer to be wrong about it and OK here, than right about it and kidnapped for sale to whichever extremist group will pay the most.' He glanced around the room, its single window high up on the wall. 'This feels like the ideal place in which to spend our last hours in Beb.'

The sudden force of the words. They would be leaving. They had to leave. With Bridie still lost to her.

'You don't think we should contact the police?'

Henning shook his head. 'It's not like at home.'

'The consulate, then?'

He fished out his phone again. He had some amazing roaming package from the WHO, which meant he could connect to networks in virtually any country in the world. 'I do have signal,' he said, peering at the screen.

If you are a British national in distress. The thought of Peter Armstrong, Anne. All the trouble they'd gone to to help her.

'I don't know,' she said. 'Are we over-reacting?'

'Maybe,' he said. 'I'm not sure what they could do, in any case. They'd probably just contact the police. Mind you, that could be helpful, if the police knew your consulate was involved.'

It was stupid, damnable. While it was just them, they could be completely mistaken and no one would ever know. The minute they involved others the questions would start, the opinions would be formed. Did it matter if they were judged to have panicked, to have shouted out about monsters at the foot of the bed in the middle of the night?

Henning flipped his phone case closed. 'Let's leave it for now,' he said. 'It's a big city. I think we've done enough.' He drained the last of his water. Got to his feet. 'What I do think is we should get some rest. We need to get going first thing.'

They moved through to Bridie's bedroom and stood contemplating its narrow single bed.

'Shall I flip a coin?' Henning said.

It felt reassuring, to hear his quiet humour again. It meant he must truly be happy they were out of whatever danger they might have been in. And if he was happy, so was she. She elbowed him in the side.

'Counting sheep is better, I think. But you'll certainly need to do something. That floor looks really uncomfortable.'

Henning extinguished the light and they fumbled forward, finding the bed, squashing together on the mattress, fully clothed, Elodie managing to arrange the blanket that had once retained the heat of her sister's body.

'Henning?' she said, feeling his breath warm against her neck. 'What are we going to do about our things at the hotel?'

'It's too risky to go back,' he said. 'I'll wire money when I'm back in Geneva – maybe Azoulay will forward them on. We'll buy some emergency supplies once we're in the capital, and blame lost luggage when we get home.'

Something about the remark rankled.

'Who would you have to make excuses to?' she said.

'Hey.' She could feel Henning prop himself up on his elbow. 'It was just an expression.' He stroked her cheek, smoothing his hand over her hair. It felt good, a gesture of simple care. 'We have a pact, remember?'

They'd struck a deal, after the first couple of stolen times together, when they both wanted to meet again but both realised they were vulnerable to being badly hurt. If either wanted out for any reason – a new love interest closer to home, or just unable any longer to carry on the long-distance assignations that were inevitable given their situations – then they swore they would put the other person in the picture straight away. No stringing anyone along. Cross my heart.

She shuffled herself back slightly, pressing more firmly into him. She thought about her photos of Maddie and Ollie, abandoned at the hotel, the pictures that had come with her whenever she had travelled to conferences and meetings and symposia.

'Do your boys know you're away?'

'They think it's work,' he said.

He hadn't told them about her yet. Said it was better to wait until they were on a proper footing. Proper footing. By which, they both understood, she had to make the leap and separate from Adam. Not that Henning pressured her. He understood. It had taken him eight years to be able to leave Marta. Eight years during which his determination to keep the family together had become the Achilles' heel with which Marta had come to control him, treating him with ever more contempt. Elodie remembered him telling her: once she understood that I wasn't ever going to leave, it was like the brakes were off; there was nothing to stop her treating me like absolute shit. As soon as the genie was out – as soon as she sensed the power she had – then the only way to get it back in the bottle was to do the very thing she believed I would never do, and which I never ever wanted.

She thought she knew her own moment of fateful weakness now, after a lot of soul-searching. It was way back, when the kids were five and three, and they were run ragged with the demands of family and work and she was being head-hunted for a research fellowship back in Manchester. And Adam hadn't even allowed her to discuss it, hadn't allowed her to express her aspirations and feelings. Had simply told her, in a way that felt like a blow to her solar plexus, that if she took the post and tried to force a move on them then it would be a divorcing matter. The thought of Maddie, Ollie, growing up with a broken family – it filled her with terror, utter fear. Her own childhood fear. What she should have done – what any normal person would have done – was leave it for a couple of days, go back to him and say: that was unacceptable, that's no way to conduct a relationship, we need to talk this through. What she did was, she thanked them politely at Manchester and turned the offer down. After that, there was never going to be a way back. Not unless Adam himself recognised the need to change.

'I'm scared,' she said.

'I think we're all right now,' Henning said.

'Not about here.' She tried to gather her thoughts. 'About the future. I got it so spectacularly wrong with Adam. What's to stop me making the same mistake again?'

'I know,' Henning said again. 'I was the same. You have to trust that you've grown wiser, that you can choose better. You can only do that once you understand what it was about you that got you into such a relationship in the first place, what it was that made you stay.' He kissed the back of her neck, his nose his lips gently parting her hair so he could connect with her flesh. 'I see in you someone I can share a normal life with. I assure you, the same is true of me. But my assurances don't matter. You have to see that for yourself.'

She'd seen no dogs since arriving in this country, but now she heard some, at least two, maybe more, barking and snarling, the noises carrying eerily on the night air. Bridie's room was so dark. She could see the luminous hands on Henning's watch, his arm tucked beneath her neck and stretched out over the side of the bed. She imagined Bridie lying here on another night those months ago. Starkly awake. Listening to the angry shouts outside her church, the repeated thuds as something substantial was smashed again and again against the wooden door. Wondering if at any moment the bolts would pull out of their fixings, and the door cave in, allowing the mob to gain entry and rip and tear and burn and destroy every book in her library, and, God forbid, do unspeakable things to her.

What had she done? Had she prayed? She would have prayed. Our Father, Who Art in Heaven, Hallowed Be Thy Name. Hail Mary, Full of Grace, The Lord is With Thee. Whispered words tumbling from her lips as the assault continued unabated. Elodie was chastened to find that, though she could remember the whole of the Our Father, she couldn't conjure up the second part of the Hail Mary. All the rosaries and penances she must have recited as a child. She'd have thought it would have been ingrained forever.

Outside, the dog fight reached a new crescendo, a high-pitched yelping as one of the protagonists switched from aggression to pain and sudden fear.

Fear. When had that come for Bridie? Is that what faith had done, blunted her capacity to be afraid? And what faith? What version of faith had come to sustain her here, with her books and her library and her teaching and her interfaith dialogue and her sense of belonging to a people other than her own?

'Do you believe in God?' she said.

'I don't know. Maybe.' Henning shifted against her. 'I saw some extraordinary things when I was in practice, things with terminally ill patients it was hard to explain. Even in my own family. Levin, when he was about seven, he woke up with a nightmare that Marta had lost her rings. The thing was, she had, temporarily – she'd taken them off to do some decorating and had forgotten what she'd done with them and was in a real panic. But that was all after he'd gone to sleep. No way could he have known. And Luca, I had a dream about him once, about a cure he needed for something that was wrong with his back. He developed the problem a week later.'

'OK, that's strange. But does it prove anything about God?'

'Probably not. But it suggests there's more to the world than we see in the everyday.'

'I've never had that kind of thing happen,' she said.

They lay in silence for a while. Their breathing was in synchrony.

'I go for out for beer with some of the boys from CERN sometimes,' he said. 'There's crazy stuff goes on at the sub-atomic level. Real hard science. Paired particles, separated by light years, mirroring each other instantaneously, with no possible way for any communication to pass between them that we know of.'

Her eyes had adjusted to the darkness; the luminosity of his watch appeared correspondingly brighter. She could even make out the second hand ticking steadily round.

'And does that make them believe in something?'

'Some of them.' He laughed. 'Most of them just say it's weird shit, and carrying on drinking.'

She thought of the unimaginable complexity of even the most simple organism, the symphony of structures from creature to organ to tissue to cell to organelle to molecule to atom and beyond. All matter, in the end, energy. All energy, what?

The orchestrating principle that could see those humming vibrating equations working together to create a living thing. And human creatures forming relationships, families, friendships, tribes, societies, nations, cultures, and beyond. Bequeathing knowledge, artefacts – music, paintings, sculptures – those books that were cramming every pew in the body of Bridie's church – a silent presence persisting long after life has gone. She craved a sense in it all, some way to get her head round what was at once comprehensible and beyond understanding.

Henning's breathing had become rhythmic, his arm lying heavily over her waist. She marvelled at his capacity to sleep. She lay there, cramped and uncomfortable, longing to turn over but knowing she couldn't. At the same time feeling contentment, the warmth of his body all along her back, his breath percolating through the hair on the back of her head.

She did trust herself. She did trust him. What had he told her once? We make these disastrous choices because we try to relive our childhood, to make it right this time around. He'd been drawn haplessly to Marta because she was a damaged soul, just like his mother. He'd wanted to make everything better, finally to win the love he'd never felt certain of as a boy. No one marries a monster. That was true, too. Adam had seemed so charming, so irresistible. But somehow, deep beneath the surface, she must have sensed in him the capacity for anger, for irrational rage. When it began to be manifest, it had been directed outwards, towards family, friends, colleagues, managers. Initially, she had colluded, sympathising and supporting him – each sporadic instance, taken on its own, seemed so plausible: a snub, a slight, an insult, bullying. But as the incidents accumulated, and increased in frequency, they became a pattern. The one constant: Adam; and the distorted way he perceived the world. It was only a matter of time before she, too, came into the firing line. And once he had discovered her fatal weakness, he no longer had any need to try to suppress and control his rage at home.

The dog fight outside ceased quite abruptly, a few more snarls and barks and yelps then silence. She wondered if the warring parties had reached a truce, had slunk away to lick their wounds and fight another day. Or whether the victor was even now crouched over the body of its erstwhile foe, sharp teeth tearing at lifeless flesh as it sated its gnawing hunger.

Henning could not be more unlike Adam. He could not be more unlike her father. Henning could be the person with whom she could finally know peace.

༜

The muezzin woke her, the tannoyed call to prayer loud in her ears – there must be a mosque close by. The sky through the single window was just beginning to lighten. She couldn't remember falling asleep, was surprised that she'd managed to do so. Her body felt stiff and achy; she was still in the same position, Henning spooned behind her, sandwiched between her and the wall.

He began to stir.

'Morning,' she said, pivoting herself to upright.

'Morning.'

She could just make him out in the gloom. She liked him like this: unshaven, hair messy, his face somehow less angular after sleep. She kissed him lightly on the lips, a bit inhibited by how she must smell.

'I feel like I've been beaten up,' he told her.

'Yeah, me too. Not the best night in the world.'

'We'd better get going,' he said. 'Get down to the bus station first thing.'

They used his phone torch initially, lighting the room enough to see what they were doing. They took turns to wait in Bridie's office while the other used the loo in the corner of her bedroom. Henning brought more water through when he returned. Dawn broke quickly at this latitude, and soon there was enough natural light to see by. She shook out the blanket, and plumped up the pillow, aware as she did so that it was a bizarre thing to do. What did she think: that Bridie would one day come back and want to sleep in this bed again?

'Are you sure you don't want to take anything back with you?' Henning asked, 'before we go?'

She sighed. Actually, she did. Now she felt ready to. Maybe just the pictures on the crockery shelves in the other room – the one of her children, and the one of Bridie and her on the Thames. The painted driftwood Bridie had kept from her Cornish holiday with Tim, that could stay here. As could Ollie's calendar; so much of the year had already gone. And the cross, Jesus crucified not just by nails, but by all the hatred and fear and vilification his fellow men could heap upon him. She cast her eyes around Bridie's bedroom, looking to see if there were anything to take back for Mummy. She was struck by a sudden sadness: there was no picture of Mummy anywhere. That would break her heart if she knew. But perhaps Bridie's forgiveness had extended beyond what she had the material possessions to display.

There was one other frame perched on the window ledge, angled away from her. She reached up and lifted it down. But it wasn't of their mother. It was a foreigner, a stranger. A middle-aged Arab, with a clipped full beard, smartly dressed in a Western suit, his posture upright, his arms hanging loosely by his sides, a smile softening his features. On the wall behind him, half in the shot, the banner display of some conference or other.

'Who's that?' Henning had come to stand next to her.

'I've no idea.'

Every facet of Bridie's life unknown to her. Every meaning unclear.

Henning took the picture from her, held it a little more closely. 'It's Tahar, actually, isn't it?' he said. 'Professor Yacine?'

She looked again. Tried to imagine him as the man they had dined with the day before, clean-shaven, his hair longer, his features a few years older.

'Yes, you're right, it is Tahar. It is Professor Yacine.'

Sixteen

AT THAT TIME of the morning, the A11 was laden with traffic. An Audi saloon stopped a little way behind her. She watched in her rear-view mirror as the suited driver exited his own car through the passenger door, then made his way towards hers along the edge of the road.

'Are you all right?' he called, peering in at her.

He was in his sixties; he looked concerned and friendly. She leaned over and wound the window down. 'It's completely dead. I've phoned the AA. Shouldn't be more than a couple of hours apparently – even though I'm an unaccompanied female.'

He grimaced in sympathy. 'I'd recommend you wait over there.' He nodded towards the grassy bank that separated the main road from a slip-road running in front of some nearby houses. 'There's a heck of a lot of people get injured when something goes into the back of them.'

It was indeed unnerving, the buffeting and the din of the passing traffic, the lorries especially, which actually caused her car to rock as they slipstreamed past.

He helped her out of her nearside front door and together they walked to his hazard-lit vehicle.

'I had a Renault once,' he said loudly, above the road noise. 'Real Friday afternoon car. Always going wrong.'

She loved her little Super 5, but it was an elder-statesman now, 110,000 on the clock and that was a petrol engine as well. Could be that this was a fatal episode. The Audi driver left her with his red warning triangle, politely rebuffing her attempt at giving him money for it. From the safety of the grassy bank, she watched as he finally managed to pull back out into the traffic steam and continue on his way. He held up a hand as he passed. It had been the briefest of encounters, but now he'd gone she felt alone, becalmed.

It could be worse, she told herself. It could be tipping it down with rain.

She sat on the ground, rested her elbows on her knees and her chin on her palms, and stared back along the snaking road, seeking out the first sign of a yellow AA van. The enforced interlude gave her yet another opportunity to contemplate the different ways her life had gone wrong.

It was her own fault – she'd been way too keen. With previous boyfriends she'd been quite cool, seeing how things went, only incrementally allowing herself to become attached. With Adam it had been entirely different. How much of it had been the ticking of the clock? Some; maybe quite a lot. But there'd been that extraordinary chemistry, like she was properly in love for the first time, finally understood the madness of infatuation. Seal's party: Elodie standing in the hallway nursing a drink, catching sight of this dark-haired guy climbing the stairs, heading to the bathroom, their eyes connecting as he glanced casually over the bannister. She would have thought it was the stuff of fanciful fiction but she really felt it, a moment of actual physical joining, as though there were, for that brief instant, solid metal rods instantaneously spanning the space between them. Then he broke the gaze and continued his ascent to the upstairs landing. She was acutely aware of him throughout the rest of the evening, wondering if he'd felt it too. Even when she was dancing, or ostensibly engrossed in conversation with Celia or Laura or Patrick, one part of her conscious mind was monitoring his whereabouts, his presence. She kept half an eye on who he was talking to, checking for any sign that he might be with someone. He didn't come across to her, even though on a couple of occasions they had the same clashes of gaze.

The thought of leaving the party without having spoken, without having at least tried to make a connection. She took Celia to one side, spoke into her ear beneath the music pumping from the stereo.

'Seal, don't make it obvious. Who's that guy, in the corner there, with the white linen shirt?'

Celia did a pretty good job of surreptitiously looking round. 'That's Adam. Amanda's cousin. Adam and Amanda!' She giggled, then lowered her voice. 'Are you interested?'

He was wiry rather than muscular. She liked that. His hair was thick and black, swept back. The sleeves of his shirt were rolled half-way up his forearms. His eyes were super-blue. He was talking to one of the post-grads from Prof Steady's lab, a mousy girl called Diane.

'Yes,' she said. 'I think I am.'

Seal giggled again. 'I can introduce you, if you like.'

'Is he single?'

'Single and broken-hearted. Amanda brought him along cos he's just been dumped. Came down here for work, but it's too much distance for the girlie up north, apparently.' She laid a hand on Elodie's arm. 'Come on, I'll do the honours.'

'No,' she said. 'Maybe in a bit.'

'Go on, El.'

'I don't know.'

'What's the harm?'

So she let herself be persuaded. His hello was crisp, like a knife slicing. She was struck by the frankness of his eyes. The touch of his skin when they shook hands caused a raw jolt of nerve energy to course up her arm. This is crazy, she told herself, no one had ever made that happen to her before.

He'd read law at Nottingham, had been working his way through the ranks in a personal injury firm in Leeds, but eventually accepted that it wasn't for him. So he'd taken up this job with the MoD. He'd never lived in London; could do with someone to show him the ropes. She left the party having given him her number. He lived just off the Holloway Road. It took her ages to get to sleep that night, tossing and turning in bed, high pitched ringing in her ears, wondering whether or not he would call.

He left it three days. The agony of waiting. She could never do the same, not once she'd got his number, not after they'd been out to the Lord Palmerston and found the conversation flowed and they had so much in common, not least the fact that he, too, had an overbearing father who had never once in his life said anything positive or affirming, and whom he pretty much hated with a passion. He didn't say anything about his former girlfriend; she didn't let on that she knew. She thought about him constantly, could never be cool enough to resist ringing him after a maximum of two days without contact.

Had it been a mistake to sleep with him so soon? Yes: because that seemed to be the catalyst – the absence of a call, the answerphone whenever she tried him, the messages left unreturned. Yes: because of the intensity of it – the mind-mashing power, her orgasm going on and on and on as though this were simply going to be her new way of being now, reducing her to a helpless immobile mass repeating again and again, 'Oh God'. She'd never experienced such a thing with any previous partner. It was as though she had finally been granted a taste of unadulterated joy, and it had left her with an insatiable craving for more.

Then the short call: how he was really sorry, he'd just come out of a serious relationship, how he needed some space.

And the spiralling despair of this wonderful, ultra-promising thing, stillborn.

The spiralling despair of anything ever working out, ever.

Twenty-nine next birthday. Life flying past at speed.

And her work, that constant; the dependable consolation for every one of her failed romances. That was mired in difficulty, the seeming impossibility of ever manipulating a viral vector to be able to transmit the crucial mutated gene.

This journey, travelling to Cambridge to the Albermori lab there, where they had recently managed to get an adeno-associated virus to integrate exogenous genes into human chromosome 19, albeit weakly. The glimmer of hope that it might, after all, be possible. The lessons she could potentially learn. Even this journey was now aborted in a dead car and a non-existent AA response. Why the hell hadn't she hung the expense and gone by train?

Finally, not far short of the stated two hours, the break-down van did hove into view. It took the mechanic, with all his grating joviality, thirty minutes to decide her Super 5 couldn't be resuscitated at the roadside. It took her thirty seconds to decide that he'd better recover her to a garage near her home. If her car had had it then she'd better not strand herself. Cambridge would have to be rearranged for another time.

It was gone one o'clock before she finally made it back

to her flat. Absolutely no point trying get to UCL and do anything constructive with what remained of the day. Always bits of admin and domestic chores to be done, but she felt wretched, miserable. Decided she would treat herself. Papa Luca's. The counter staff always capable of raising a smile with their flirtation and banter and general love of life.

⛤

'Elodie?'

She looked up. Took a moment to comprehend that he could be here, so out of context. She didn't know if he'd been coming in anyway, or had seen her sitting at her table on the other side of the plate-glass window and made a deliberate detour.

'Tim.' It was more acknowledgement than greeting.

'Amazing,' he said, smiling uncertainly. 'How are you?' He put a hand on the back of the chair on the other side of the table. 'Are you waiting for someone?'

She thought about lying, thought about pretending a friend or a lover were just minutes away. But the half-eaten crab linguini said otherwise.

'Just having a shit day,' she said. 'I thought I'd spoil myself.'

'Sorry to hear that,' he said. 'May I?'

She didn't know if she needed this. She didn't need this. She could just say: I'd rather you didn't. But she couldn't see herself doing it.

'Sure, go ahead.'

He hooked his jacket over the back of the chair and sat down. Looked at her with that stupid grin on his face.

'You live round here, then?' he said.

229

'Yeah. You?'

'Near Archway.'

She knew he'd come to London, had got himself a transfer as part of the business of leaving Bridie. Had never thought that, among these millions of people, they would ever run into each other again.

'So how are you?' he asked. 'Are you still researching?'

'Yeah, still at UCL.'

'Cured malaria yet?'

'We're not trying to cure it. We're trying to prevent it.' She took a deep breath. 'Look, Tim, I don't think we should pretend. I'm still really angry with you, what you did to Bridie.'

That caused a stilling of his face. She sat, slightly amazed at herself, her habitual aversion to conflict somehow overcome this one time. A waiter came across, asking Tim if he would like to order. He looked at her questioningly. 'Just a coffee – a latte, please.'

'I know, of course you are,' he said, when the waiter had gone. 'How is she?'

'You know she's gone to France – to live in a convent – don't you?'

'I had heard,' he said, his tone flat. 'Do you think she'll go through with it? Become a nun?'

'I don't know, Tim. You broke her heart. What happened, the operation and everything, I don't think she could see a future. Actually, more than that, I think she thinks this is the only way to atone. Not that she has anything to atone for. That's what drives me completely mad. You were a complete shit, you know that, don't you? How long were you guys together? You were engaged, for Christ's sake. What the fuck

230

were you thinking? How the fuck could you do that to her? How the fuck can you even *live* with yourself?'

He sat there, listening to her, absorbing her anger. The more she spoke, the more furious she felt. She saw Bridie: crumpled at the Gurtenfestival. She saw herself: throwing Sanpellegrino lemonade in Tim's face, propelling herself to her feet, slapping him across the cheek, hard, the sharp retort drawing startled looks from the chirpy waiters and the other lunchtime diners. All the pent-up rage – with him, with her father, her mother, all the useless drips of men it had never worked out with, with the fucking mosquitos and the viral vectors and the mutated gene that had looked so utterly promising but that simply would not be controlled – all the rage released like a torrent through a disintegrating dam wall.

'I'm sorry,' she said, sagging back against her chair, only then realising she'd edged right forward with the aggression of her fantasy revenge.

'Don't worry.' He brought his hands to his face briefly, pressed his fingers against closed eyelids, let them run down over his cheeks, his jaw. Looked at her again. 'I'd feel the same, if I thought what you thought.'

'What do I think?'

He sat there, staring at her. A muscle above his eye was flickering, making the skin shiver.

'She never told you what happened, did she? Not really.'

'Don't try and make this her fault,' she said, a further flash of anger stropping her words. 'You get to live another day, find some other woman to have a family with, and she's basically fucked.'

'It's not that easy, you know. I'm not in another relationship.

Most decent people have paired up by now. Everyone left has problems, it seems, of one sort or another.'

Adam. That stupid, insultingly short message: how he'd just come out of a serious relationship; how he needed some space.

'Perhaps you should have thought of that, before you dumped her.'

Tim's coffee arrived. She watched him tear open a sachet of sugar, tip it out, the brown crystals clumping together briefly on the surface of his drink before absorbing sufficient liquid to weigh themselves down, slipping and vanishing and sinking unseen to the bottom. He took his spoon and stirred methodically. Spoke as though addressing the cup.

'It wasn't a miscarriage.'

The spoon going round and round, drawing traces of brown into the frothy white milk, whorls of colour tracing its path.

'What do you mean?'

He met her gaze. Sadness in those dark eyes.

'We were going to save for a couple of years, then one more mega trip before we settled down. I said we could still do it, take the kid in tow, as long as we did it before they started school, but she was adamant she didn't want that. She wanted to be completely unshackled – that's the word she used – one more chance to be out there, on our own, footloose and fancy free. It was such crap timing. She'd lost all her maternity entitlement, too, when she switched jobs. And we'd have either had to bring the wedding forward without explanation, or get married with a massive bump and everyone knowing and gossiping and laughing behind her back.'

He withdrew his teaspoon, laid it on the saucer with the

tiniest of ceramic chinks. Small bubbles of froth clung to its metallic surface, shrinking and collapsing as the steam evaporated.

'She had an abortion?' She said the words the way you say *we're going to crash* a second before smashing into the oncoming car.

'Termination, they called it.' He let out a breath. 'I was dead against, but you know how she is when she's made up her mind. I had to take the fee in cash to the clinic, handed it over in an envelope like we were doing some kind of sordid deal.'

'Fuck, Tim.' Bridie, pale as alabaster, sobbing uncontrollably in that side room in the Royal Infirmary. Elodie's heart rending at what her sister – beautiful, beloved Bridie – had lost.

'No one need ever know, that's what she said. It'll be tough for a bit but we'll just deal with it and carry on like before, and have our family when we're good and ready.' Tim turned his coffee cup a quarter turn, the handle rotating to point across the table towards her like a compass, wrapping his hands around its body as though trying to absorb its heat. 'I should have said no. I *did* say no. But I didn't stick to it. It was her body, I didn't really have a say. In the end I went along with it, even though in my heart of hearts I knew it was wrong.'

'And the – complication?' Elodie's words had an unreal quality, like she might be speaking them in a dream, or in some play she was putting on. 'That happened during the abortion?'

Tim nodded. 'They couldn't deal with it at the clinic – it was just some tinpot private set-up with no blood bank or intensive care or anything. They had to transfer her by ambulance all the way to the infirmary. It took forever. I was in the back with her, she was bleeding everywhere. They had her legs up and drips going and she kept drifting in and out and they kept shouting at her to stay with them. I still hear the sirens going sometimes. The way we were thrown about round the corners. She was practically gone by the time they got her there.'

Elodie laid her fork down. She felt light-headed. The noises in the restaurant – the hiss of the espresso machine, the clunking of plates, the laughter of a lunch party out back – seemed intrusively loud. Bridie: telling her how she and Tim were arguing all the time, how the fun had gone out of the relationship. How guiltily sorry Elodie felt for her.

'You could still have stuck by her,' she said. 'Even if she did choose to do it. It was still both of yours, that baby.'

Tim shook his head. 'I did stick by her. I tried to. She blamed me, El. She said every time she looked at me it brought it all back. She said she could never stay with me, could never marry me, not with what I'd done.' He strained forward. 'I didn't *do* anything. But somehow in her mind she made it into a totally different story – one where she was the innocent party, and I'd been the one to drive it all along.' His hands, which had clenched, unfurled slowly. 'I don't know. Maybe it helped her feel better or something, having me to blame.'

It must have been a good couple of years since she'd last seen him. They'd been in the Morningside flat; she remembered him making her cheese on toast with Worcester sauce. He looked quite a bit older, more than time alone would allow. Thinner. His hair, if not unkempt, was certainly less smart. The stubble seemed less a fashionable look than a sign that shaving had become too much trouble.

'I'm really sorry,' she said. 'I've been really mean. I had no idea.'

'It's OK,' he said. 'Perhaps I shouldn't have said anything. Perhaps it would have been better to let you carry on thinking what you thought before.'

'No,' she shook her head. 'It's always better to know the truth.'

Her mind was all over the place, summoning a hundred different memories, re-evaluating them in light of what she'd learned, testing them, finding that they held water. Most of all, Bridie's guilt – which had always struck her as being disproportionate to the supposed sin of extra-marital sex – now made perfect sense. Elodie wanted to be alone, to have time to turn these new perspectives over in her mind, to work out how she felt towards Bridie. She was aware of anger – a feeling of being conned – a sense that her sympathy, her pity, had been falsely evoked. The way Bridie had milked their parents' outrage – they knew nothing about the pregnancy – presenting herself as the abandoned party, Tim as the arrogant bastard moving on to pastures new. Yet Bridie's tragedy was no different for its self-inflicted – for its differently self-inflicted – origins. It was the being lied to. The way even she had been duped into seeing Bridie as the victim.

'Why on earth couldn't she tell me?' Elodie said. 'I can completely understand not wanting Mummy or Dad to know. But we've always told each other everything.'

Tim finished taking a long sip of latte. 'She was ashamed, that's what I think. Too ashamed even to admit it to herself.'

She couldn't eat anything else, not now. She signalled to the waiter. Tim started to search his pocket.

'No, I'll get this,' she said. 'It's the least I can do.'

Bill paid, they loitered on the pavement outside the restaurant, neither of them seemingly sure what to do. She craved solitude, a chance to come to terms with the world as it now was, but she felt a new guilt towards Tim, all the ill-feeling she'd borne towards him. He didn't look so good. It was his confidence; his habitual self-confidence was diminished. He struck her as bewildered somehow.

'So where do you go from here?' she asked him.

He looked up the street. 'I was just taking a walk, basically. Killing time. I guess I'll head back home.'

'You not at work?'

'No.' He looked embarrassed. 'I've been off for a while. Things haven't been so good.'

'Are you ill?'

'Yeah, sort of. Just a bit down, actually.'

His shoulders, which over the years must have crunched into a thousand scrums at number eight, were sloped. She tucked her hands into the pockets of her jacket.

'Have you talked to anyone? About what happened?'

'Nah. I'll be all right,' he said.

All she had was admin, domestic chores, the emptiness of her flat. The dismissive message from Adam, the stalled research, the coming to terms with the fact that her sister had deceived her over the biggest thing in their lives.

'It's years since I've done any proper daytime drinking,' she told him. 'How about we go to the Lord Palmerston and get ourselves seriously lashed?'

࿊

The mistake would have been to invite him in for coffee. She didn't do that. They were both completely pissed; his offer to escort her home was just another instance of his innate chivalry, a quality she was reminded of again and again as afternoon morphed into evening and the drinks kept flowing and he unwittingly demonstrated – in conversation, reminiscence, repetition – the thoroughly honourable way he'd been dealing with the traduction of his character. The way he seemed at pains to understand and explain Bridie's behaviour in terms of her deep shame.

She didn't invite him in for coffee. He just sort of came in, naturally.

The mistake would have been to have made an advance, to do anything to lead him on. She didn't do that. He found the Giants baseball cap hanging on the pegs in the loo, brought it out with him, said something like did she remember him getting that for her, all those years ago in San Francisco, and landed it on her head with a fond, almost wistful look, telling her he'd always found her attractive, and that if he hadn't been with her sister he would definitely have wanted to have been with her.

The mistake would have been to have taken his hand after they finished that first, pulse-thumping, transgressive kiss, and lead him to her bedroom. She didn't do that. She said we can't do this, it isn't right. And he agreed. No, we can't. But they did it anyway.

The mistake would have been to have seen it as the start of anything, the beginning of a long-destined love affair. She didn't do that. It would be impossible, in the way it is impossible for the sun to rise in the west. Unacceptable, in the way that it is unacceptable to grind the sole of your shoe repeatedly into the face of your sister as she lies half-submerged in mud.

It was not the start of anything, it was the end. A meeting of two souls in lonely benighted stretches of their journeys, their paths intersecting just long enough for them to find solace and comfort with each other.

The morning would have been excruciating, having to navigate round each other and say all those hollow, kind things that would gloss what they'd done with a coat of brilliant white. They didn't have to do that. He was chivalrous to the last. He let himself out at some point during the night, leaving a note on the breakfast bar with his mobile number and the comment that he realised she would probably never use it.

She didn't think she ever would have done, but she did keep it, tucked inside her purse, for a few days. She threw it out with the recycling the day she got the answerphone message from Adam saying he realised he'd made a mistake, and if it wasn't too late could they get together and go for another drink or maybe a Thai and who knows maybe go dancing after and he hoped she'd give him another chance.

Seventeen

ON THIS OCCASION, her knock elicited a response from inside, the Arabic word or phrase unfamiliar to her but the tone unmistakably one of granting entry.

'You're sure?' Henning asked.

'Yes,' Elodie said, turning the handle.

'OK,' he said. 'I'll wait in the taxi. Please don't be long. We need to get out of here.'

She entered the room, closed the door behind her, leaving Henning on the other side. Professor Yacine looked up from the pile of papers on his desk, the pencil in his hand arrested mid-comment.

'Ah, good morning,' he said, confusion evident in his expression.

'I'm so sorry to barge in on you,' she said. She held up the keys to Bridie's church. 'I completely forgot these last night.'

'Ah, not at all.' He rose to his feet, smiling now. 'I also forgot - too much good conversation. That's very kind of you to bring them. Can I offer you some coffee?'

'No, thank you.'

He took the heavy iron keys from her, and laid them on his desk. Her hand felt light suddenly, relieved of their weight.

'We're on our way to the bus station,' she told him. 'Henning's waiting in the taxi.'

'Of course, of course. Well. Once again, it was a pleasure to meet you.' He started out from behind his desk. 'And you will, please, let me know if you have word from your sister, won't you?'

She nodded silently. Reached into her shoulder bag. Brought out the picture frame.

'That's you, isn't it?'

He took the photograph, studied it intently for several seconds.

'Utrecht,' he said, stroking his jaw as though trying to remember what it had felt like to have a beard. 'Two thousand and nine. I was presenting a keynote address. It was a collaboration with a Dutch media organisation – we had published translations of the Qur'an and the Bible side by side in Arabic, Dutch and English. The man behind it, he had astounding vision – he was a not a believer himself, you understand, but he had the remarkable insight that what united people of faith was far greater than what divides us. His project sought to start to heal centuries of mistrust, Christians and Muslims mistranslating each other's holy texts and condemning them as the work of the Satan. When you read them next to each other it is plain they are both the work of God.'

'I found it in Bridie's church.'

'Yes, I did wonder.'

'Did she take it?'

'No, it was a publicity shot.'

He paused, as though checking with himself that his memory of the occasion was right.

'Was she there?'

He nodded once. 'My English is serviceable, particularly for conversation, but when it comes to shaping the written word precisely, that takes a native speaker.'

'She worked on the project with you?'

'She expended a considerable amount of time and effort. It seemed only fitting that she should hear the presentation first-hand.'

What would she have been doing in 2009? Up to her eyes in grant applications, probably, the three-yearly scrabble to secure further funding to continue the frustrating and painstaking work she'd become locked in to. Ferrying the children around, trying to keep the house running, trying to keep a marriage going. Things with Adam: 2009 was the year the wheels came flying off – what had been sporadic difficulties up till then becoming an entrenched war of coldness in which her every attempt to bring reconciliation was met with hostility and misinterpretation. That was the time she'd got the first realisation there was something seriously wrong, that Adam was no longer in control of himself, was no longer capable of relating as a normal person would. Bridie in Europe, at some interfaith conference. Their father had died some years before. She didn't come home. Nor did she tell Elodie, or anyone else, that she was just across the sea.

'Where is she, Tahar?' Elodie asked him.

His eyes – deep dark brown – held hers for some moments.

She wrapped her arms across her chest, each hand cupping the opposing elbow. Spoke bluntly, aware of Henning's desire to be out of Beb. 'You had a relationship, didn't you, you and Bridie? That's why she had your picture.'

He looked down. 'That would have been transgressive, both in terms of the cultures from which we come, and in terms of the vows she took.'

Chastity. Obedience.

'It would have been far more provocative then helping

students improve their English, and running a library for them, wouldn't it?' she said.

'Immeasurably so,' he said. 'In a place like this, with its deeply conservative culture, already suspicious of the progressive influence of the university on their youth, it would have inflamed passions to a frightening degree.'

'Where is she?' Elodie asked again.

She became aware of hubbub from the corridor outside; students beginning to gather for the first class of the day.

'I think,' Tahar said, 'that as and when she wants to be found, your sister will surely let you know her whereabouts herself, will she not?'

She felt a flash of anger. 'Only if she's quite well, and not in the throes of some breakdown.'

'And this would reassure you?' he said. 'If you knew that to be the case?'

'Of course. She's her own woman. I can't force her to be in contact, not if for some reason she doesn't want to be.'

Tahar leaned his bottom against his desk, allowing its solidity to support him.

'I leave here at the end of the month,' he said. 'I've been appointed to a chair at the Lebanese International University. Beirut is a cosmopolitan city where cultures intermingle freely without causing any rise in anyone's eyebrow. It is also a very big and bustling place, where it is easy for someone to reinvent themselves.'

'And that's where Bridie is now?' Elodie asked.

'I didn't say that.' He straightened his back as though stretching an aching muscle. 'All I am saying is that it is the sort of place where someone like your sister might in due course wind up. And if she did then it is the sort of place where she would be likely soon to be able to feel at home.'

It would have to do. 'If you were by any chance to have any contact with her,' she said, 'would you tell her that her sister came looking for her, and that she sends her love?'

'Of course I would,' he said. 'If I were to have any contact.'

He came with her to the door, paused with his hand on its handle.

'Thank you for returning the keys.'

She looked at him. 'What's going to happen? To her library? Now that she's gone? If you're going, too?'

'That will be a matter for Bishop Bonouvrie. If he'll allow it, there are any number of students who will open it again – after a suitable period to allow the temperature to cool – and see that it's well run. It's too valuable a resource to be let go to waste.'

Beneath the inscrutability there was a depth of kindness there. A peacefulness emanated from him.

She held out her hand. 'Au'voir.'

'Exactly so.'

They shook hands.

'Au revoir,' he said.

She heard him close the door behind her. She set off to rejoin Henning, and to begin their journey home. As she walked away, she wondered whether she actually would, at some point in the future, meet Tahar Yacine again.

Eighteen

THEIR TERRACED TWO-BED – more a one-and-a-box-room, really – was full to bursting with all their stuff, would explode with the arrival of a child. It had been their place, the home they'd bought together only six months ago. Every inch of floorboards they'd stripped themselves, taking turns at wielding the sander, their ears defended by spongy plugs, their faces shielded by masks and goggles but still the dust got everywhere and gritted their eyes and clogged their noses. Adam spent so long kneeling on the hard boards he bruised a nerve at the side of his knee and gave himself foot-drop. They painted the front door Chapel Green. Brought some order to the patch of jungle beyond the back door. Put window boxes on the sills outside their bedroom window, which she never did get round to planting. It was down the road from the sports centre, a short walk from the Arsenal, easy into town for work and theatre and music and pubbing and clubbing. They loved the address, just off Piano Lane. We live near Red Square, they'd tell people. It was perfect, though it cost them dear in terms of the mortgage and the disapproval of her family.

She couldn't believe she'd made the same mistake as Bridie. They'd never discussed contraception; she wondered if Bridie, too, had felt guilty about taking anything herself, had left it all to Tim. Elodie was on three yearly research grants, no maternity pay. Adam's was the only stable income. They looked at every permutation. No way could they afford anything bigger in town. They would have to move out - Herts, maybe even Essex - swap the city on their doorstep for rattly train commutes. Adam didn't want to keep it, said they should wait till she had tenure and their financial position was secure. She told him no way, even though it meant saying goodbye to everything that had been slipping inexorably through her fingers since the moment the second Clearview line had turned blue. She didn't tell him he should have been more careful.

And Bridie. Bridie had completed her novitiate, had announced she was going to take her vows and enter the order that had restored her life.

She should have taken Adam, she knew that, but she was still wounded by his reaction to the pregnancy. She presented it as one last shebang, a way of sending Bridie off in style. She even believed that herself. Two tickets to Glastonbury, fallen into her lap courtesy of friends whose circumstances had radically altered, and, to cap it all, finding that Faithless were on the line-up. One last festival - the last hurrah. One last time with her sister before her sister became a nun. One last time with herself, before she became something she didn't even yet know, living in some dormitory town and finally accepting that her life belonged to work and kids and Adam.

Sure, he didn't mind. Sure, she should go off and have a bloody good time.

Sure, I'll come. If you'd like me to.

Saturday evening, Pyramid stage. They endured some crap Irish punk band. People were drifting away in their droves, seeking something better in the smaller venues. Then, at last, the end of the set, and the changeover. The distant but familiar figures running on to the stage, the striking up of the anthemic synth intro to *Insomnia*, Sister Bliss's tiny keystrokes causing hundreds of decibels to roll across the fields in a siren call. The hordes flocking back, the crowd swelling. Maxi Jazz, his urban-edged voice suddenly booming out a staccato disquisition on a shattered life. On and on it went, defying belief, a high-wire act of street poetry: shards of squalor and drugs and despair, all the while the sense of a soul crushed by loss – of relationships, of family, of hope – struggling to keep a fingertip hold on meaning. The anticipation in the crowd: knowing what was to come, craving the boom of the bass, the start of the party, yet at the same time not wanting this extraordinary polemical rap to end. And then, finally, the explosion. The banks of lights discharging in perfect synchrony with the onset of the deafening dance chords, the kick of the drums. Tens of thousands of people jumping up and down in unison, an endless field of waving arms. The intoxication. The sense of awe. The being part of this thing that united this great mass of humanity. Everywhere, memories of the best of times being burned indelibly on people's brains.

And, in her excitement, looking to see where Bridie had got to. The heave and surge of the crowd. The momentary fear that she'd lost her. Then seeing her many yards away, at the edge of things in a clear area of grass, her gaze locked on the giant screen. Dancing, yes, but half-heartedly. As though going through the motions.

Later, one a.m., lying side by side on their backs in the tent, the sounds of the never-still festival at last beginning to diminish.

'So what did you think?'

Bridie's voice, disembodied in the dark. 'Faithless? Yeah, they were good. They always are.'

A few seconds silence.

'What?' Elodie said.

'I don't know. I'm just not in the mood.'

There was some horrible anticlimax about it. Yes, the sounds and songs and style had been the same. There'd been the same thrilling cohesion in the crowd that they'd known at the Gurtenfestival. But here at Glastonbury it had been ephemeral, no sooner said than done, leaving behind it a deflation more complete than that which had been there before.

The hedonism all around. The music, the booze, the comedy, the drugs, the sex, the laughter, the friendship, the camaraderie – all that desperate groping for something. What would be left, when the thousands of abandoned tents had been taken down and boxed up and reincarnated as shelters in refugee camps in war-zones around the globe? When the litter-pickers had finished combing the fields and had coiffured the land back to being Worthy Farm? When the security fences had come down, and the residents of Pilton and East Compton and Pylle had retaken possession of the homes they'd rented to wealthy festival-goers for thousands of pounds a day? When the charter helicopters had flown, and the best suites at the Charlton House Hotel lay unoccupied once again?

'So are you really going through with it?' Elodie said, into the dark.

'Yes.' Bridie had no hesitation. 'I've found real peace there. We had no idea as kids, El, it all just seemed so boring. At the convent, we live by the liturgy of the hours, and it is the most beautiful rhythm, each day structured around different sets of prayers and readings and worship and reflection. It stops anything else gaining hold. Nothing can become too important when your focus always comes back to God.'

This is my church. This is where I heal my hurts. God is a DJ.

'You never used to think he existed,' Elodie said. 'You never used to. You used to say you'd grown out of fairy tales.' She could feel her heart picking up tempo, pulsing the tinnitus in her ears.

Bridie sighed. 'I said a lot of things. That was pride talking. I had a monumental amount of pride.'

'What's so wrong with that?'

Bridie didn't respond. Even as she asked the question, Elodie already knew the answer.

'You made mistakes,' Elodie said. 'We all make mistakes. That's what life's about, isn't it, learning and growing?'

'What I learned,' Bridie said, 'was it had all been there – it had all been there for thousands of years – the whole blueprint. If I'd known it, if I'd followed it, I wouldn't have had to have made the mistakes I made in order to learn the lessons for myself. God knows how flawed we are, what appallingly bad decisions we come up with if left to our own devices. He tried giving Moses the law, but that was about as successful as telling a kid not to eat the chocolate bar you're going to leave him alone with. So God came himself to show us how it should be done. And to forgive us when, even then, we still manage to screw it up.'

'You could never forgive Dad, though. Or Mummy.'

'I know. Pride again. I was so angry with them.'

'Have you managed it now?'

'Not yet, not really.' Bridie sounded subdued. 'It's a long process. But I am trying.'

It wasn't so much the belt, it was the humiliation. Having to lower jeans or lift up skirts and being whipped on the buttocks even when they were in their teens. And Mummy. The thud, the crash, the crockery missing from the dresser the next morning.

'Bridie,' she said. 'I've got something to tell you.'

'I know.'

'What?'

'I know. You haven't drunk all night. Congratulations. Really.'

She felt suddenly close to tears. The way Bridie had said it. She'd known it would be hard. But even so.

'Listen, El, I'm kind of nervous about this, but I've got to say it. You don't have to do what I did. You don't have to make mistakes in order to learn the lessons.'

'What are you saying?'

'You and Adam, living together.'

'Don't you start.'

'I'm not starting anything. I'm trying to help. As your sis. I did all that, and look where it got me. You've got a chance, to do things right, do things properly. Don't listen to me, listen to God. Go back to church and listen. There's real wisdom there.'

'Mummy did things properly. Look where it got her.'

'OK, OK.' Bridie shifted. Elodie could hear the sloosh of water as she took a drink from her Evian bottle. Heard her replace the cap with a click. 'You've got a baby coming, though. Surely it's worth getting it right for his or her sake.'

She almost said Adam isn't Tim, but then Tim wasn't Tim either – or wasn't the Tim Bridie had made him out to be. She felt a flash of irritation, being reminded of Bridie's duplicity.

Felt hotly indignant that she should presume to advise her, Elodie, on how to conduct herself. She was acutely conscious of the life inside her, how that would never again be Bridie's to know. Even so, she felt a rising rage at Bridie lecturing her after what she herself had done.

'I saw Tim, you know, in London.'

She thought she could sense Bridie stiffen.

'When?'

'Last year. He lives quite near my old place. We bumped into each other in a café.'

'You never said.'

'I've hardly seen you.'

'So how was he?'

'Not great, actually. I'd say he was depressed.'

Outside, footsteps were approaching. The light from a torch beam played on their tent, penetrating its material, illuminating the inside briefly. A male voice called, 'Ellen?' Elodie was about to shout that it was the wrong tent but he evidently realised the same thing simultaneously. The torch light disappeared. She could make it out by the shadows it cast as the lost guy weaved his way through the adjacent pitches.

'You should have said something,' Bridie said.

'What difference would that have made?'

'Why are you being like this, El? Of course it would have made a difference. I still care about him. I might have written or something.'

'Do you really think that would've helped? Hearing from you?'

'Maybe. He's someone else I'm trying to forgive. I've often thought about writing.'

'Look,' Elodie hitched herself up on her elbow, 'you're just embarrassing yourself. I know what happened, Bridie. He told me all about it.'

'What do you mean?' Bridie's voice was suddenly normal volume, the semi-hush of night time confidences banished.

'That you finished with him. That you couldn't stand the sight of him, that it kept reminding you of what had happened.' She peered into the gloom, trying to make out her sister's face. 'Everyone felt so sorry for you, poor jilted Bridie. In reality, it was the other way round, wasn't it?'

'It was complicated.' Bridie's voice had hushed again, a deliberate calm that irritated Elodie further. 'You have no idea.'

'Oh, I have more than an idea.'

'Meaning?'

'Meaning I *know*, Bride. About the baby. The abortion. Everything.'

The silence went on for a long time. Elodie could hear Bridie's breathing. From a long way distant she heard a man shouting *Shut up!*, the admonition carrying way further than the noises that were bugging him.

'I suppose he told you it was my idea, too,' Bridie said.

'As a matter of fact, yes.'

'And you believe that?'

'Shouldn't I?'

'It was him. He pushed me into it. Said it wasn't the right time, we shouldn't let it spoil our plans.'

'That's funny,' Elodie said, 'because that's exactly what he said you'd said.'

'For God's sake, El. Why would you take his word over mine?'

'Because when he said it, it sounded like the truth.'

Bridie sat upright. The angry hornet of her sleeping bag zipper. 'I'm not listening to this.'

She started moving, landed a knee on Elodie's leg. 'You've always been jealous of me, couldn't stand the fact that I'd made the break and you couldn't. Hated the fact that I had Tim and you were incapable of staying with anyone longer than five minutes.'

She was over by the flaps; Elodie could hear her fingers scrabbling against the nylon as she tried to find the zip. The furious ringing in her ears.

'Something else for you to forgive, while you're sitting in your precious convent,' she said. 'Tim said I was better in bed than you ever were.'

The blow, when it landed, was a slap, not a closed fist, but it stunned her all the same. Later, she would marvel ruefully at how Bridie had managed it, connecting unerringly with her cheek in the dark. It took her ages to stop shaking, to compose herself sufficiently to reseal the tent flaps Bridie had left open in her wake.

She wouldn't have thought she'd slept at all, but she must have, at some point in the pre-dawn, because when she came to, with a dreadful gnawing in the pit of her stomach, Bridie's clothes had gone from the corner of the tent, and her rucksack from under the awning. She didn't stay for any of the Sunday, just gathered her stuff, and the rest of Bridie's gear, and took herself off home, back to Adam, and their Victorian terrace with its sanded floors and its neat back garden and the new life they were starting to build.

He was very supportive, telling her that, from the little he'd seen of her sister, he didn't like her much, and thought she was probably unhinged. That they could neither of them choose their family. But they needn't let them ruin their future together.

Mummy and Dad went. She pretended, for their sakes, that she'd received an invitation, but that it clashed with this important international conference where she'd been given the task of presenting the UCL group's work, her last contribution before going off with the baby. They said it was the most beautiful, humbling ceremony. What they didn't say: Bridie, the prodigal daughter, who had never done anything as immoral as give birth to a child out of wedlock. They brought her back a dedication card, from which she learned that Bridie had taken for her patron, Saint Sebastian. Bound to a tree, arrows piercing his body in a dozen locations. They displayed theirs in pride of place on their mantelpiece. She stuck hers in a drawer in her desk. A few months later, Madeleine Mary was born. It would be years before she had the time, energy, or inclination ever to dig it out again.

Nineteen

Dear Mummy

I'm back in the capital, and should be on a flight home within the next day or so. I know you're going to be upset, but I didn't find her. I've lots to fill you in on, but please don't be too dismayed. I can't explain now, but I think she's all right, that wherever she is she's OK. I met some people she knew well in Beb, and they told me much more about her life there and what happened. Things did get pretty sticky for her, what with being a Westerner and a Christian missionary to boot, and she was doing a lot of good work with the youth in the city which some people found threatening and objectionable. There's intolerance and suspicion bubbling up everywhere at the moment, and Bridie got caught up in that. The safest thing was for her to go into hiding. I feel sure she will be back in touch when she's ready.

Thanks for the updates on the children, Maddie especially – I have been worrying about her. Perhaps leave it to me to explain about Aunty Bridie – keep it general for now – I'll have to think how best to broker it.

Mummy, listen. I do admire what you did, sticking with Dad all the way through, and I'm glad, in the end, that things came good for you and that you feel you did the right thing. Things with Adam are fundamentally different, though. A friend of mine told me once that any relationship can be saved, all it takes is three things – two willing people, and maybe some professional help if things have got that bad. Dad was, in the end, willing, and although it was never enough, the help he got took him a long way. Adam has never had the insight – he's still stuck blaming everyone else – his father, his mother, the kids, me most of all – for the way his life has turned out. We're going nowhere.

I didn't really want to get into all that here, I'm sorry. I'm still sorting things through in my head. We'll talk more when I get back.

In the meantime, try not to worry about Bridie, I really think everything's going to be all right.

Much love, Elodie

Dear Maddie

I haven't heard from you. I want you to know I love you, and I understand that things are confusing and difficult in life at the moment, and quite probably you're feeling sore with me (and quite possibly the rest of the world). Maybe you're feeling neglected or abandoned. I'll be back very soon, and hopefully we can go for a pizza together and start to sort things out.

Much love for now, darling
Mummy xx

Dear Ollie

Poor old Barkington Duck! Still, he was a dog toy, and he was meant to be something Pogo was allowed to get his teeth into, so we can't really blame the poor old *pooch. Better that Barkington bites the dust than one of your trainers!*

I'm pretty much ready to come home now, and I can't wait to see you. I've done my best for Aunty Bridie, and she's got the help she needs at the moment, so there's no need for me to stay any longer. Talking of Aunty Bridie, your calendar is in pride of place on her desk, and she's clearly put it to good use. We'll have to see if we can find her another good one for next year.

Be good for Nana and Daddy.

Love you loads, Mummy xx

Adam

I'll be back pretty soon now, hopefully get a flight tomorrow but I will update you once I know for definite. Aside from everything else, I've been doing a lot of thinking out here, and we should make some time to discuss the future. I'm not willing to go on living estranged under the same roof. Something will have to change.

Elodie

☙

The waiter brought a glass of still, iced water alongside each cup of coffee. She guessed it was a matter of course in this country, given the unremitting heat and the need, alongside caffeine, to maintain hydration. She found it was good, being able to slake her thirst first, leaving her free to savour the rich, slightly bitter café au lait in leisurely sips.

'I'm so sorry your trip came to nothing.' Anne had on a pretty floral headscarf, the pattern of which matched her long dress. Her dark glasses were completely opaque. 'You must be deeply disappointed.'

'Not really,' Elodie said. 'I may not have found her, but it was helpful in so many other ways. Thank you for everything you did, you and Peter.'

Anne gave a self-deprecating laugh. 'I'm not sure we did anything.'

'Oh, you did,' Elodie said. 'We didn't need them in the end, but it was so useful to have the consulate credentials just in case. And putting a call in to Monsieur Azoulay. You were very kind.'

'He was very fond of your sister,' Anne said.

'Who?'

'Monsieur Azoulay.'

She paused, momentarily puzzled. Thought back to the hotelier's non-stop babbling. 'I didn't know he knew her.'

'Didn't he mention?' Anne paused, as though doubting herself for a moment. 'He sounded very happy when I told him who you were. Sister Sebastian taught his son English – that's what he told me. He credits her with him getting to the States. He went to MIT, I think, or somewhere prestigious like that. Monsieur Azoulay was *very* proud.'

She remembered the hotelier showing her the photograph. Why had he not been open with her about the role Bridie had played? Bridie: sheltering from the scandal, the disapprobation, rotating through various safe-houses hosted by liberal friends among the Beb citizenry. Perhaps, from time to time, that very hotel had been one of her sanctuaries.

'Your friend, the chap from Sweden? Is he not around?'

She looked at Anne. 'He's from Geneva. No, he's at the airport, sorting out our return flights.'

'When do you head back?'

'Tomorrow, all being well.'

'I expect you'll be glad to get home.'

Elodie drank some coffee. The aroma as she lifted the cup to her lips. Her sense of smell seemed to have been heightened out here. Even last night, jotting some thoughts in a notebook, she'd been able to detect a faint, woody, carbolic odour emanating from its pages. Perhaps her olfactory system had been awoken – the pungent spices in the markets, the proximity of unwashed bodies, the animals and the dung and the exotic dishes being cooked on open fires at street stalls. A sensory assault after London's blandness and pervasive petrol fumes.

'When will you see your children again?' she asked.

'We'll make a trip home at Christmas,' Anne said.

'Don't you miss them?'

'Terribly, sometimes. Most of the time, really. But it's so much easier than it used to be, what with Skype and FaceTime and the like.'

Could she do it? Could Maddie and Ollie? Spend whole terms with nothing but periodic link-ups on the laptop? Emotional reunions at Geneva airport; tearful departures at the end of every holiday?

'I'm wondering whether to board mine,' Elodie told her. 'Next year. There's an opportunity that's come up. Maddie's trying out for the national squad, you know. In swimming. It could really help her.'

'How wonderful.' Anne sounded genuinely thrilled. 'I was a bit of a swimmer myself, back in my younger days.'

The image of Maddie, sleek tight-fitting Speedo swimsuit and cap, tumble-turning and kicking off and flexing herself like a dolphin for the maximum distance under water until she had to break the surface and resume the front crawl, her arms thrusting left-right-left-right, slicing into the water, lancing it almost, time after time, propelling herself by sheer force of will as much as by muscle power, straining with every stroke so as to beat that personal best or catch that pacemaker or trounce that rival. Her determination, her single-mindedness – these were some of her greatest assets, vital ingredients if she were ever to succeed. They worried Elodie, who could see something of Bridie in her; she feared that Maddie was creating an edifice out of rough-hewn rocks that, if she couldn't surmount it, she would end up dashing herself against. But maybe that was what sport was for. It must be healthier to strive for a goal, however unattainable, than to keep forever defining yourself in opposition to your past.

She became aware that she'd lost the thread, that Anne was waiting for her to say something in return.

'I'm sorry?'

'It was nothing. I was just saying I used to be a swimmer myself, when I was younger.'

'I had you down as a team player,' Elodie confessed. 'Hockey, or something like that.'

'You're right, actually, that was my real love.' Anne smiled a little self-consciously. 'How clever of you to guess.'

She was aware that she didn't want the conversation to end. That there was something more she wanted from Anne, though she wasn't sure exactly what it was. 'Wouldn't you prefer it if you lived in the UK? If you got to see your children all the time?'

Anne waved a hand, disturbing a fly that had settled on the rim of her cup. 'Peter would still want them to board, I suspect. It's what he did. I long ago accepted I can't change who their father is – or their mother, for that matter.' She laughed. 'Does that sound a ridiculous thing to say? It is ridiculous, but we do, don't we? Go about life thinking we can change other people, ourselves even? Peter's a diplomat, and being married to a diplomat, being the child of a diplomat, that brings all sorts of things along with it. Once you've accepted that, you just roll your sleeves up and get on with it. The trick is always – always – remember the silver linings. Spend your time contemplating the cloud and that way madness lies.'

Adam was Adam, and she was – well, who was she? Was she like Mummy, staying put in the grimness, hanging on for the sake of the pretence of a family life? Or was she someone else, someone who respected herself enough not to sacrifice herself once she'd given it her very best shot, and her best shot had proved never, on its own, to be enough? What lessons would Maddie, Ollie, learn from her?

Elodie looked across at Jack, sitting, as he had done when they'd gone for lunch, at a separate table on the far side of the terrace. He seemed engrossed in the cars driving past, his head repeatedly swivelling as he tracked their progress past the pavement café. Always the jacket on, despite the perspiration.

'What if there aren't any silver linings?' she said. 'Or not enough, anyway?'

Anne pushed her sunglasses up over her forehead, leaving them resting on her headscarf, the pale blueness of her eyes. 'If you can't create them, then I suppose you move on. But it's always another cloud you're going to, isn't it? You don't get one without the other. It would be foolish to think otherwise.'

Henning. Geneva. The WHO. It scared her, if she were to get it wrong. The thought that, in a year or two's time, she may find herself exactly the same, mired in another cloud of her own making. All the pain and upheaval she would have caused, and for what?

Elodie wanted to pay for the coffees but Anne wouldn't hear of it. 'It's on HMG,' she said, leaving a banknote tucked under her saucer. At the other table, Jack got to his feet.

'Now,' Anne said. 'Where can we take you to?'

Henning found her by the pool, lying on a lounger belatedly trying to soak up the sun before turning to the English autumn.

'It's all sorted,' he told her, sitting on the edge of the lounger next to hers.

She shaded her eyes with her hand. 'Both of us?'

He gave a nod. 'Mine is at ten, going direct, yours is quarter past three via Paris.'

She flopped her head back, let her arm fall by her side. She was going home.

'And guess what?' he said.

She peered through slatted fingers. He brought his hand out from behind his back. Dangled the WHO lanyards in front her.

'I left them in my suitcase. They were never in Beb.'

She shook her head, felt a flash of crossness. The blind panic in that Beb hotel room, thinking that they'd been stolen by persons unknown. She grabbed the photo IDs and pulled them from Henning's hand, letting them fall on the tiles in a pool of plastic and ribbon.

'We should have a special meal this evening,' Henning said. 'To celebrate our last night.'

Something about the words. The crossness vanished, replaced by a sudden guilt, and a sudden fear. She reached across and took his hand. 'I know this trip hasn't exactly been fun. It's not what either of us thought it was going to be.'

'That's why I propose we get out there and do something nice. Perhaps your friend at the consulate knows a decent restaurant.'

'I'm sure she does.' Anne, dining out; did Jack sit at another table when it was just the two of them? What about when Peter was there, too?

'I know I've been preoccupied,' Elodie said. 'I'm so grateful. I couldn't have managed on my own.'

She could tell he wanted to ask about Geneva, the WHO job, beginning a life together. She desperately didn't want him to. Perhaps he could sense that.

'They're having fun,' he said, looking over at the far end of the pool, where the two American kids were laughing and splashing in the shallows, their mother lying on her back, her novel interposed between her eyes and the sun.

'They were here when I arrived,' she told him. 'I'm kind of glad they've not gone. I'd begun to think I might have imagined them.'

'I'm sorry?'

'I don't know. It just seems so long since we set off for Beb.' She shook her head. 'It makes me realise how short a time we were actually away, the fact that they're still here.'

He pretended to take her pulse. 'Are you all right? Perhaps the sun has got to you?'

She laughed. 'I know. I'm not making any sense.' She leaned in conspiratorially. 'I always wondered what brought them here. What they were doing having a holiday in this hotel, in this country, in the middle of all the stuff that's going on in the world. I've never seen them with anyone, you know.'

'You should go ask them,' Henning said.

She watched the kids for a bit. They had a blow-up ball, with one of the Disney princesses on it, she couldn't make out which at this distance. It seemed that whoever had the ball had to run away from the other, who would chase them through the shallows, sometimes doggy paddling through deeper water, and when they were caught then the ball changed hands and the chase continued. The mother was oblivious, wrapped up in her reading, or maybe lost in thought, the book a convenient prop to legitimise her disconnection.

'I think I'd prefer not to know,' she told him.

They did eat out. They found a place called the Restaurant Ten Years a few streets away, and had a cracking laugh at the idea that this was probably an indication of how long it would actually take to eat the meal, so mountainous were the helpings of couscous.

'We had a night of madness in Beb,' she told him at one point.

He looked at her quizzically.

'The hotel owner, he knew I was Bridie's sister, you know. Anne said he was a great admirer of hers. There's no way he would have let anyone into our room.'

Henning made a face. 'The world is full of great admirers who become great betrayers if scared for their own skin.'

'I feel bad we did a runner. Left without paying our bill,' she explained, seeing his confusion.

'I told you,' he said, 'I'll wire him the money. I don't like it, though. Someone was definitely in our room.'

'Maybe just the cleaner,' Elodie said. 'Picked up my photos

and put them down the wrong way. Disturbed the computer by accident.'

'You seem so certain all of a sudden,' he said.

'I think I just feel better. It's like I've come out of a bad dream and found the world is actually exactly how I remembered it.'

'OK, well that's good,' he said. 'I guess the lanyards spooked me. I feel stupid for leaving them here.'

They made love when they got back to the hotel. She was back in that place where desire lives, was as eager for him as he was her. The first time was quick, urgent, and she couldn't reach orgasm before he came. She massaged his back, his shoulders; sitting naked astride him, gently rubbing herself against his buttock until she was thoroughly aroused, and the feel of her, the thought of her, had conquered his quiescence. Second time it was like a homecoming, deep and slow and full of tenderness.

Afterwards, lying against him, she said, 'I know I shouldn't ask. Is sex with me better than it was with Marta?'

He was silent for a long time. She could hear his heartbeat in his chest. 'It feels whole,' he said, eventually.

She traced a fingertip over his breastbone, around his nipple.

'Two damaged souls,' he said, 'coming together to try to find healing in each other – that is a very particular form of sexual energy. There is something toxic about it. There's none of that with us.'

She was aware of a tiny bit of resentment, of feeling slighted. She quickly quieted it. What he said made perfect sense, and meant he understood. What she'd had with Adam in the early years, before the madness had crept in and made their home its home – that towering all-consumption had, at its heart, a fatal dis-ease. She would never feel the vertiginous heights again, that exposed rawness, the discord in the wall of sound. She never wanted to. What she had with Henning – what she hoped he had with her – was symphonic. He was right. It was whole. They were whole.

Twenty

THERE WAS PRECIOUS little to do there, just a shabby bureau de change, a store selling leather slippers and artisan jewellery and various date-based confectionery, and a café. They ordered themselves coffees, after he'd checked his bag in, and sat themselves at one of the round tables. Compared with the bustle of any UK airport, it was sparsely occupied. She watched a cleaner pushing an extra-wide dry mop over the tiles of the main hall, a rim of dirt and dust and cigarette butts and wrappers being propelled along at its leading edge. An extraordinarily fat man in a flowing white robe, his round face centred by a bushy black moustache, was progressing in stately fashion across the concourse, at least a dozen burka-clad women in his wake.

'Will you be all right?' Henning said. 'I can leave a book if you'd like.'

'I'll be fine,' she said.

He read a lot, she'd noticed. She didn't generally – there was never any time, not with working, and the children, and the house, and the dog, and the hundred other things that seemed to fill her every waking moment in London. She didn't know that much about him, not really. Their relationship amounted to a half-dozen snatched rendezvous – mutual conferences, her pretending to have a symposium to go to, him hiding out for a week during the summer in a hotel not far from Gower Street. She'd been a cat on a hot tin roof when out and about with him in the parks, the museums, the restaurants, fearing that at any moment they would run into someone she worked with, or a friend from someplace, or – heaven forbid – someone much closer to home. Adam had made it clear that as far as he was concerned she could do what she liked away from the house, but it still felt illicit, dangerous, to be with Henning on such intimate soil. Should she tell Adam, she wondered? Regularise the arrangement? Something in her baulked at the idea. Partly she didn't want him to know the first thing about Henning's existence; it would sully everything. And she didn't trust him, the way his mind worked. It would be the perfect excuse, she could see him turning it on its head, twisting it into being an affair, allowing him to shatter the family and claim innocent victimhood, fuelling an anger that would smoulder and flare for years to come. More than that, though, this strange fractured life wasn't actually what she wanted for herself anymore.

The tannoy announcements were in Arabic, repeated in French, then finally in English. The international language. The language of escape. The passport away from this place for so many seeking a life elsewhere.

Henning's flight was going to be delayed by an hour.

'Less time for you to wait on your own,' he said.

Time enough for us to talk, was what she could hear underlying his words.

She looked at him. Self-composed. Handsome. She liked him, a lot; liked his gentle humour, the wise things he often came out with, his self-sufficiency. A life with Henning would be liberating – two adults, partnering side by side, not intertwined, enmeshed, choking the life out of each other even as they clung and bound themselves more tightly till only an axe could cleave them.

Gene therapy. The massive optimism that had accompanied the first successful treatment of a single patient back in the nineties, only to be followed by twenty years of total lack of progress, the challenges of designing vectors to insert the exogenous DNA in just the right place, with just the right switching to ensure expression, defeating their group at UCL as it had defeated every other lab round the world. There'd been a few isolated breakthroughs in the past few years, so maybe sometime in the not too distant future techniques would become sufficiently advanced. But she didn't know if she had the stamina for it anymore – not after so many years of abortive attempts and frustrating failures.

The WHO recruitment drive, a now or never chance for a complete change of direction. Henning said she was a shoe-in for one of the posts. A new life, in a new city, a new country. No more lab work, no more experimental grind. A chance instead to shape, to catalyse, to influence and encourage.

Would she move in with him directly, or rent herself a place to start with? Check that there really were more silver linings than cloud?

It would have to be her own place. She would need Maddie and Ollie to have their own space, introduce them to Henning gradually, give them time to adjust, opportunities to reject and rebel.

Geneva. The WHO. The UN. The International Committee of the Red Cross. The International Federation of Red Cross and Red Crescent Societies. Medicines Sans Frontières. The World Council of Churches. Geneva was a beacon city, a centre of hope, a nexus of collaboration to counterbalance the confrontation engulfing so many parts of the world, the true seat of the internationalism that she and

Bridie had been swept up in, in the naivety of their youth, when LiveAid had seemed to promise so much. There could never be a concert to transform the world. Where were the concerts for Iraq, for Afghanistan, for Syria? Only years and decades and centuries of patient work, dogged perseverance in the face of setback, drawing not demoralisation but resolve from the depravity of that which had to be changed.

If there were any place in which to make a completely fresh start.

'Henning,' she said.

He looked across.

She smiled. 'Yes.'

His brows dipped briefly. 'Really?'

She nodded, emphatically. 'Absolutely. Yes.'

It was like a dam had been breached. They talked of where she might live, all the places they would go, how they would lead their children through the changes that were to come.

'It will be hard for yours,' he said, 'especially to start with. You're absolutely sure?'

She smiled again, as much to reassure herself as him. 'I can't change who their father is, nor their mother. We're just going to have to roll our sleeves up and get on with it.'

The extra hour flew. Henning's flight was boarding. She walked with him to the passport control. They embraced and kissed, despite the embargo on public displays of affection advised in the WHO briefing dossier for the country.

'See you in Geneva,' he said, giving her a grin.

She resolved, next time they met, to re-establish their intimacy from the word go.

'Yep. See you in Geneva.'

❧

She bought herself another coffee, and an hour's wifi, and got her laptop out of the cabin bag at the café table. It booted straight from hibernate, as she always left it. She sent emails to Mummy and Adam confirming her flight times. Then she brought up her browser tab.

She could delete Missing Abroad from her favourites. Before she did so, she scrolled once again through the thirty-two faces of the lost. Chris Rowland, his Celtic complexion liver-spotted from two decades in the Brazilian sun; Lucas Garrett, grinning gawkily outside the Queen's London home; Kerry Andrews, still blowing her eternal kiss to the person behind the camera; David Saunders, the off-shore breeze from the ocean behind him never letting his hair rest. Then Bridie, moon face in the centre of her habit, staring out of the screen at her. Ten seconds before she would fade away to be replaced by the first of the missing once again.

Where did it happen? In Tahar Yacine's office; at his apartment; in Sister Sebastian's library? And how? The end of a long session discussing the nuances of translation; or at the close of an interfaith meeting debating the identity of the one true God, the others in the group dispersed back to their homes, Tahar and Bridie standing uncertainly before each other, one of them – Bridie? – taking that step forward, tilting her face upwards and half-closing her eyes. How long had they spent wanting that moment to come, but believing it never could – all the taboos, the vows, the commitments, the cultures barbed-wiring the no-man's land between them? And once they had kissed? Once they had left their respective lines and found each other in the middle? How many weeks, months, years, till their secret was known, and the ordnance began to rain down?

Bridie's picture dissolved, and the cycle of the missing started again. This litany of faces she had come to know so well. She was already sure, but she watched through again to be certain. Only thirty-one. It was Guy Baverstock, forty-nine, failed to return from a diving holiday in Mozambique. His picture had been taken down, it was no longer there. She trawled the site, but there was no update, no feedback, no end to his story. Had he returned, safe and rueful? Had his body been found in a shallow grave a couple of hundred yards inland? Had he turned up in a Maputo hospital where he'd been admitted with a breakdown, or amnesia, or in a coma from a near-drowning? She could google for news, or email Missing Abroad and see what they could tell her. But she didn't. She didn't want to know for sure. She preferred to be allowed to imagine, to create a happy end.

Would Mummy agree to taking Bridie's photo down, to remove all reference to her from the site? Elodie was returning empty-handed, save for the few mementoes she had taken from the library. Those, plus the picture of Tahar she'd found in Bridie's room. She tried to imagine showing it to Mummy, telling her about the future Bridie had chosen for herself. She couldn't see herself doing so, not yet. Broken vows, the espousal of an inter-faith relationship? Maybe in the fullness of time.

The photo was also in her cabin bag. She took it out, and held it for a while. His thick black hair, his hint of a smile. The pride with which he was standing in front of the conference banner. How little she knew of him – whether he'd been an inveterate bachelor, or whether there had once been a wife, children, a life before. At least she had an idea of the gentleness of his soul, and a picture to remind herself.

She didn't know who had stolen into their hotel room. Fancifully, she wondered if it had been Bridie herself – still in Beb, being smuggled from place to place until safe passage could be arranged, holed up on the top-floor of the hotel, being let into their room by M. Azoulay. But she didn't think that likely. Bridie had gone, could even be in Beirut by now. Far more likely it had been Azoulay himself, garnering what he could from their possessions. Would Tahar bring Bridie the news in person, or on the phone, or by means of a letter or email? Whatever, she would soon know about Henning, Tahar's account of him unquestionably telling her that there was a new man, a new direction in her sister's life.

She put Tahar back in her bag and turned to her laptop again. She deleted Missing Abroad. With her remaining minutes, she went to the Guardian website to catch up on news from back home. Reading the headline article with a mounting numbness, she sat looking at the poorly focused picture of the priest, seized from the refugee camp on the Syrian border where he was undertaking humanitarian aid, and was threatened now with beheading by jihadi terrorists. For a moment she thought it was Fr Tellier, so much did he resemble Bishop Bonouvrie's curate, the same outsized black plastic-framed glasses. But the kidnapped man's name was different and his nationality said to be Australian. She stared at his neck, mesmerised by how thin and vulnerable it looked. Tried not to imagine black-clad arms holding his head, his torso, in a vicious vice; the blade slicing brutally through windpipe, major vessels, severing the spinal cord between two vertebrae until the head was held aloft in a torrent of blood.

Tried not to imagine the terror of those final moments. Tried not to ask whether there would be faith-filled acceptance or abject fear. She clicked to extinguish the browser, closed her eyes for a moment, and offered up a silent prayer.

෪

Emerging on to the runway to begin the walk to her plane, she felt the full force of the blistering heat for the final time. The concrete of the taxiing apron served only to reflect and amplify the sun's radiation.

The same blue-overalled workmen, leaning on shovels, watched the trail of passengers heading towards the aircraft. There was a furious shimmering of air behind the idling jets. How long had it been since she'd arrived? A week, only a week. It seemed far longer, as much as half a lifetime ago.

She always travelled well, except for take-offs and landings. Always playing in her mind: the aircraft suddenly lurching, a wingtip striking the ground, a violent slew, objects hurtling like missiles through the cabin, a fireball engulfing them as a ruptured fuel tank explodes. When she was younger she used to pray. When she travelled in her youth, she left last wills and testaments on someone's answerphone – having done it once, the superstition was set, and it was tempting fate to fail to comply. Now, she sat back in her chair and breathed deeply, in and out, as the engines crescendoed and the brakes were released and the Airbus lurched forward to begin its thunderous lumber skywards. People came to her: Maddie, Ollie, Mummy, Henning, Bridie. Jumbled impressions: Anne in the restaurant, Peter Armstrong behind his desk, Tahar Yacine welcoming them in, Bishop Bonouvrie in his vestments, the hotelier in Beb beaming his truly genuine smile. The terrific rumbling ceased and her stomach yawed and they were airborne, and the engines surged and the flaps swivelled and the plane gathered height, soaring up above the sun-baked land below.

She gazed out of the window. How rapidly things on the ground became shrunken and diminished until they were like insignificant toys – matchbox cars on the road; clusters of squat, flat-roofed dolls-houses; regimented olive groves like nurseries for Hornby accessories. The plane banked and turned and left Anne, and Peter, and Jack, and the Restaurant Ten Years, and the Hotel Splendid, and the American mother and her children behind. It gained ever more altitude, effortlessly overflying barren desert landscapes, impassive mountain ranges, and fertile river valleys. Eventually, another conurbation – just a blur of man's imprint on the earth – that might, perhaps, have been Beb, with its gas fields and its struggling university and its abandoned English library. Down there, somewhere, were human beings doing things out of hatred; many others doing things out of love. And most, like Bridie and her, contending with the mess and muddle that lies between.

NEW FICTION FROM SALT

GERRI BRIGHTWELL
Dead of Winter (978-1-78463-049-2)

NEIL CAMPBELL
Sky Hooks (978-1-78463-037-9)

SUE GEE
Trio (978-1-78463-061-4)

V. H. LESLIE
Bodies of Water (978-1-78463-071-3)

WYL MENMUIR
The Many (978-1-78463-048-5)

STEFAN MOHAMED
Ace of Spiders (978-1-78463-067-6)

ANNA STOTHARD
The Museum of Cathy (978-1-78463-082-9)

STEPHANIE VICTOIRE
The Other World, It Whispers (978-1-78463-085-0)

RECENT FICTION FROM SALT

KERRY HADLEY-PRYCE
The Black Country (978-1-78463-034-8)

CHRISTINA JAMES
The Crossing (978-1-78463-041-6)

PAUL MCVEIGH
The Good Son (978-1-78463-023-2)

IAN PARKINSON
The Beginning of the End (978-1-78463-026-3)

CHRISTOPHER PRENDERGAST
Septembers (978-1-907773-78-5)

JONATHAN TAYLOR
Melissa (978-1-78463-035-5)

ALICE THOMPSON
The Book Collector (978-1-78463-043-0)

GUY WARE
The Fat of Fed Beasts (978-1-78463-024-9)